# To the Thug I Loved Before

Monet Dragun

**Lock Down Publications and Ca$h
Presents**
**To the Thug I Loved Before**
A Novel by *Monet Dragun*

# Lock Down Publications
P.O. Box 944
Stockbridge, Ga 30281

**Visit our website @**
www.lockdownpublications.com

Copyright 2020 Monet Dragun
To The Thug I Loved Before

First Edition November 2020
Printed in the United States of America

*This is a work of fiction. Names, characters, places, and incidents either are products of the author's imagination or are used fictitiously. Any similarity to actual events or locales or persons, living or dead, is entirely coincidental.*

**Lock Down Publications**
**Like our page on Facebook: Lock Down Publications @**
www.facebook.com/lockdownpublications.ldp
Cover design and layout by: **Dynasty Cover Me**
Book interior design by: **Shawn Walker**
Edited by **: Nuel Uyi**

# Stay Connected with Us!

Text **LOCKDOWN** to 22828 to stay up-to-date
with new releases, sneak peaks, contests and
more…
Thank you.

# Submission Guideline.

Submit the first three chapters of your completed manuscript to ldpsubmissions@gmail.com, subject line: Your book's title. The manuscript must be in a .doc file and sent as an attachment. Document should be in Times New Roman, double spaced and in size 12 font. Also, provide your synopsis and full contact information. If sending multiple submissions, they must each be in a separate email.

Have a story but no way to send it electronically? You can still submit to LDP/Ca$h Presents. Send in the first three chapters, written or typed, of your completed manuscript to:

LDP: Submissions Dept
P.O. Box 944
Stockbridge, Ga 30281

*DO NOT send original manuscript. Must be a duplicate.*

Provide your synopsis and a cover letter containing your full contact information.

Thanks for considering LDP and Ca$h Presents.

Monet Dragun

# To the Thug I Loved Before

*Dear Diary,*

*Today this nigga had me fucked up! I watched him talk to all these hoes because I'm invisible to him. They don't know him like I do. He thinks my kindness is a sign of weakness. I literally want him all the time. Just can't stop thinking about him. I always dream about him. But here I stay, in the friend zone. I'm not like the girls that flaunt themselves around him as if he's king. Yeah, he's the most popular dude on campus, jock and street nigga. But he's also my best friend, so how am I supposed to break that bond? To let my feelings get in the way? Man, I can't do that to him. To us. But my feelings are too strong to just put them off into thin air. Every day I see him, I get those butterflies in the pit of my damn stomach! Am I not good enough for him? I'll never understand. I love him, but he loves me as a friend. I know it'll always be that way if I break what friendship we have. But I can't let this go; the love is too strong in my heart. So I have to either tell him that or let that shit go. Either way, I can't go on like this much longer. I really love JaKobe. So it's either sink or swim. I know he has some type of deeper feelings about me, I can feel it when I catch him looking at me with those beautiful brown eyes. Or sometimes he'll say things that'll just confuse me. But I know this: I have to tell him, but I can't lose him. It'll tear me apart . . .*

Monet Dragun

# Chapter 1

## Going Back to ATL

*Jaidah O'Neil*

"Flight 102, welcome to Atlanta, Georgia—The Peach State! Please enjoy your stay!" the flight attendant said with a beaming smile.

I stepped off the plane with my big Gucci shades plastered on my face. I took in the bright sun and fresh Atlanta air. "Damn, I missed being here." The private jet was wonderful, and I naturally got used to the luxurious lifestyle that I lived. After six years of being away from home, it was good to be back home; I needed this. Eventually, I had to come back and take a little break from modeling. Just for the time being. I deeply missed my family and my city.

Pushing my long thick curly hair back as the wind slightly blew it all over the place, I rolled my suitcase to the limo. My driver immediately got out, laughing at how independent I was. My driver took the suitcase from me, and pulled off his shades. "Thank you," I said, as I pulled off my red leather coat. The Atlanta heat was hitting me like a ton of red bricks.

"You're welcome, Miss O'Neil—Did you have a nice flight?—I hope Delta treated your private flight well," my personal driver said, as I threw my coat in and slid into the limo.

"Yes, I did. Thank you, Jackson!"

Jackson smiled as he closed the door. He waltzed to the driver side of the limo, and got in. I buckled up as I pulled my phone out of my Louis Vuitton handbag. The bag was a gift from his headlining fashion show. Jackson pulled off as I was in the back comfortably. "If you'd like a cold glass of champagne, it's already been made for you, miss."

"Thank you once more, Jackson," I said with a smile as he rolled up the tinted window. I turned off *airplane mode* that was on from the flight. Then I went straight to Twitter, seeing my post being retweeted by my fans. The tweet was of me letting my ATL fans know that I'd be in my hometown. Also, my pictures from the NY fashion week were spreading around like flies. I smiled at the comments. Logging out of Twitter, I went to Instagram. I noticed that my recent pictures were getting more than a hundred likes.

The joy of having so many fans was mind-blowing. Shaking my head, I extended my hand to press the button on the side of the door to roll down the window. I looked at some of the passing buildings. I missed the *A* so much. Being away from home was hard, but in time I learned to live with it. The first person I had to go see was my dear momma—Momma O'Neil. She didn't know that her only daughter was coming down, and I just wanted to surprise her, being that she hadn't seen me since I was nineteen. Besides, I was just starting off my modeling career.

Jillian O'Neil—my mom—let me follow my dreams to the fullest, and trusted me to go off to Milan, Paris, Fiji, and other beautiful cities around the globe. She knew I had modeling potential, and didn't hold me back nor let my dreams fade away. After the visit to my mom's, I had my mind set on going to see my friend, Monica. I hadn't seen her since college and modeling camp.

I pulled my eyes from the scenery, and pressed the intercom button. "Um, Jackson? Can we stop by Dunkin' Donuts? I'd love me a caramel latte," I said nicely through the intercom. Jackson rolled down the front window.

"Of course, would you like me to go to one close by your mom's?

I nodded. "By my mom's place would be nice."

Jackson nodded as he turned down the Peach Tree Ave. We passed by a park. The same park I'd go to everyday after school with JaKobe. Just seeing it made me remember back when JaKobe and I used to play one on one against each other.

Smiling, I placed my hand on the side of my face as I looked at the girl and guy of yore. I instantly thought of our one-time friendship.

Letting my eyes gently close, I could hear our childish voices echoing in my head:

*"JaKobe, I don't see why you even like her, honestly. She's a hoe. Anything that walks she going to put her thang down on that pole. Come on! O, you're smarter than that. I don't see why you always have to think about your looks? Hell, I did make you over. Didn't I?" the young me spoke, as I bounced the basketball a few times. He was much taller than I was, but I still had some defense.*

*I flipped my hair out of my eyes, the sun beaming in them. The sun also caused sweat to run down JaKobe's forehead and mine. It was hot as Satan's playground while we ran up and down the basketball court.*

*JaKobe paused as he held the basketball. Then, as he caught his breath, he began to talk: "Why wouldn't I?" he said through gasps. "She's one of the finest girls in school. And I heard nothing about her 'hoe ways'. I know you gave me a make-over, sheesh! I just need to step my game up, and her ass—Hella fire! Woah!" He gave me a duh tone, pushing me back as he dribbled the ball.*

*"Actually, she is not the finest girl in school. Have you seen half of the girls at Nomad High?" I said in a nonchalant tone, stating the obvious.*

*"Listen to yourself. Ha! She wouldn't see me if I was standing right in front of her." He pushed me back, and shot the ball. Making a three pointer, I stuck my tongue out at him. I still didn't get why he never understood. Why did he never catch on to my hints?*

*"Listen to yourself, JaKobe Harrison! You always dog yourself out. Oh my god!" I snatched the ball, and checked it to him.*

11

*He checked it back, and got into defense mode. The moment I was about to go in on him, he looked up at someone. I turned around and rolled my eyes.*

*"Eck!" I gagged playfully on my finger. I dropped the ball. He didn't even notice what I did. Of course he didn't. I was completely invisible to him anyway.*

Hearing the thump on the window, my eyes shot open. Jackson's voice pulled me out of my deep thoughts. "Would you like to go in?" I sighed and nodded. Jackson got out and opened the door for me. I extended my long legs out of the limo, and stepped on to the dark pavement. The bold cameras instantly started flashing, as I stood up dusting off my dress. I slid on my sunglasses, as I gave a broad smile. Yes, I was used to it, but I also hated it so much.

"Jaidah, how did you feel about the statement Naomi Campbell said about you and the other younger models, since she was one of the first supermodels?" one paparazzi man said.

"O'Neil! O'Neil! Have you heard about what Banks said? Will you be working with her?" I shook my head with a smile as some fans held their hands out, asking me for my autographs.

"Okay, guys! I've had a long flight. And I'd love some coffee. So let's take a group pic, and make sure you tag me in it!" They all yelped with happiness, as I posed with them while camera phones and selfie sticks swung into action, snapping photos of us. After I got done with that, I walked in along with Jackson by my side. The Dunkin' Donuts was peaceful as I waited to get my order taken.

"Oh my god! Oh my god! It's Jaidah O'Neil," some people enthused. I sighed lowly with a smile. Anyone knew what it felt like when coming back to one's hometown. This is what it was going to be—getting a lot of love.

The limo eased to a halt, and we were at my mom's house. It was in the suburbs, in a very nice neighborhood. Jackson pulled the door open for me to get out of the car. I eased out, and looked around my surroundings. Just to breathe in my neighborhood air brought a tight smile to my face. Jackson brought all the bags to the door. I strutted up the path, and looked through the screen door as the smell of food and people's voices came from the house. Taking a deep breath, I looked at Jackson and said, "Thank you, I'll call you when I'm ready to go to my hotel." He smiled as he gave me a hug. "Most welcome, and okay." I took yet another deep breath as he walked away. Extending my hand, I grabbed the door handle and pulled the door open. I smiled as I shook my head. *My momma never locked this,* I thought. And it was true.

"Hello, family! The princess is here!" I screamed, as I entered the house.

"Who is that?" My mom came around the corner, and she placed her hands over her mouth as she walked over to me. Tears came to her eyes, as she looked at me with admiration.

"My baby! I missed you so! How are you? You look so beautiful!" my momma, Jillian, said all at once as she looked me up and down, giggling.

"I missed you, mama! I haven't seen you in years!" I said, as I gave my mom a very tight hug.

"Baby, I missed you too. Look at you! That modeling didn't eat you up, body looks healthy!" I gave my mom a fake smile when she said that. I was about to counter that when I heard a deep voice.

"Ohhhh! Jaidah? Is that my sister, Jaidah!" I heard my elder brother—Bradley—say. Our mom pulled away from me as my brother came up to me.

"Geez! You got tall, and you finally grew some facial hair!" I said.

Bradley rolled his eyes, and pulled me into a hug. "Shut up. I'ma grown man!" he said, giving me a stern face. I pushed his head back as he laughed. "I missed you though, shorty McFooty," he added in a teasing tone of voice. I gave him an ugly face, causing him to laugh. He knew all too well that I hated that nickname.

"You make me sick," I said, laughing. We started laughing while walking into the kitchen. Our mom was in there like the chef she was. Jillian owned a fine restaurant in Atlanta. There was no reason for us to not be able to cook. As we sat down, Bradley nudged me in the side, causing me to punch him playfully.

"So? Have you talked to JaKobe?" Bradley questioned out of the blue. The only reason for that was because he and JaKobe were good friends as well. If truth be told, I was madly in love with my brother's best friend. Even before JaKobe and I became friends, I'd taken a shine to him, then we soon became friends.

I hated it, but it was better being friends than ruining a relationship.

"No, I haven't talked to him since we had that falling out before I left, while he went off to college," I said with a casual shrug. Bradley shook his head in disappointment.

"Well, you know he stay in the A?"

I turned to him with a frown.

"Why? He went off to LSU in Louisiana? So why would he come back down here? He had a full ride and was bound to go pro, what happened?" I asked with curiosity, as our mom began to cut her eyes back at us.

"Well, he did go pro, but he got injured. So, yeah."

I hummed a low, "Okay." I kind of felt bad, but JaKobe had gotten cocky and dropped me as a friend. *So could this be karma?* I was just sitting there in thought before I spoke up. "Why you tellin' me this?" I asked Bradley with attitude.

"Why you got all that venom in you? Damn. He is coming for dinner. We didn't know you was making a surprise visit, you know!"

I rolled her eyes. "For real? Well, I won't be here. I'll eat my food, then leave."

# To the Thug I Loved Before

Our mom turned around with a stern look. "In God's heaven, no, you won't! You haven't seen your family in how many years? Stop letting that boy run you away. I invited him, and you're here, so let that be it. Don't you even talk back either, Jaidah!" I pursed my lips as Bradley cracked a laugh. In all honesty, I hadn't seen JaKobe in years, and I didn't want to deal with him. Every time I saw him on TV, I immediately turned it off.

Bradley went on, whispering: "You need to let that day go. Okay? A grudge isn't good. Just because y'all stopped being friends don't mean you need to be a hard ass." But I couldn't just let go. Bradley didn't know the whole story between me and JaKobe. And I planned on keeping it that way. JaKobe and I had sex. And he was my first; my first time at the frat party—freshman year. The reason we fell out? Because he decided to run game on me like I didn't mean anything to him. It took me a long time to get over that. A long time.

"Old wounds never really heal, Bradley. And JaKobe Harrison has never changed. He's dead to me." And with that said, I got up from the stool and grabbed my things.

"I'm going into my old room and putting up my things for the night, mama," I said sweetly, as Bradley shook his head. He couldn't figure out how I could be this cold.

"Okay, hunny," my mom responded. I sighed as I began to haul all my things upstairs.

I looked back at my brother and said loudly, "You ain't gon' help me? Laziest brother in the world!" I said with a playful face.

"Don't worry, you got it! Make sure to bend your knees, G!" I smacked my lips, flipping him off while our mom wasn't looking. I proceeded up the steps. How was seeing JaKobe going to affect me? No one knew what went down except my mother. And how he did me was just full out wrong. I didn't even tell my father. Everything could be going right for once, just for once, in my life. Then everything goes left just by mentioning his damn name.

\*\*\*

*I stood in the mirror, checking out the new deep red velvet dress I had purchased earlier; it was so beautiful on me and exaggerated all my curves. I turned to the side and smoothed the dress against my somewhat curvy hips. I couldn't believe how good it looked on me. I swore it was going to be oversized and bland. But instead, it hugged my body in certain areas beautifully and hung elegantly in other areas. It was absolutely stunning.*

*"I think I found the one."*

*I smiled to myself, and backed away from the mirror and decided to strike a runway-worthy pose. I stood on the tip of my toes, slid the dress up my thigh, and imagined the perfect shoe to match. Just seeing the shoe on my feet reminded me of back in the day.*

*"Thinking about me?" I could hear JaKobe's voice say.*

*I looked through the mirror to see JaKobe standing in my doorway. I rolled my eyes and continued to admire myself in the mirror. JaKobe smirked and crossed his arms. He knew I was still upset, but deep down I loved him.*

*"Jaidah, when are you gonna get over what happened in the past?"*

*I looked at him.*

*"Why are you here, JaKobe?" I said, rolling my eyes at his tone.*

*"You know why I'm here."*

*"No, I don't."*

*Although I knew the reason, I decided to play as though I didn't. Just couldn't believe he was standing in my bedroom asking questions after everything we'd been through.*

*"So, you're going to pretend you're not upset about how things went the last time we saw each other?" he questioned.*

*"I'm over that. Now if you'll excuse me—"*

*I brushed past him the moment he tried to get closer to me. I refused to fall victim to his soft, smooth, seductive charm. My thoughts were interrupted by his strong hand grabbing mine.*

*"Forgive me?"*

*"It's been years. Shid, I hate you with a passion, JaKobe. That's hard to get over, not right now."*

*He dropped his head and nodded; he had to respect that I just wasn't ready to forget everything and move on. He let go of my hand, and leaned in for a kiss. Just before our lips could meet, I heard someone calling my name.*

"Jaidah!"

My eyes fluttered opened, and I was met by the bright green numbers on the clock that sat on the nightstand. I rolled over, and felt the other side of the bed, hoping someone would there. But I was met by the cool empty feeling of loose sheets.

"Jaidah!"

I looked towards the door, hearing my name being called, and I thought this was a part of my oddly nice yet strange dream. I squinted in hopes that they'd adjust to the darkness. I noticed my brother standing in the doorway with a throw blanket around his shoulders.

"What?" I finally answered.

"Were you asleep?" my brother asked.

"No, I was just observing the inside of my eyelids at 2:30 a.m. What do you want?"

He ignored my smart remark, and sat on the bed without asking if it was okay for him to invade my space.

"I thought I heard you talking in your sleep, bad dream?"

I shrugged. I didn't wanna go into detail about the dream I just had. It was way too soon.

"Ehh—maybe, maybe not," I said.

"One of those, huh?" he said.

"Unfortunately."

17

"Well, whatever it is seemed to really bother you even in your sleep."

"It's complicated," I replied, trying to get him to leave it be.

"How?"

"So complicated that I'm unsure if the dream was a nightmare, or simply amazing."

He rubbed his arms and yawned, thinking of all the dreams he had that left him wondering the same.

"Well, whatever it was, if it's meant to be, it'll be and if not— you know the rest."

"Thanks," I said, unsure of what to think.

Bradley stood up, and kissed me on the forehead before walking out of the room. I sighed, and glanced at my phone, thinking of the times like this when I'd wake up to a silly text or something worth staying up for. But now everything was different. I opened my email, and continued looking through the ones I hadn't gotten to earlier. This had become the highlight of my late nights—work all the way!

# Chapter 2

## Dinner with A Villain

*JaKobe Harrison*

Tracy kept bobbing her head as her eyes occasionally gazed up at me. She had that rhythm and jaw suction that had me on edge. I couldn't help groaning. She had a way of doing something with her tongue and throat as well, but I wasn't about to buss that quick. Grabbing her thick curls that were tucked into a ponytail, I pushed her head down further. Her eyes looked up to mine. As I kept the blunt balanced between my lips, pulling it from my lips, I blew out the smoke, and bit my lip while holding onto the nut I was soon to release.

"Damn!" I groaned loudly, as my head hit the back of my couch cushion. Her mouth had a way of doing things to me. Something serious—and she knew that shit.

"Mmm, buss all in my mouth daddy," she moaned out on my hard piece. My eyes fluttered closed, as my load shot out into her mouth, my come oozing all the way down her throat. I let out a loud grunt as she licked it all up. I finally came down from my high, and brought my head back up, looking at her.

"Damn, Tracy!"

She giggled, and she got off her reddened knees. She was about to sit her naked body in my lap. But I pushed her back. She knew that was all I needed before I got back to the trap.

"Really?" she whined.

"Yes, you know I got som' shit to handle at the trap, girl. I got you later. You know we'd be going at it all day. Just keep that shit wet for me." She rolled her eyes. I shrugged, as I pulled up my boxers and got up off the couch, feeling good. She turned around, and was about to give me a kiss, but I swerved around her.

"Pause! Don't you think you should brush yo' teeth? Or clean ya face? You know ion' kiss you after you suck me off." She rolled her eyes, as she turned around, going in the opposite direction.

"Whatever," Tracy said, swinging her twenty-four-inch Brazilian weave over her shoulder.

"You gon' stop rolling them shits at me too! Watch, I'ma fuck your ass up later," I said loudly, while I scratched my chest. Going up the steps of my house, I looked at my watch; it was about a quarter past four. I had to get in the shower and do my hygiene.

Mrs. O'Neil don't like when people are late to her functions. I walked into my room, and went over to my dresser, pulling off my gold chain and putting it in the jewelry box. I stopped when I saw the promise ring I had when I was in college. The thing was so old; I don't know how it got out of my memory box. It was from Jaidah O'Neil, my once best friend, who I was really close to until I fucked that shit up. I sighed while looking at the ring, then tucked it back into the box before Tracy popped her big nosy ass into the room to see what I was doing.

I ran my hand down my face as I shook off the thoughts of Jaidah. That was long ago, and I'll never get that old thang back. I shook off the bullshit feelings, and made my way into our bathroom. Rubbing my thick beard as I shut the door, I pulled down my boxers, and stepped out of them. I grabbed my Dove shampoo, opening the glass shower door. I placed the bottle in the shower caddy. I turned on the shower, then made sure the water was all the way on hot, as I slid the glass door back again and stepped in. The hot beads of water hit my skin as I closed the door.

I got my hair wet as I closed my eyes. I started to think of Jaidah, and I don't know why. I haven't talked to her in years. She went her separate ways: I went to college; she went to Spain. As much as I hated it, I let her go, and she did the same. I opened the door again, grabbed the shampoo bottle, and I squirted some into my hands. I rubbed it in my hair as the smell hit my nose.

I closed my eyes as the memories came flooding back; memories of the argument that destroyed our bond we once had.

Those memories invaded my mind. "Shit!" Only this time I couldn't shake the memories off as her beautiful face flashed across my mind.

*It was hot outside as I walked from the football field. I walked with my bag on my shoulder as the Atlanta heat beamed down on me. I hadn't seen Jaidah since the frat party or her induction into the sorority. And, believe it or not, I was truly avoiding her. I was making a good effort not speaking to her, even though the feelings I had for her never changed.*

*After we had those drinks and had sex that night in the hotel, I didn't know how to feel about her. For one, I didn't like playing girls because there was no need. But, I was feeling Tracy. I wasn't into Jaidah like that because she was my friend, my best friend at that. That had made a drift in between our relationship because she was a virgin. I wasn't.*

*"JaKobe!" That voice—I just kept walking down the sidewalk. She called again.*

*"JaKobe Harrison! I know you hear me calling you!" she shouted, as she finally caught up to me. She started to catch her breath, as I stopped and rubbed my bare smooth face.*

*"What's good?" I spoke nonchalantly. She gave me a look as she ran her hands through her hair,*

*"Why the attitude? We haven't talked in days. You didn't even hug me on grad day! We didn't even take pictures or nothing! And I hope it's not because of, you know—I mean, it was really special—" I held my hand up to stop her, as she fiddled with her nails.*

*"Listen, I only did that because of a dare. I was drunk. You were tipsy. What we did was risky. I ain't mean for it to go that far." She looked stunned as we both stood there, just staring at each other, and it was ticking me off. "Is you gon' say something or nah'?" Her eyes shifted to mine.*

*"Are you serious? I know we're friends! But, you don't have to be an asshole! You know the old JaKobe wouldn't have done this to me! How could you—how could you do this to ruin our—"*

21

*"Just shut up! I'm tired of you throwing that shit in my face, yo'! All you did was give me a make-over! What's the big fucking deal? I had sex with Tracy. You happy you could ruin us?"*

*She scoffed.*

*"So what was I? Just some joke? I should have never given you that damn make-over! You hated yourself, now you think you're the hottest shit wall king! I hate you, JaKobe Harrison! We don't ever have to be friends again! Go be with Tracy! You took my fucking vir—"*

*"I ain't take shit! It was just fucking! I put my dick in you, and that's all it was to me."* A tear slipped down her cheek, I didn't have time for this.

*"The reason no one liked you is because you are arrogant, selfish, selfless, and a straight up dick!"*

*I rolled my eyes. "Are you done?" Her eye twitched, and her hand came flying across my face.*

*"And to think I fucking love you! Have a good fucking life when you be with Tracy and go off to LSU! You don't have to talk to me ever again in life." She turned, as tears ran down her eyes. She stormed down the street, as I stood there looking at her. I held my cheek, as my eyes brimmed with hot tears. I wiped them away as I walked in the opposite direction. It was better off this way.*

I turned off the shower and stepped out, as I rubbed my hair with a towel. I opened the door, and all the steam seeped out. I walked into my closet, and pulled out my outfit choice of the day. I threw my towel on the bed, and walked over to my dresser with my clothes in hand. I pulled out pair of boxers, and slipped them on.

My phone started to buzz a couple of times; it was Brad and some more people. I pulled on my black pants, and my door opened.

"I'm going out, did you leave it?" Side eyeing Tracy, I grabbed my wallet.

"What are you doing today anyway?" I asked with a brow raised.

"Just going out with some friends, that's all," she said, wiggling her fingers, waiting for me to give her the cash. I pulled out a couple of hundreds and fifties.

"Here, girl." I fanned her off as she giggled and hugged me, then kissed my cheek.

"Thank you, babe."

I nodded as I pulled on my shirt. Tracy placed the money into her purse, and fixed her hair. "Did Chino contact you about the merge? You know if that sell don't go right, hell gon' break lose. Shit! Honestly, you need to just kill his ass. 'Cause I bet he tryna plot on you." I sighed and rubbed my chin hair, as she stood there bombarding me with this talk about Chino.

"Nah, and stay in yo' place, Tracy—I got this shit, shorty," I said, pulling my Tommy polo on, and followed suit with my jacket. Then I moved to the walk-in closet, and went towards my jean section. Tracy popped her head around the corner of the closet.

"Oh, well, I was just saying if you gon' do this shit, don't let him be no step ahead of you. You'll be good, though. But I'll see you later. Bye, babe."

"Okay," I said, while sliding into my jeans. I tied my bandana around my head next, then looked myself in the huge mirror. "Looking fresh as fuck!" I smirked while I grabbed my phone and slid it into my pocket along with my wallet. I heard the downstairs door open and slam shut. I sighed again.

"When is her ass going to ever get a damn job—tryna come up off my trap!" I pulled on my chain, and was about to step out of the room, before my phone started ringing. I pulled it out of my pocket. It was Brad.

"What's poppin'!" I said, as I put the phone to my ear.

"Yo', my mom said being a gourmet, she knows you can't cook shit. Bring something good."

I laughed, and so did Brad.

Walking out of my room and down the steps, I said: "I'm a hood ass nigga, but I'm taking a cooking class! We like to cook too, bruh. Ya' mom ain't got no chill, bro."

"Yeah? From who, chef? Food Network channel?" he cracked.

"Ha-ha, you got jokes. Sick ass nigga. I gotta hit this lick first, then the spot. I'll be there in a few minutes, though. I will definitely pick up ya' mom's favorite." I locked up the house as he said, *okay*, and we hung up. I walked towards my black Mercedes and hopped in, driving off down the street.

\*\*\*

Pulling up the lick deep in the trenches, homie dressed all black with a pit bull posted next to him and waved his hand for the gate to be opened. He stayed with an AK-47 on his side if shit ever went heavy. Five-o never came through these joints, so anything can happen in the dirty streets of ATL. I didn't give a damn who Chino was in these streets; he knew 'bout me and the understanding we had: *Don't touch my homies, and I don't touch his.* We had our spots, but I knew in my gut this nigga wasn't true to his shit. I wanted my money, and he had my product. So, that was the understanding. My product was too good to get it from anywhere else. I had all the connects, so there was no way he could ice me out. Get rid of me, and all that shit gon' fail.

The iron gate finally opened fully, and I drove forward as I could hear all the rocks and gravel hit the bottom of my car. I gave the man a nod; he did it in return. A beefed-up man came from the side of the house, walking towards me. Cutting my eyes at him, I reached for the back duffle in the back seat, but never kept my eyes from off the man. Best believe that .45 stayed in my lap ready to blast if shit ever got heavy; a nigga was ready. He tapped his knuckle on my driver side window. I didn't even lower the window. The only thing he needed to see was the contents in the bag; he didn't need to hear my voice.

I unzipped the bag, leaning it for him to see. He nodded, and gestured his head towards the front building on the lot. "Bet," I said, while putting the car in gear, driving to the front spot. Soon as I parked the car, I slung the bag on my shoulder. I shut the car off, then hopped out and beeped the car to lock it. This bag was going towards my next business venture. I had boss moves to make, and ain't no nigga or bitch gon' stop that.

After walking up to the doors, I was immediately buzzed in. I pushed the door open, walking through the hallway that led to his office. You could smell the thick smoke from the drugs being pushed. A door was open on the side of me, as a couple of naked women with masks on were cooking dope. Chuckling, I pressed on to Chino's tiny office, tapping on the door with three knocks. I announced my name before grabbing the door knob and walking straight in.

"Yo, this Kobe." My voice boomed through the sound-proof halls.

His thick southern accent called out, "Come in, dawg." Twisting the knob, I swaggered into the office room. His woman stood by him. She had an hourglass shape. Her hand rubbed through his locs, as he smoked his stank ass cigar.

"I got the brick, you got my stacks," I emphasized with a raised eyebrow.

"Damn, homie! I got your bag. Baby, get them Gucci duffles over in the Chester cabinet." His eyes never left her ass, as she switched over to the cabinet. She pulled the key out of her bra and unlocked it, as she pulled the doors open and took out two Gucci bags. He turned his head back to me. "I told you I'm 'bout my business. Like I said, I ain't gon' touch yon homies if mine wasn't touch." He paused. If Chino thought this was intimidating me, he could try that shit again.

"Chino, listen, my boys ain't touch yours. Trust me, if shots was fired, it wasn't mine. Hear me? All I came for was my damn money. You shorty got my shit, so just hand it over so I can be out. You get yours, I get mine. Just that simple."

"Bruh, I wanna hear none of that shit. You feel me? One of my muthafuckin' corner boys got blasted, and my niggas telling me it's yo' click. I'on like be played with." Chino spoke these words with his lip turned up. I wasn't fazed at all. His hand eased on his Glock, and I chuckled.

"Like I said, it wasn't us, I hold onto my word. You ain't shit without me. But I'm not going to speak on that. You the one that need this hot shit." I raised the duffle in my hand, and his whole facial expression changed. "Yeah, that's what the fuck I thought. Now let's keep this shit cordial. Feel me? Now I'll keep ears in the streets to see who really popped your boy. Cool?" Chino kissed his teeth and nodded. I lightly tossed the bag towards his desk. He looked towards his shorty, then she looked at him. Chino nodded, and she switched over to me the heavy bags.

"Cool," Chino agreed, taking the bag from her and gripping the handles

I turned to walk away. "Aye. Next time you pull a gun on me, make sure you ready for that hot shit." No other words were made, so I pressed on to my next destination.

*** 

After hitting the lick and putting my money in the safe, I finally got the chance to stop by Cosco. I picked up momma Jillian's favorite dish—Potato salad and sweet potato casserole. I got her a cake too, along with her favorite wine. I pulled up to her big house, and walked up to the screen door. As I opened it, the music filled the house, and the smell of food was like heaven.

"Uncle O!" Bradley's kids said as they ran up to me, almost making me drop the food.

"What's up, rugrats! Where ya' pops at?" They pointed to the kitchen. And they let me go. Bradley had three kids. Two twin boys and one girl who was the oldest.

I walked into the kitchen, and was greeted with hi and hellos, "Hey, mama Jillian!" She looked at me and rolled her eyes,

"Hey boy, get your hands out my food! You are just like one of my own. Greedy out of Thai world." I laughed as she popped my hand, then gave me a hug. We talked as I placed the food by all the others.

"How have you been?" she said, as I gave her the wine and cake.

"I've been decent. Still trying to get my knee how it used to be. But other than that, I started my own football camp for kids and teens."

She smiled and nodded. "That's what I like to hear. You still with that Tracy girl? Why would her mom give her a man name? I still don't know till this day."

I laughed and shook my head. "We coo', Mama Jillian."

"Okay," she said, as someone in the house called her name. She gave me a smile as she told me to enjoy myself. Then walking off, I looked and saw Brad. I snuck up behind him and licked my finger before I put it in his ear, making him jump.

"Nigga, you nasty!" he said, as we both busted out laughing.

"Boy, watch yo' mouth in my house!" we heard his mom say. Our mouths instantly closed as we stifled a laugh. His dad was on the grill, tearing shit up.

"Why Tracy didn't come?"

I shrugged. "She ain't wanna come. So I ain't make her."

Brad nodded. "Probably shopping or drinking damn lattes. Anyway, it's good 'cause don't nobody like her no way. Don't see why you even stayed with her."

Brad's girlfriend—Tia—kissed his cheek as she went to mingle with some other family members. *Why they ain't married yet? I don't know.*

"That's everyone else's opinion not mine," I said in response to Brad's statement that no one liked Tracy. He looked at me, then laughed.

"Still stubborn as ever, yo'."

I was about to say something when I heard the kids shouting someone's name.

"Auntie B!" they yelled.

"Cousin Jai!" I heard someone else say. I frowned as Brad's word became incoherent. I was trying to figure out if I wasn't going crazy. And they weren't calling out Jaidah O'Neil's name. I looked at Bradley, and he had a blank expression on his face as he whistled.

"Brad, I know Jaidah ain't here?" I said, pushing his shoulder.

"Hey, babies! Y'all got so big. I brought y'all gifts too."

Brad looked at me, and raised his eyebrows as he smirked. I looked through the crowd, and there she was. She still looked the same. Just slim-thick. She looked up, and I couldn't believe my eyes. We hadn't seen each other in years.

She stood up from giving her nieces, nephews, and cousins a hug. Her hair flowed out of her eyes as she looked at me. She smiled, and that was it; no *hi*, *hello*, no nothing. Should I say something to her? Or just fall back.

*** 

"Okay, everyone!—All kids at the kids table—Adults, you know where to go—And no smacking ya' lips, kids—Y'all know the deal!" Jaidah said, as her mother told her to do. She had on this right ass romper, and she looked real good in it. Everyone separated, as the ladies were making the plates. After that, we all sat at the table and blessed the food. I just so happened to be sitting right across from Jaidah. Ain't that some shit?

"Hello, Jaidah."

She looked up from her plate, as she swallowed hard.

"Hi," she said, as she kept talking to Claudia and Bradley. But I knew it was all fake. I ate my food, as everyone mingled. But deep down inside I was pissed.

"Humph, so how was Spain? *Hot?* I know your nappy hair puffed up like crazy." Her brother looked at me. I was trying to be funny but—shit!—I was mad.

"Actually, it's really beautiful there, ya know! Full of nice people. And—no, my hair didn't puff up. What about you? How was LSU? Didn't you get kicked out for dealing, lost the full ride, right?" The tone of her voice was dry, with a tinge of curtness. She was about to get some potato salad before she looked at me with a stank face. The meal had a price tag on the side of it, and Jaidah laughed. "Still can't cook, I see. Got a whole woman that couldn't show you nothing. Still burning water?" She giggled, then gave me a stale face.

"Same as your burned edges and that raggedy crooked wig on yo' damn head," I scoffed.

"Oh? Same as the burnt noodles on top of your head, right? Why your dumb ass put that dollar store dye in your head?" I cracked a laugh. It seemed like the only ones who could hear us bickering was her mom, pop, and brother.

"No, at least my breath don't smell like ass."

Jaidah rolled her eyes. "Nah, homie. That's the potato salad you brought. Who cooks your meals? Tracy? That hood rat probably makes you TV dinners every night. She can't even boil water to make yo' dumb ass ramen."

I sucked my teeth. "Damn, just can't get over yourself. Still on a nigga dick like back in the day."

Jaidah snapped her head at me. "My momma told me to never lie down with dogs, you'll get fleas."

"Oh, last time I checked you got played and laid down like a *fool,* right? What happened then? You still lay on your back? Fucking clown."

She stopped eating, dropped her fork on the plate as she glared at me and yelled, "I will slap the shit out of you. You ain't shit, clown!"

"You two stop it right now!" her mom said.

"No, mama. Fuck him. I lost my appetite. I'm going outside before I *kill* him." Jaidah snatched her phone, and shot out of her chair, as she pushed the plate away from her.

"Jai? Baby," her dad began, "just come here. Don't let that get to you."

Monet Dragun

"C'mon, shorty McFooty, just sit down and eat," her brother cooed.

"I said *no*. If *he's* here, I don't wanna eat at this table. Just makes me sick to my stomach. Excuse me—" As she spoke, her voice cracked. Her brother looked at me. And I kinda felt bad. I did go a little too far. I shouldn't have said that about her *first* time.

"You're an idiot for real," Brad said to me. Then he faced his parents. "Ma and pop, I'ma go check up on her." They nodded as he got up from the table and went to where Jaidah ran off to. Seeing her again had me all screwed up inside and out. Maybe I had to fix this, maybe we need to be friends again. I ate my food, questioning myself. I never question myself.

# Chapter 3

## Sorry? I Ain't Sorry

*Jaidah O'Neil*

*It was two weeks before the frat party. And I was going to tell him how I felt for once in my life. I sat on the stoop of our dorm as I had a book in my hand. The urban book was called 'Loving Gutta,' to be exact. I heard my name being called as JaKobe walked to the corner where I stayed. He could see me sitting out on the stoop, looking off in the distance at nothing in particular. It was only because he looked so good. He began to jog and was at my house in no time. My big curly hair flowed as the wind picked up speed.*

*"Jai!" I looked his way as he waved at me, with a bright smile. Those perfect white teeth glistened in the sunlight.*

*"You're early," I spoke, as he nodded. Oh, this boy made my heart skip a beat. His tattoos complemented his sculpted face.*

*"Yeah, I was over at Dustin's house," JaKobe spoke. I rolled my eyes in disgust.*

*"Why you making that face, ma'?" he questioned.*

*"Because I don't favor his ass too much. He gets you in trouble all the time, and he got you in these streets. Plus, he's playing Tavi, and that's my bitch." Again, I rolled my eyes, as I groaned, and he sat next to me. He was hanging with the wrong crowd. And I didn't like it,*

*"What? I don't be out here in them streets, girl. I told you that. Stop believing what everyone telling you. I'm your best friend. You should believe me. And shit, Tavi has her ways too. She's no angel, and she's playing him too." Jakobe shrugged but continued. "They go out, but she fucking around with niggas twice her age. Don't say nothing, though." I still didn't approve.*

*"What do you mean don't say nothing? That's my girl, you know. Dustin isn't my friend, but you get what I'm saying." Dustin and Tavi were not our problems. If they wanted to go,*

*cheat, fuck around on each other, then that was fine by me. Only person I care about is my damn self and JaKobe.*

*I had my own problems, and JaKobe did too. But I was so caring about others and sometimes not myself. That's what JaKobe didn't like. But here he was not giving a damn about me but his own self. All the same, he still didn't see how I felt about him,*

*"I know that, but what can we do? We can't fix it, they need to." He rubbed his thumb across my chin. I tried to hold back my rapid heartbeat. Sometimes I couldn't get enough of my best friend, O. Everyone thought it was weird that he hung around me all the time and never made a move on me, but it ain't none of their business at all. It was actually a real friendship. But I had become in love with him.*

*"Fine, fine. What are we going to do today?" I asked, as I played with my blonde curls. He shrugged, and I looked at a passing car, which was blasting music to the max.*

*"Whatever you want to do is fine, Jai," he replied, giving me a big smile.*

*"But I asked you first," I countered, as I pouted.*

*"I mean, if we're going to do what I want to do." He smirked, as I looked at another passing car.*

*"Stop being nasty, weirdo," I giggled, but secretly bit my lip. I lightly punched his arm and smiled.*

*He shrugged, before a goofy grin appeared on his face, "You're the one that asked me what I wanted to do." The way that he smiled when he laughed was just indescribable. I treasure the moments when he smiled, because you can rarely get a smile out of JaKobe. "Fine. I'll come up with something that we could do that doesn't involve the nastiness." I grinned, as he laughed midway in the sentence.*

*"A'ight. I'll give you time—Just think of something before we get into the house," he said, as another car went by, receiving a chuckle from me. I took a deep breath, and I was going to confess—*

*"Uh? JaKobe, can I ask you something?" I said, as I fiddled with my curls.*

*"Yeah, wassup, mama?" he said, looking my way, as the sun beamed in my eyes, causing me to squint.*

*So how you rolling into the frat party? You got a date? And— Have you ever seen us being more than friends?" I asked in one breath. That kind of threw him into a loop, but I had to be honest. I had to tell him before I exploded,*

*"Jai, to be honest—" he began, before my phone rang and my mom's number rolled across the screen. I sighed and looked at him.*

*"Maybe you should get that, Jai, could be important," he said. I nodded. What he was about to say was out the window now.*

*"You may be right, you know!—Just hold that thought, we can talk after I get off the phone," I said while smiling.*

*JaKobe nodded with no response. He proceeded to answer his face time call that came in there and then. "Yo? Yeah, I'll be there in a minute. You want the gram, right? Bet, cool." By this time, I had had finished my phone conversation with my mom. "And Jaidah," I heard JaKobe say to me. "We might have to wrap this up quick, I don't have a date. We can go, friend and friend—" I nodded, looking off at the passing cars of the students either going to classes or coming home. Telling JaKobe was going to be harder than I thought it would be. So, I decided against it.*

\*\*\*

Why? Why didn't I just tell him that day? We hadn't had a falling out. We wouldn't go to any frat party. We didn't have sex. We were just friends. But my love for him ruined it all. All I had to do was, tell him and see what he felt inside. I sat on my parents' patio with my ear buds in my ears, thinking of all the old bull shit.

Beyoncé's 'Sorry' blasted through my ear buds, as I had my arms crossed over my chest. My phone vibrated, and I picked it up as I read the text from my best girlfriend—Monica. She was a model too. I had a text from Rashad, an incredibly famous photographer. But I didn't even read it. I had no feeling for work at this time.

I really didn't feel like texting anyone at the moment. But the text mentioned that I could stay at her apartment rather than waste my money at a hotel. I drank some of my wine cooler as my brother came out, looking at the kids as they ran about in the yard. I sighed as I looked straight ahead. He took a seat next to me, as I looked at him side eyed.

"Jai?" he called out. I truly hated that nickname mainly because JaKobe gave it to me,

"I'd love it if you called me by my full name," I said sarcastically.

"Come on! What he said was really foul. And I don't like y'all bickering. What really happened between the two of you?" He pulled my ear buds out of my ears. But one you could still hear the music.

I sighed deeply, still not looking at him. "If I told you, you'd hate him, and want to kick his ass. And I don't want to ruin y'all friendship. So just leave it alone. Okay, Braddy?"

"You for sure? 'Cause, I swear, I wanted to sock him in his damn mouth and slam his head in that damn potato salad. Yo' comebacks were fire, though! You had his ass sweating! I just wish he had some sense. Everyone and they mama know Tracy a snake murk ass bitch." I tried to stay with a hard face, but he made me laugh. He always did.

"Yes, I'm sure. But enough of me. How are you and your baby momma? Why ain't you wifed that girl yet?" He sighed and rubbed his thick beard. "You know I love her like a sister I never had," I added.

"We good. I just been so busy with music and—"

"Stop lying, you know you love that girl to death. What's the real reason?" He sat back in the patio chair, and looked at his kids.

"I'm simply scared. What if we don't last, you know! I really want us to last forever." I smiled, noticing he was deeply interested in her. I remember when they first started dating; I knew they would be together forever.

"Wife her before she slips away. That's all I have to say." He looked up at me, as I turned and looked at his kids. The patio door opened, and Bradley looked up. I knew who it was already,

"Aye, Jai? Your pops want you." His voice made me want to vomit. Bradley sighed and got up, planting a kiss on my forehead,

"Talk? Alright," JaKobe whispered. I didn't respond. I just nodded. Bradley sighed and slapped JaKobe in the chest hard, making him a little winded. My brother entered the house, and closed the screen door so no bugs would fly into momma house. I sat there with my arms crossed as I looked ahead.

"Auntie, look at me!" Dylan said, as she did a cartwheel.

"Jaidah?" JaKobe called, but I ignored him. I wished he'd just leave me the hell alone.

"That's good, baby girl! Do it again for auntie."

"Jai, come talk to me!" JaKobe sighed, as he was trying to get my attention.

"Auntie, you wanna play soccer with us?"

I was about to stand up, but JaKobe touched my wrist.

"Jai—" That name made me sick.

"What? What do you want, JaKobe? Stop fucking calling my damn name," I said, finally looking at him.

"Can we talk at least? I didn't mean what I said. I was just upset. But you said some stuff too." I sat down and started laughing.

"Babies, just go play with your cousins and brother for now, okay?" They nodded and ran off.

"Jai, damn I know you hear me, man."

"Don't call me that! Like for real, you bring up my damn virginity like it was a joke? '*Oh, last time I checked you laid down like a fool, right? What happened then? You still lay on your back?*' You think everything is a fucking joke! You know what a joke you are!"

He looked at me and scoffed. "Still ass stubborn like back then."

"Ha, nigga, stop talking about back then. You're the one to talk? Did you know that little miss Tracy is a gold digger? So I'm the fool? Really? You letting a girl take your fucking money, ain't that some shit? Money that you should be using for yourself; well, drug money, I might add. But hey, that's what the fuck you like and the fuck you like to do. But that's none of my business. All you want is a bitch to kiss your ass and tell you how pretty you are like a bitch. Fuck outta my face!"

"You don't know shit," he said calmly.

"Speak the fuck up! You had balls at the table, right?" He looked at me and saw all the pain on my face. I was not the same soft Jaidah from back then.

"I'm sorry, but seeing you made me feel somehow." I scoffed at his fake ass *sorry*. "But we should be friends, you know—Let the past go. And start over."

I nodded. He had the fucking nerve to say I should let go of the past just like that!

"Okay, I'm sorry too." I gave him a fake smile, and he believed it.

"Alright, so—"

"Tss! Fuck that sorry, I ain't sorry. Maybe we can be cool when yo' ass learn the truth. Until then you can kiss my chocolate ass!" I stood up and left him there dumbfounded. I spent a little time with the kids before I'd leave. The whole time I could feel his eyes on me. But I didn't care at all. If he wanted to continue to be naïve and selfless, then that was him. I was going to continue to live my life with or without JaKobe Harrison.

\*\*\*

I was sitting on the bed. I was at Monica's house and staying in her guest room. I had several fashion magazines in my bed, in search of inspiration. I decided to start on my small project. Even though I was still on somewhat of a vacation, I still wanted to gain ideas for the clothing line that I was coming up with Kia Dunkin. She had her own company. She saw my passion for modeling and fashion when I was young, and took me under her wing. Fashion is such a broad topic, wherein new trends are reinvented and created every day.

I flipped the pages, and landed on a beautiful mermaid dress inspired by African culture. The door opened and in walked Monica.

"What you up to?" she questioned, as she sat on the edge of the bed. I grabbed the magazine, and ripped the page out. Not only was the dress beautiful, but it was also something I felt would never go out of style. I handed it to her, and she smiled while nodding in approval.

"Oh, your line. This would be perfect."

I nodded, and she looked at me.

"What?"

She handed me her phone and showed me a picture of Tracy copying my style and hugged up on JaKobe.

"Why are you showing me that?" I said with attitude that I really didn't mean to show.

"Because that bitch is fronting like you constantly, and she is playing him."

I shrugged. "I don't really care. And you shouldn't either, Monica."

Shaking her head, she sighed, and her eyes shifted back to the picture. "You should really busy her ass out. Maybe he'll go back to who he used to be. You can't dwell on the past. I know you still love him. But it's none of my business. I'm going to bed. It's been a long day." She grabbed her phone, and walked out of my room while saying good night. I was kind of stuck. I told my inner being repeatedly that I didn't love him. But I guess you can't keep lying to yourself. I sighed and pushed all the papers back, as I picked up my phone, going to my Twitter, and other social media accounts.

My phone chimed, and I pulled my notification bar down, reading the text.

*305-549-2134: Hey, this is Rashad from the photographer agency. We'd love to have you back, Jaidah! Call me back, I'd like to take some personal head shots of you."*

Rashad was a very sexy man. He's always looking at me in a different light. Maybe I needed someone. Someone who was never like JaKobe. But getting a man was not going to help my heart. I had to fix my own broken heart.

# Chapter 4

## Collateral Damage

*JaKobe Harrison*

Leaving Mrs. O'Neil's house felt iffy to me. Seeing Jaidah, I knew I screwed up all the way up and then some. Just to think of how it all went down, I blamed myself because I was a complete asshole towards her. I really wanted it to go fine, for her to just to change her mind. So, we could be good again like the old days.

*"Jai?"*

*"What, JaKobe? You really broke my heart. And you play like we are cool. You can't just try and make things right like we don't have bridges burned already!" I looked at her, I could just see all the pain in her eyes.*

*"Stop being like that. You were always stubborn. You can keep holding a grudge against me."*

*"Ha, you think I can't? You led me on. How do you expect me to forgive you after that, JaKobe?"*

*"If you give me a chance, I can fix it. I'll do better. Like I should have back then. I'm speaking up now, Jai. When I saw you walk in the house after all these years, you just don't know what that did to me. We haven't spoken in years and to hear your voice made a nigga heart ache. You just don't get how much I missed you."*

*"Now you want to speak the fuck up. The damage is done, nigga!" I looked at her and realized this wasn't the same soft Jaidah from when we were kids.*

*"I'm sorry, but seeing you made me feel somehow." She scoffed at my apology. "Can we just talk? We should be friends, you know—Let the past go and start over. I know you miss me as much as I miss you." I stepped closer, grabbing her waist, trying to pull her as close as possible.*

*"Okay, I'm sorry." She gave me a big smile.*

*"Alright, so, where do we go from here?" I asked.*

*"We try to figure this out. JaKobe, if you truly want me back, you need to see your faults. And maybe we can get past and I can't let go of the hurt you gave me. I don't want to hate you at all. But you need to fix this. That's the only way we can get back right."*

If the conversation went like that, we'd be good. I fucked up more than once with her. I wish that was how our conversation went. But I had to face it that we fell off a long time ago. And there was no coming back from that. I pulled into my driveway, seeing that *"Miss. Spend A Lot"* was here as well. I parked the car right beside her, and got out with the food that Momma J said I could bring home. I was going to bring my mom her plate the next day, because it was too late now. And I knew she was sleeping.

I walked up the brick steps, as I fiddled with my keys. I found the right one and keyed myself in. The house smelled of the *Bamboo Rain* air freshener as I walked in. I slid off my timbs, and walked into the kitchen, putting all the food in my fridge. I scratched my hair as I pulled out an ice-cold beer. It was a long day, and I felt like I needed one.

I walked away from the fridge after closing the door. I popped the cap open, and was just about to put it against my lips when I hit my bad leg against the wooden panel.

"Muthafucka!!" I hissed and yelled as I slammed the bottle down on the counter to rub my leg. It was stupid of me that I haven't been going to my therapy sessions. But I thought the pain was gone; I was completely wrong. Being deep in those streets really messed me up for a long run. When the pain was gone after a few minutes of rubbing it, I grabbed the cold bottle and walked up the steps to my bedroom.

I heard Tracy's voice coming through the cracked door. Soon as I opened the door, she quickly hung up the phone.

"What's up? Who was that?" I questioned, as I sipped some of the beer and placed it on a coaster while I slipped off my jacket.

"Oh, no one important," she said, smiling at me. I raised an eyebrow at her, but didn't question her because I didn't have time for her mouth.

"Humph, alright," I said, shrugging as I continued to strip out of my clothes. When I was down to my boxers, she called out my name.

"Oh! I forgot this came for you today in the mail," she held out her hand holding the pink envelope. I nodded as I grabbed it. She got up, walking into the bathroom. Tracy wasn't the kind of woman to ask you how your day or anything else was. I rolled my eyes as I looked at the envelope. Important message enclosed.

I frowned as I ripped it open. I heard the shower cut on. I grabbed my beer and read the letter as I sat in the edge of the bed.

*Dear Mr. Harrison,*
*We are notifying you that your house payment is three weeks past due. We are giving you till 8/7/20 to pay your overdue charges or your house, car, etc. will be foreclosed:*
*Amount of 2,336.97$ is due—*

I stopped reading it and sipped some more of my beer. I got up from the bed, busted into the bathroom and pulled the glass door back. I looked at Tracy as she snapped her head at me.

"Oh my god! You—"

"Why don't you pay the damn bills? All I asked you to do was pay the bills and you can't even do that! The fuck Tracy, what the hell did you do with the money I gave to you for fucking bills?" Her eyes looked in every direction but mine.

"You can't hear now?" I said, pissed off as ever.

"I did pay them."

"That's a lie, yo'! What the fuck did you do with that bill money? Knowing damn well I haven't been playing football right now! So, I'ma ask again, what the fuck did you do with my money? 'Cause your ass don't work!" She rolled her eyes,

"I paid those bills so you can shut up," she said, mumbling. I licked my lips and walked out of the bathroom. I went into my room and in our closest, pulling out every new bag she had. I heard the shower cut off as I was pulling stuff out: Michael Kors, Chanel, Givenchy, Jimmy Choo, Gucci, Versace, and fucking Wal-Mart bags. All the damn money I give her towards her shopping, and she can't do one simple thing? Like pay damn bills!

"What are you doing with my stuff?" she yelled as I threw everything on the bed. But I ignored her. I was not about to be put out of my place because of her. "JaKobe! I know you hear me! What are you doing?" She was more nervous now.

"I'm taking this shit back! I'm getting my fucking money back and paying the gat'damn bills! Now move, man!" But she wouldn't. She was about to cry over some damn clothes.

"Baby?"

"Don't baby me! Why the hell did you buy all this shit like you Queen Sheba or some shit! You ain't rich, far from that! Now why you buy all this!"

She sighed. "I bought it for my niece for her birthday." She was fucking lying again. She didn't even associate with her siblings 'cause she thought she was all high and mighty,

"Fucking liar!"

She grabbed me. "Okay, okay! I bought the stuff and then I'm going to sell it. And use the money for—" I slammed my hand on the dresser top,

"Use the money for what! And you better not lie! I'm already pissed the fuck off!"

She fiddled with her thumbs. "I can't tell you."

I shrugged. "Then you can get out. Just that simple. How about that?"

She grabbed my arm. "I don't wanna leave. You know I love you and I'm sorry. I'm using the money to start up my own salon. I swear."

"Well, lying wasn't the way to do it. I'm taking all this back and paying what it was supposed to be paid with. I'm pissed off to the maximum. So you can sleep on the couch, don't even think about sleeping in the guest room. You can sleep your lying ass on the hard sofa." I turned my head from her, and grabbed all the bags. I was sick of the lying. If she was to lie again soon, I was going to be done with her ass for good.

I felt her grab me, and I yanked away. "Don't touch me, yo'!" I pushed her out of my room and locked the door. If anyone found out about this, they'd call me a fool. Like Jaidah did. I shook my head, and went into the bathroom and stopped when I heard Tracy's voice.

"Babe! Open up! I need some clothes" I shook my head, closed the bathroom door and got into the shower. I needed some type of stress reliever. Because I know I wasn't getting it from Tracy ass. She was the damn stress, and now all I could think about was Jaidah even though I didn't want to. But I did think about her. Then everything bad that I did to her came rushing back.

"Maybe I am just a fool." I got out of the shower a few minutes later. I had a towel wrapped around me, and I sat in my bed, lying back.

"Damn! I can't get her off my mind." I closed my eyes, and that night popped into my head:

*I looked at Jai, and she swayed her hips to the music. She was out-of-this-world gorgeous. And I wanted her bad. I had a few drinks before I came to the frat party. I was drinking there as well. But I felt a little weird inside. I couldn't fail her. And, after she told me what happened to her sister, I knew I had to mend her heart in some way.*

*But another part of me didn't want to. I looked at Tracy, and she was grinding on some dude, making me jealous. "Why you staring at her? Go dance, dude!" Mike shouted, as he shook my shoulders.*

*"I wasn't staring." I lied. I was staring at Jai, that tight dress had her body on ten.*

*"Lie again." He chuckled. "But, did you tell her?" I nodded and took a sip of my drink.*

*"It felt good telling her. Now I just gotta' finish the bet."*
*He raised an eyebrow.*

*"Is she ready for all that, though? I don't think you should do that stupid bet, man?"* He was right, but I kind of figured she wanted to do this with me for I don't know how long. Her body was so tempting. But she was my friend. I didn't even notice she was coming my way.

*"Make up ya' mind, bruh. I gotta go. Felicia is, ya' know, waiting on me to fill her up."* I shook my head at their bipolar relationship, as Jai was inches from me. I had already decided what's was going to go down tonight—

My eyes shot open. And I rubbed my face. I could never escape that night. I could never escape all the pain I caused her. I was going to have to earn her friendship back.

\*\*\*

**The Next Day**

After taking back all the shit Tracy bought, I went to my momma house because I needed to visit and bring my momma her plate. I wasn't going to tell her about Tracy because she didn't like her in the first place.

"Aye, momma, ya' chile is home," I said loudly, as I came into the house, closing and locking the door behind me. My mom was sitting on the couch, drinking a nice glass of wine while watching one of her soaps.

"Hey, son! It's high time you came over here. You were supposed to come last night with my plate. You know Jill is my best friend." I smiled as I put the plate in the refrigerator and walked back into the living room. "Boy! Take ya' shoes off in my house!" she snapped.

"Alright, ma, my bad." I nodded and kicked my shoes off by the door.

"So how you been feeling, mama?" I asked.

44

"I've been doing okay. Your father is at work." She sipped her wine.

"Have you been taking your medicine, mama?" I said, looking at her, then the TV. She nodded and patted my hand.

"Don't worry about me, boy. I've been taking care of myself very fine. But have you? Jill told me what happened yesterday with you and Jaidah."

I knitted my eyebrows together, but nodded.

"A'ight, ma. I can see where this is going." She gave me a stern look.

"Boy, do not get disrespectful with me! What you said to that girl was flat out wrong! You treat that Tracy whore like a queen. But when you finally see Jaidah again, you do something dumb! When will you finally realize the truth? When something bad happens?"

I sighed.

"Mama—" She cut me off.

"Don't mama me! You are so stubborn, and what you said to Jai was just damn wrong. You should be ashamed of yourself."

I nodded.

"I'ma make it right with her."

"Okay," she said, as she turned back to the TV. I talked with my mom before I left her place. I had to take care of a few things at the football camp and the office.

"You're leaving? When will you be back? You know your sister has been a hot head lately."

I nodded.

"I know. I don't know if I'll have to fire her, mama. She just been too—"

"Hard-headed? Like you? Hmm."

I laughed and nodded. I gave her a hug and a kiss before I stepped out of the house. I'd call up my pops later. But right now I had to figure out some things.

\*\*\*

I walked into the tall brick building, and was greeted by the receptionist.

"Hello, Mr. Harrison, how is your morning going?—Oh, and you have a few fax and calls waiting for your response," she said in a pleasant British tone, and a million dollar smile.

"I'm doing great, Ailsa. Thanks for asking, and you seem to be in a great mood, so I know Duncan has asked you out, huh?" She nodded and passed me the papers.

"Of course! He was so sweet with it."

"That's great to hear. Now, is my sister in her office?"

She bit her lip and nodded.

"Oh, uh, yeah," she mumbled, and I knew something was up; she was covering for my sister, why?

I nodded and made my way upstairs,

"No need to even be nervous. This just might be my sister's last day—" Going straight for her office room, I grabbed the knob to the door, but it was locked. "What?" I said to myself as I jiggled the lock.

"Jada! Open this door!" This is not how my business is supposed to be working. The sound of commotion made me pull out my keys. This business was for kids to get ready for their dreams. Not for her shenanigans.

Before I could even stick the key in, the door flew open. "Uh! Um, JaKobe? What are you doing here so early?" I pushed the door open, and some man was in my office, fixing his clothes.

"It's not what you think, O!" I just had to keep my anger in check. But my damn sister was having sex with some random dude in the office. My place of business that I was going to give to her when I got my football career back in check,

"I don't know who you are! But you better get ya' shit and step!" The dude nodded and ran out the door. I slammed my door, and shoved Jada into the seat.

"The hell is this about?" She shrugged, and sat there with her arms crossed. Jada was only twenty-one years old, and she was already on a bad path unlike me.

I was young as well. I was going to be twenty-five in November. Jada wasn't even close to that yet.

She looked up to me too much. But then again, I was dogging out Jaidah.

"You can't keep doing this! Random guys? Really when are you going to actually settle down and have someone that actually cares? You need to worry on beauty school and worry about finalizing your management degree. You're so smart. You're better than this, you have to do better. And I mean it! I was thinking of giving you all of this. But you ain't proving shit to me. Mom and dad are gon' whoop yo' grown ass if I tell them. So, you need to get it together and fast! I am not about to tell you this again, I mean it Jada Lera Harrison! You're so close to being fired!" She rolled her eyes, and crossed her arms over her chest. Like she didn't have a damn care in the world.

"Okay, I get it! You don't have to call out my government name. Geez! I will do better. I'm already embarrassed." She hung her head low,

"And you should. Next time you use my receptionist again, we gon' have serious problems. Now, get back to your desk and do some work. This place is for kids! Did you forget? Damn!" I looked at the papers I had in my hand, and it said that Elhae, a new artist, wanted to have a photo shoot with some of the kids. It would be great publicity.

I pushed past her, walked over to my desk, picked up my phone and started to make a few calls. As I looked down at all of the papers, one name stood out: Rashad Evans, the best photographer in Atlanta. And one of my close friends.

Monet Dragun

# Chapter 5

## You Think I'm Hollywood?

*Jaidah O'Neil*

"So? Basically, he had the monkey balls to say some shit like that to you! He is dead ass wrong for that." I looked out of the window, as we drove to get us some breakfast.

"He sure did—But he goes home to a gold-digger who wanna be me so bad—But I checked his ass real quick," I said, looking at my nails that needed a filing,

"I still can't believe he still with her. So, he even see the shit she post on social media?"

I shrugged.

"Hell, I don't follow the long neck heffa. So I wouldn't know." We stopped at a light, and she passed me her phone. I unlocked it and went to her social media.

"You follow her?" I asked, laughing.

"Yes! I want to be nosey and get the low-down tea!" she said, snapping her finger and turning the street. We were going to our photo shoot. I busted out laughing at the photos I scrolled through. This girl was crazy. Why was she trying to dye the ends of her hair purple? Girl, you can't do me.

"Well, continue being nosey. 'Cause she can never be me, period." Before I could pass the phone back to her, I gasped. "Uh uh! Wait, she is using the Purple Unicorn too? She doing way too much."

She laughed and shook her head. "Yes! He don't even follow her. She be flaunting money and stuff. Like knowing damn well she broke as a joke and getting all that money from JaKobe. JaKobe is so stupid. But you know what? I think she's a lesbian."

I snapped my head at her. "No! How you know? Bitch, you lying!" I said, shocked.

"Jai, I'm bisexual and you know this—So I think I know a low down bitch when I see one," she said, rolling her neck. Monica and I were friends since we were in diapers. She had never come onto me and never tried to. Monica liked men as much as women. And she came out to me. I was the first person she told. It was hard for her to do so. But we were such good friends, besides me and JaKobe when we were close.

"Well, you know I be forgetting. Bitch, you be having more men than anything." She laughed at my comments.

"I mean, I have interest in a woman. But we're just talking, you know!"

I nodded. My phone buzzed, and it was Rashad telling me our spot was now open. We were early and on our way. We never were late to our shoot; that would cost us money.

"I understand," I said, not looking up from my phone as I was texting.

"Humph? You not even paying me any mind. Who got your attention?"

"Huh? Oh, no one," I lied. She rolled her eyes as we pulled into R.E. Studios. I passed her phone to her, as I grabbed my purse. She fixed her hair in the mirror. Then she pulled the key out of the ignition, and we both got out of the car.

Monica sported a mini shirt dress with the sides cut. It was maroon and velvety. She had on her black and gold Calvin Klein cat shades on, with exquisite heels that complimented her dress all the way. Monica was the definition of *slim-thick*. But she didn't let her figure go to her head.

I was slim all the way down to my toes; nothing more, nothing less. We walked up into the studio, and the receptionist looked up at us with a smile. "Hello, welcome to R.E. Studios. Names, please—And do you have an appointment?" she said in a pleasant tone.

*Monica Hayes*

"Yes, Monica Hayes and Jaidah O'Neil. We have a photo shoot appointment for 4:15," Monica said with a smile. The receptionist typed away at her desk computer and looked back up at us.

"Okay, just found it. You two are right on time. Just go straight to the back and make a left. Mr. Evans is waiting for you. He just got done with the 3 o'clock shoot." We both nodded and waved at the woman as we headed to the back.

"Thank you, Clarissa? Right," I said, looking at her name tag and saying it perfectly.

"Yes, and you're welcome—Have a wonderful shoot," she said before we walked off. His studio was beautiful. He had portraits of all the celebrities he did work with. Rashad also had beautiful white furniture and art pieces everywhere. This man was a true artist.

We turned left like she said, and were met with beautiful French doors. Monica was already in front of me, so she opened the door. "Girl, his studio is the shit," Monica whispered. I nodded in agreement as we walked in. Rashad was sitting at his desk, looking at his Dell laptop. The door softly closed behind us, causing him to look up. His eyes immediately landed on Jaidah, like I wasn't next to her.

*Rashad Evans*

"Oh! Hello, ladies. I was waiting on you two. You're right on time. Have a seat. I'm just editing these last head shots." They sat on the plush cream sofa. I noticed both were gazing at the luscious and luxurious racks of clothes.

"Okay, so my team is about to come in and do y'all make-up and wardrobe. So to answer your unasked question, *yes*, those are the clothes for this shoot." I smiled. I could see Jaidah eyeing my fit. And my fit was definitely on point. I had on the complete outfit from the Yeezy collection. The holly shirt gray, ripped shirt, white jeans, and the Yeezy Boost "Oxford Tan". Shid, I even had on the hat. Personally, I could say that I looked good. Besides, by the way Jaidah was looking at me, she thought a nigga looked good too. I could see Monica nudge her in the side; that's when we broke eye contact. Jaidah huffed as she snapped her head at Monica.

"What?" Jaidah said in a whisper.

"Why you are staring at him like that?" Monica said with a smirk. I shook my head, playing it off like I didn't hear them, as I chuckled. They didn't pay any attention to me, but I did pay attention to her particularly. Jaidah shook her head as she pinched the bridge of her nose; her cheeks were turning a bright rose red.

"What you shaking your head at, Jaidah?" Monica laughed.

"Leave me alone," she said playfully, as I rolled my eyes. Truthfully, Jaidah and I had been talking but not too deep. Only because she didn't want it to go that far.

"Okay, ladies. We're ready for you." They stood up, then headed to the small, closed off section. The ladies had pulled the racks of clothes in. "Okay, I want Jaidah in the Brian Lichtenberg outfit, and Monica in the Scot Louie. I want the make-up to be natural, no need to pile the make-up on their faces. I want these shots to be of the lighting and natural look." The stylist and make-up artist complied, as the women were directed to their chairs to start the process.

"How would you like Jaidah and Monica's hair?" my chief hair stylist said. She parted through Jaidah's hair. Jaidah looked up at me with a smile. There was no way she could hide her blushing face. She was so red in the face. Just my general presence made her feel warm inside.

"Well, she has the beautiful purple curly hair. So let's keep it that way, and Monica's hair is to be straight bone. It fits her high cheek bones well." They nodded and soon finished up with their hair.

*Jaidah O'Neil*

I was put in a purple Lichtenberg bra top and matching pants, with a feathered black fur. Monica had on this beautiful black and white bra top, with a patterned black and white dress.

"Let's get this thang crackin'. Jai, you're up first—"

I stood on the purple background and posed as he took the pictures.

"Okay, tilt your head down a bit, there we go! Beautiful." I showed off the clothes nicely and made myself look gorgeous.

\*\*\*

"That was a fun shot!" Monica said.

"Glad you had fun, ladies—But um, Jaidah, can I talk to you?" Rashad said. Monica looked at me, nudging me forward.

"Yeah? What's up?" I asked. The way he looked at me just gave me butterflies.

"Yo' Jai! I need to make a call. I'll be in the car." Before I could say a word, Monica was headed for the door. Now I could give him my full attention. Rashad sat on the sofa, then I took a seat next to him.

"So are you doing anything this weekend?" he questioned, getting right to the point. I shook my head.

"Not at all, why?"

Rashad smiled and his hand touched my bare thigh, making the heat shoot through my body. My heart thumped as he looked at me.

"Listen, the moment you came back here, I couldn't stop thinking about you, Jaidah. So, will you go out with me? We've been putting each other out on the back burner for a while now. Ya' know? I'd love to take you on a date. I want to move forward with you. But, I can tell you won't let me in." He looked into my eyes. I started to fidget with my fingertips. Rashad knew how I could get. He reached out to grab my hands softly. "Just talk to me," he said gently.

"Rashad, it's just some things I've been through. I don't want to go hurting you and—"

"Leading me on?"

I sighed and nodded.

"How do you know if you won't try?" he said, inches from my face.

"Because this always happens. Rashad, you such a good guy and I don't want to hurt you or put you through bullshit just because—" He grabbed my chin softly and kissed me, his tongue grazing my bottom lip. His tongue entered my mouth as our heads moved in sync.

He pulled away, and our eyes opened, just staring at each other. "So? Will you go out with me? I'm not who you think I am. I generally like you for who you are." His hand ran down my shoulder as he bit his lip.

"I'll go out with you—Just tell me what you want from me— Tell me before I start falling for you deeper than I already am," I said, as my eyes searched his.

"I don't want nothing from you. But your trust—I see you in the media, in Hollywood, and in the magazines. And all I be saying to myself is damn I wish I had that girl from Hollywood." He was inches from my face. My heart was thumping even faster.

"I'm not all that special," I said, as our foreheads finally touched.

"But to me—To me—You are."

*Beep.*

"Mr. Evans, your five o'clock is here. Should I send Mr. Harrison up?" Inside I was flipping out. He pressed the button and looked away from me,

"In about five minutes, yes." Rashad said to his receptionist.

"Okay," she replied.

Rashad focused his attention back on me.

"So, Hollywood? Do I have a chance with you?" he said.

I nodded. I was feeling him.

"Trust me, I don't give up on what I want. And what I want is you." His lips touched mine again.

"You have a client, and I should get going. I'll call you. And I'll put the picture on my Instagram page and the rest of my social media."

He smiled, and so did I.

"You know, if I didn't have a client—" his lips grazed my ear and neck, "I'd show you how much I really feel about you."

"Slow down there, tiger. My friend is waiting on me, so I'ma get going. Okay, Shad—" He nodded, and we both got up from the couch. I gave him a hug before I walked out. I walked out of there feeling happy. If he was who he said he was, he deserved a chance. I couldn't make every guy to be like JaKobe. I'd never have any relationships if I did that. My heels clicked against the wooden floor, as I walked towards the front door,

"Goodbye, Clarissa. You'll be seeing me again."

She smiled. "Goodbye, to you too, Jaidah!" I walked straight past JaKobe as he watched me walk away. I wasn't going to dwell in the past anymore. JaKobe was my past. And I was planning on keeping it that way.

Monet Dragun

# Chapter 6

## The Truth Will Set You Free

*JaKobe Harrison*

"Goodbye, Clarissa. You'll be seeing me again." She smiled, that one-in-a-million smile.

"Goodbye to you too, Jaidah!" She walked straight past me. She knew damn well I was watching her as he walked straight out that door, acting like I was invisible.

"Mr. Harrison, he's ready for you now."

I nodded and got up. What was Jaidah doing here in the first place? Yeah, I know she's a model and all. But why she come out with that glow and shit?

*Why am I acting jealous? That's not my girl. Get it together, O.*

I walked down the hall, sauntering into the Rashad's studio room. He was looking at his phone as he sat at his laptop. He looked up, and nodded at me.

"JaKobe, my man. So you came to discuss the photo shoot with the kids?" I nodded, walked up to the cream sofa and sat down. As I pushed my cap to the back, he got up from his seat and sat in the plush red chair. I couldn't help but notice some pink lipstick on his gray shirt collar.

*I know this nigga wasn't kissing on Jai, or was he?*

"So? This was the idea I had. We have a nice function, ya' know, raise money for them. And take pictures of them in there. More publicity for you and your biz, ya' feel me?"

I nodded. I began to rub my chin hair before I spoke.

"I was thinking we should get an artist to perform. I know them well. And they favor Drake. Plus, I'm cool with him. So we can get him, and take pictures of him with the kids as well." He nodded, typing some stuff down.

"This is going to be dope," Rashad said. "Should we have this at the end of the month?" he added.

I nodded. But I still had this question on my mind,

"Yo', who was that bad chick that left your office before I came in here?"

He looked up at me and frowned.

"Oh! Jaidah O'Neil, the chocolate princess that just left?"

I nodded. "Yeah, her."

"Man, she fine. I photographed her and her friend, Monica Hayes. They both some bad models. But Jaidah—Yo', she is something truly special."

*Yeah, nigga, I know.* "You feeling her, dog?"

He hesitated for a moment, but then nodded.

"Yeah, I am. Do you know her?" he questioned.

"I don't know her," I lied. He nodded and finished up some stuff. His phone buzzed, and his ass smiled at the text. I shook my head. "Aye, I know you got some shit to finish up. And I got somewhere else to be. Text me the rest of the details. I'm out, fam." He got up and dapped me up, giving me a bro hug.

"Aye, for'sho."

I gave him the deuces and walked out of his establishment. I made it to my car as my phone buzzed. I took it out of my pocket, and it was Bradley. I was kind of expecting it to be Tracy. I haven't talked to her or seen her all day. I had been out since early this morning. Maybe I'll make her a dinner or some romantic shit.

My phone continued to buzz before I answered it. "Yo'!" I said as I got into the Jag.

"Aye, you should shoot to my crib. My lil' rugrats are asleep and my girl got me on baby watch while she out getting her a spa day with her little sister and mama. So, you should come through. Before they wake up and torture me." He laughed.

"You know you love them kids. But I gotta handle some business, so I can't. But you know of Jaidah talking to some nigga name Rashad?" I asked as I frowned up. I pulled off and was heading to the store to get a few things.

"Uh? No, why?" he said, kind of avoiding my question.

"Yeah, you knew! Man, why you covering it up?" I said, driving down the road.

"Because you got a girl, don't you? Why you worried about what my sister doing?"

I sighed.

"I ain't worried about no one—I'm just asking," I said, giving him a testy attitude,

"Aye, check all that. What my sister do is her business. She been through a lot with guys. And I can honestly say Rashad is cool people. If she wants to be with him, then she can. My sister is fully grown. She don't need my or your permission! Now I wanna know what went down with y'all. Y'all was like two peas in a pod. Did you do something to her to make her hate you so gat'damn much? I mean we boys, so what'chu do?"

I wasn't going to tell him, because I was the one who did his sister dirty. If I was to say anything, it would most def be a fight.

"Nothing, I ain't do nothing. Me and Jai just grew apart. And we just fell off. But I gotta' go. I gotta get some shit going." I rushed him off the phone.

"Yeah, whatever, man. There better not being nothing more than that. Well, one baby just woke up so that mean the whole house about to be chaos. Peace."

"One." The phone beeped, and I slid my phone in the cup holder. I ran my hand down my face, as I continued down the street. I turned on the radio and let the hard melody of Snoop Dogg's raps fill my ears.

I just couldn't bring myself to tell him what really went down. I shook my head, as I finally pulled into the grocery store. But I had to hurry up before I got swarmed by fans. I parked my car in the parking lot and made sure I was a little in disguise. I slipped on my shades and turned off my car as I got out. I fixed my hat and clothes.

I grabbed me a basket and walked up to the door. The sliding doors opened, and I walked in, going straight to the vegetable and fruit section. As soon as I did that, I heard my name being called.

"Oh my god! It's JaKobe Harrison!"

I sighed to myself but with a smile. They all ran up to me and gave me hugs. The boys wanted to know about me coming back to the football team. And the girls where in awe. Even the grown women were acting up. I was going to be here for a while.

\*\*\*

I decided to make the food at Tracy's house because I knew she'd be at mine. I was just going to call her over here or go pick her up. So she can look real nice. When I pulled in, I just parked in her driveway instead of the garage. I didn't have the parking garage lock anyway.

After I got swarmed at the Marino's for about a good thirty minutes, I got my groceries and everything else I needed to actually do something sweet for her. Even though she got on my nerves at times, she was still my girlfriend. She never did this for me, but I did for her; well, some times. I walked into the dark house and turned on the light.

I put all the things in the countertop. The house was quiet and peaceful. It was pitch-black when I came in, so I just kept one light on just in case she came in. I had bought chicken, and stuff for pasta. I had mushrooms, peppers, onions and more. I got the recipe off of the Food Network Show. I had got stuff to make brownies—the box brownies, not that homemade stuff. I was going to take my time and actually try and cook. Hopefully won't burn up everything.

I washed my hands, and started getting everything ready. I had pulled up the recipe in my phone, and was following every direction. I was surprised my damn self that I ain't burn shit up. The chicken was cooking nicely, as I started cutting up the vegetables. I was getting down, and was about to turn on some music. I had to flip over the chicken and put a little seasoning on it. I was getting happy because—for once—the relationship was going to turn out well. I was going to fix all of this. I walked over to the cabinet to grab some olive oil. Then I got some cream out of the fridge.

When I walked back to the counter top, I paused when I heard some noises coming from upstairs. I stopped what I was doing, and looked around. "What the hell was that?" I put the knife down, and walked towards the stairs. I heard even more bumping as I moved further. "If a damn burglar in this house—" I walked up the steps slowly, as I kept hearing the loud bangs. I didn't think nothing of it. It sounded as if someone was rambling in the damn upstairs bedroom.

"What the fuck!" As I got to the top of the steps, the banging got louder, and then I knew it wasn't a fucking thief. I walked to her room, the door was closed. My heart thumped as I was so close to it, I pressed my ear to the door. The banging was coming from that room. Sex sounds. "Oh fuckkk, yes, daddy! Gat'damn harder! Uh! I'ma cum—Just like that— Ahhhh! Yes, yes, yessss! Fuck!—"

I heard it all. And I was pissed off to the max. All the signs were there, and I didn't even see the shit! I grabbed the knob and twisted it slow. The door crack opened, and the soft music filled my ears, alongside the moans and the banging of the head board. I pushed the door open, and looked at the sight before me:

Tracy—on the bed. Face down. Ass up, held down by a bitch. An actual bitch who was fucking her in the bed.

I stuck in one spot. I dropped whatever was in my hand. But they didn't stop or hear what it was.

"Oh! Yes, Karma! Right there, you hitting my spot, baby girl!" Tracy shouted. I couldn't believe this, my girl was getting fuck by another girl.

"What the fuck is this!" I shouted finally, snapping out of the sicken trance I was in. They stopped, and Tracy snapped her head at me. I walked in, and the girl jumped back. I pushed her and mushed Tracy's head.

"It's not what it looks like!" she shouted.

"Oh! Oh! It ain't? Then what the fuck is it? A damn magic trick! You're cheating on me with some loose pussy bitch! That's what the fuck it looks like!"

The girl was about to say something, but I grabbed her by her weave. "Get the fuck out!"

She stumbled, and looked at Tracy. "Baby, you know I'll be back—" the woman named Karma spoke.

"Bitch, get the fuck out before I kill you!" She scrambled for her things, and I looked at Tracy as she looked at the woman then back to me.

"JaKobe, I didn't want you to find out like this! What are you doing here?" she screamed as she tried to push all of the toys off of the bed. I was so disgusted right now.

I laughed. "To do something loving for your gold-digging ass! And you go around and cheat on me! For how long? How long have you been cheating on me? Trading my dick for pussy! How long you been a carpet muncher and been kissing me? Huh! For how fucking long?" I screamed, hurt to the core, panting. She grabbed a pillow and hugged it as she covered herself. As if it was a teddy bear!

"I've been in the closet since college. I didn't really figure out I was into girls until I met Karma at a club when I was nineteen. Yes, you and me were dating. But I wasn't fulfilled. I was hiding the real me from myself. I couldn't do it anymore."

"Wasn't fulfilled! Really! So? Instead of trying to at least tell me the truth, you meet some bitch at a club and cheat on me! Instead of talking to me and at least giving me a chance to accept you, you go and cheat! How many times did you cheat on me and with how many guys—I mean girls?" She looked at everything but me. "I fucking said *how many*!" I screamed, picking up the Cîroc bottle and throwing it against the wall, shattering it and making her scream.

"More—More than Karma—And I'm in love with her. She does things that you can't. I'm sorry, JaKobe!

I felt my heart breaking. *Is this how Jaidah felt? This is what I get, this is what the fuck I get!*

"More—? More? as in what exactly?" I wanted answers.

"More, like: sex parties, twenty women, and one guy—I really didn't mean for you to find out this way," she said with tears. I stood there shocked.

"Wow! You know what? So you were buying shit for her. Okay. Okay. It's cool! It's all good!" I grabbed all her shit that I bought and began breaking it.

"Stop, JaKobe! I'm sorry!" she cried, but I wasn't hearing that. All the stuff I did, and this is what happens? This is how she does me!

"Wanna cheat and fuck bitches!" I threw heels and purses, tearing up everything in anger, grabbing jewelry and twisting it, throwing stuff out the window. I stomped on everything like she did my heart. "We are through! Over! But I bet you already knew that, huh!" She nodded. I knew she didn't care though. Then she spoke, and my hurt sunk in even more.

"But—I did love you." I turned around fast in rage mode and was inches from blasting her ass. She held up her hands, and I stopped with glossy eyes. I couldn't hit a woman. I turned around in utter hurt. She sat there crying, and I didn't care either. I walked towards the door.

"But guess what? I never loved your ass." Her sobs got louder, and I walked out of the room 'cause if I stayed I would have killed her. All the food I cooked, I threw it on the floor. All the wrong I did to Jaidah—This is exactly what I get. I walked out of the house and pulled out my phone. I texted Bradley, asking him for Jaidah's number.

Monet Dragun

# Chapter 7

## When That Hotline Bling

*Jaidah O'Neil*

My TV was on the Music Choice app. It faintly played August Alsina's latest album, as I laid on the phone talking to Rashad. We had been on the phone for a few hours now. And the way he was talking so sweetly to me made me feel like a little schoolgirl.

"Where do you want to go Friday night?" he said to me, as I twirled my hair around my finger.

"I don't know. I like Mexican food, Italian food, I can go on. I'm a girl who likes to eat."

"Just my type, how about Italian? It's romantic and I know the perfect place." The way he said it, you could totally hear his New Yorker accent.

"What's your type anyway?" I asked, as I looked at the magazine down on my bed. His voice broke my trance.

"I like girls like you: kind of short, brown skin or light skin, slim and fit, smart, gotta be real sharp with me, and beautiful. But looks don't matter to me. But you're just out-of-this-world gorgeous to me. You're very sweet, and your personality is so fun. Whatever guy did you wrong is an idiot,"

"You're such a sweet talker," I said, smiling.

"Only for you, actually. You make me feel some way. I can't really explain it. So don't ask." He laughed softly.

"Okay, so what are you doing now?" I said, looking around the room.

"By the music in the background, I can tell you want me to come over."

I began to blush.

"No, well—Monica isn't here. She's on some date, and I'm just here by myself," I said through the phone.

"Mmm, what do you have on, if you don't mind me asking?"

Butterflies began to form in my stomach. "I have clothes," I said smartly.

"Really—Come on. Stop playing with me. What you got on?"

I bit my lip. "Tank top and panties." He made a low groan over the phone. "What?" I said, trying not to laugh.

"I just imagined you sprawled all out in the bed. Please tell me you have a bra on?"

"Well—"

His deep voice cut me off. "Well, nothing. When can I come over?"

"Must you?" I asked, playing with him.

"Lord. I ain't trying go there with'chu. Enough of these mind games. You know you can't handle what I got." I bit my lip once again.

"You sure about that?"

"Hell yeah. I can do things to you that you'll love. I could have your body feelings all types of ways."

I moaned lightly, and I heard shuffling over the phone.

"You gon' stop playing with me. Where you live?"

I was about to tell him, but the line beeped on the other end. I smacked my lips. There was always something killing the mood.

"Hold on. Someone is in the other line."

"Okay, hurry up. I wanna see you."

I smiled and swapped the phone over to the other line.

"Hello?" I said, irritated that my call was interrupted.

"What's up?" the person said nonchalantly, but I didn't have time for games.

"For real who is this? I don't have time to be playing on the damn phone!" I waited for the person to respond. I was about to hang up when they finally said their name. I scoffed as I rolled my eyes. How in the holy hell did he even get my number!

"It's JaKobe. Can I talk to you please?" I got up from my bed, as the wind blew the curtains through the French doors. Monica's apartment was huge. Her room was in the first floor, and mine was in the second. Basically, my room was like my own little

66

apartment. The room was very spacious, and I had my own bathroom.

"JaKobe, how did you get my number firstly?" I said, standing up with my hand in my hip.

"Is that all important right now?" he said with a faint attitude.

"I'd check that attitude. You called me, remember? Now what is it that you want and how did you get my number? I'd answer quickly before I hang up nicely in your face. And block you without thinking twice about it." He sighed, and I tapped my nails on my hip.

"I got it from ya' brother. And you were right."

"Excuse me? I'm going to kill Bradley! And I'm right? Right about what? Last time I checked I didn't care what you did!" I switched the phone to the other ear.

"You were right about Tracy. You were right about everything. Now I had a little too many drinks. Can I come over?"

"Drinks equals trouble. How many have you had?"

"Too many to be driving. But I can function. I know how to handle my liquor."

I laughed loudly.

"Last time you said you can 'hold your liquor', bad things happened between us," I said without even caring about his feeling at the moment.

"I remember us both drinking that night. How long you gon' hold the shit against me, man?"

I laughed again.

"As long as I damn want to. Now I had someone on the other line—"

"Your little nigga Rashad?" he replied with venom in his tone.

"What's it to ya'? You should give a damn what I do? So what? Little Tracy Morgan cheating on you? She take all your money and blow it on strippers like her pictures on social media?"

"Fuck you, Jaidah!"

"You wish."

"So we're going to have a damn argument? I'm not in the mood for your antics, Jaidah. I just want to talk."

"Ha! It's a little too late for a "talk", don't you think? Tracy cheats on you, and you two break up? And now you wanna talk to me. Boy, bye! Why the fuck you wanna ring my hotline when shit goes wrong for you? Who the fuck do you think I am? A damn puppet? I don't play on your strings!"

"You still on that virginity bullshit? Man! Fucking blow me with all that!"

I was going to get mad, I wasn't going to get even, and I wasn't about to play his little games.

"You say that like I'm going to be fazed by it. You talking like you're the best shit walking. Exactly why we'll never be friends! Bad shit is going to keep happening to you. Maybe I have a little ugly voodoo doll of your burnt noodle head ass. Maybe I'll keep stabbing you in the heart like you do me. That's why your career failed, that's why your relationship failed, and every damn thing you try and do will fail. Wanna know why? Because you treat others like shit! And trust me—What you do onto others will be done onto you. Remember that, now goodbye. A real nigga with real game is on the other line. And yes, his name is Rashad."

*Click...*

I took a long deep break and felt good. I noticed I hung up on Rashad. Before I could even think and press the button to call him back, his name popped up in the screen.

Rashad was calling.

I hit the green answer button, and his deep voice hummed through the phone: "Why you hang up on me? That isn't very nice, ya' know? Only if I could punish you!" I looked up at the moon and stars. Still silent on the phone. "Hello? Jaidah? What's wrong?"

"You know that guy I told you about? The one that broke my heart when I was in college?"

"Yeah, that roach ass nigga? If you think I'd do you like that—I'd never play with your emotions."

"My virginity that I once had—" I said, swallowing hard,

"Yeah, that. Why you bringing that up? Who was that on the phone?" I knew JaKobe was one of Rashad's clients.

"It was him."

"Do I know him? Do I need to kick somebody ass?" Rashad said strongly.

"No."

"You sure?" he said sweetly.

"Yes. My address is 1276 Forcrest Lane, apartment number 46. I'm trusting you, Rashad. So, don't be late."

"You want me to come now?"

I smiled.

"Yes, now, silly—"

He groaned again, and it was even sexier this time.

"Can you be naked for me? I swear I ain't on nothing. You're just a work of art, and I wanna use you as my canvas." This man and his damn words!

"What kind of paint brushes will you be using?" I could tell he was smirking.

"My tongue—If you'll let me. I'll bring all the colors and goodies I'll be using. But the question is: will you let me satisfy you? We have known each other for a pretty long while. I won't rush you—"

"Be here soon. I'll be how you ask and even have my hair in a ponytail."

"Oh my god, sweetie! You got a nigga on hard, and we ain't even did anything. I'll be there in ten, and I'm not playing games with you. I hope you know that."

I licked my lips as I fell back in my bed, looking up at the ceiling.

"I'm not playing games either."

"Girl, I'm in the Benz now. I'm on my way."

I smiled. Now I knew he stopped everything he was doing for me at a drop of a dime.

"Hang up then," I said, biting my nail, and smirking. He laughed, and the phone call ended. I tossed my phone on the other side of me. I was in for a big one!

\*\*\*

As I sprayed *Love Spell* Victoria Secret perfume all over my body, my phone vibrated. I slipped on my satin robe and tied the slick sash around my waist, as I walked over to my phone. Looking down at it, it was Rashad, and I had a few texts and missed calls from JaKobe. I cleared them and then opened Rashad's text:

Rashad: *"i'm downstairs. Buzz me in..."*

I smiled and pulled my straightened out hair into a ponytail. I tossed my phone back in the bed, and walked out of my room. I skipped down the stairs, as I walked through the foyer. The buzzer went off, and I buzzed Rashad in, knowing it was him downstairs. I rubbed my lips around as the faint taste of strawberry entered my mouth.

A few moments later there was a knock on the door. My heart thumped as I walked over to the door and looked through the peephole. I unlocked the door, and opened it to an eager Rashad. He looked me up and down, and I stepped aside as he stepped in.

"Damn, you look good, Baby girl." He placed a sweet tender kiss on my cheek, and walked closer to me.

"Thank you, you look good always," I cooed.

"Not as good as you. Where can I keep the stuff?" Rashad said as he licked his lips.

I grabbed his hand as I led him upstairs. When we got up to my room, he pulled out everything and put all the candy syrup bottles on the dresser. He looked back at me and grabbed my hips softly, and began to kiss my neck.

"Can I take this off you?" Rashad questioned.

I nodded softly, as he untied the sash and pulled the slick robe off of my shoulders, making it fall to my feet. His soft lips left kisses on my shoulder blade, as he made sure to leave faint marks in my skin. His hands roamed my body, as he squeezed my breasts and ass. Before he pulled away, he smacked my ass lightly. "Body so damn fine! Lay down."

# To the Thug I Loved Before

I laid on the black sheets as he hovered over me.

"What are you going to do with me tonight?" He didn't answer me yet. He just continued to feel me up as he kissed my neck so good. I grabbed the back of his head, letting him know what he was doing felt exciting. His hand made its way to my sweet spot, and his thumb grazed my clit softly, making me bite my lip and moan.

"Nothing but sticky pleasure," he enthused, kissing my lips so good that he made my eyes flutter close. He pulled away as I slightly moaned. He walked away from the bed and came back with a blue and red bottle of candy syrup. He opened it and squirted it in my chest and stomach, making me giggle.

"It's cold."

He smirked, and he kissed me again. Rashad used his tongue as a brush on my skin, making swirls and designs, his tongue trailing down my skin as I shivered.

"I'ma treat you so good you ain't gon' know what to do with yourself tomorrow." His head went down to my wet coochie, and my mind and body went into bliss. What was this man doing to me?

Monet Dragun

# Chapter 8

## Nigga, You Know What's Up

*JaKobe Harrison*

I sat in my car. I had the hood up, and I was smoking a mild swisher. I knew I shouldn't be mixing liquor with drugs. But hell, my life was hell.

Turns out my ex-girlfriend is gay.

Jaidah don't want shit to do with me. She gotta nigga. I was just trapped in my own mind. I fucked up from the jump. My phone buzzed in my pocket, and my eyes slowly rolled as I fished it out of my pocket.

Tracy.

I went to the text and deleted it, not even caring what she had to say. My phone buzzed again, and I looked at the contact name:

Brad.

I slid the incoming text message down, and read what it had to say. It was just Jai's address. I mean, what was I supposed to do? She checked me up, down, left, and right. Looking back up to the sky, I thought of her.

That purple hair.

That curvy body.

That smart mouth.

She was everything a nigga wanted. But that nigga had her. Then I thought about what she said just an hour or two ago.

*"You say that like I'm going to be fazed by it! You talking like you're the best shit walking. Exactly why we'll never be friends. Bad shit is going to keep happening to you. Maybe I have a little ugly voodoo doll of your burnt noodle head ass. Maybe I'll keep stabbing you in the heart like you do me. That's why your career failed, that's why your relationship failed, and every damn thing you try and do will fail. Wanna know why? Because you treat others like shit! And trust me—What you do onto others will be*

*done onto you. Remember that, now goodbye. A real nigga with
real game is on the other line. And yes, his name is Rashad."*

I scrunched up my face as I thought of them two cuddling up
on the phone. I took a long drag of the blunt. I let it settle as I let it
blow out of my nose. It was messed up how she said bad things
would just keep happening to me. But look at my life now. It was
all screwed up. My football career was damn near washed up, my
love life was flushed down the drain, and I didn't have my friend
that I missed honestly every day.

My lips held the blunt between my lips, as I started up the car
and backed up while I took a glance at her address. I typed it into
my GPS and let the cyber woman's voice take me there. I don't
care if I am drunk and high. I still had sense. Did I care that nigga
was there?

I hit the brakes and thought for a second. "Shit," I said out
loud, as I looked at the dirt road. I just remembered that I told him
that I didn't know her. I just couldn't pop up over there and he
answers the door. I'd probably hurt his ass and lose my promotion.

"Good going, JaKobe. Just good fucking going." I pulled the
blunt from my lips and blew out the smoke. I was just all
conflicted inside. I leaned back in my seat as I pulled off. I cleared
the GPS and just decided to drive home and sober up. I wasn't
going to mope over Tracy; that's just something I didn't do. It
wasn't in my nature to really care.

Everyone thought I was so mean. But they didn't know the
real me, not like Jaidah did. It was pissing me off that I thought of
her ever second of the day and she didn't think of me at all. I
shrugged off the feeling, and turned on my radio. I made my exit
into the highway. The cool night air blew through my hair, as I
cruised down the highway.

The sounds of sirens filled my ears, and I looked into the
rearview mirror and saw a cop car behind me. "What the fuck!" I
blew out a flustered breath, and eased over to the side of the
highway by the ramp. I slowly came to a stop and waited for him

to get out. I grabbed a piece of gum out of my pocket and popped it into my mouth, chewing it.

I muttered under my breath: "I wasn't fucking speeding. The hell yo' fat donut eating ass pulling me over for." His door opened, and I made sure to get my license and registration out of the glove box. He walked up towards my car as he looked down on me with his shades on.

"Hello, sir," I said as he stood there.

"Hello, license and registration please. Oh, and can you turn the music down?"

*Why the fuck I gotta turn my music down?*

"Here," I passed it to him, and he looked at it with his flashlight. "Is there a reason you pulled me over?" I said, lightly chewing my gum.

"You were speeding," he said kind of harshly.

"Officer, I just got off the bend. I wasn't speeding."

"So you're calling me a liar?"

"No, I'm telling the truth. I wasn't speeding. I just exited from the valley. How was I speeding?" He tucked my license and paper into his pocket and put his flashlight into my face.

"Get out of the car, sir." I grabbed my phone because there wasn't about to be no damn police brutality on me.

"Why did you pull me over? I was not speeding. I've seen this in the news to many times. I have a father that's a lawyer and a mother who is retired from the police force. I know better to not speed. Especially coming off that bend because a lot of people try to beat the traffic that way."

"Are you under the influence?"

"No."

"Why are your eyes dilated? Black people like you do drugs at this time of the night."

"Black people like me? Officer, I went to college. Graduated top of my class and I'm well-known in my community. For helping young lives like y'all supposed to do. So, please tell me, how am I like my fellow black community? And I'm recording this by the way." His face changed.

"Turn the phone off."

"You can't do that. This is called freedom of speech. Why are you bothering me?"

"Step out of the car, sir!"

"You pulled me over for no reason."

"I won't say it again."

"Why did your hand go to the clip of your belt? Haven't you heard of Black Lives Matter?" His nose flared.

"I don't care about black lives."

"Should I be calling my lawyer? This is police—"

"Step out of the goddamn car, sir!" he shouted.

"Did you forget I'm videoing this?" I showed the phone, and he calmed down. "I'll gladly send this to the press." He stepped back from my car.

"Sir—"

"I have your badge number too. You'll be hearing from my people. Hopefully you won't get fired. May I have my license and registration back, please?" He took it out of his pocket and handed it to me.

"Black nigger!"

"Recorded, may I go?"

He walked away from my car and got into his, speeding off. I stopped recording, and threw my phone into the passenger seat,

"Pig!" I shook my head and drove off. I think Jaidah got a damn root on me.

\*\*\*

The next day I was up, and leaving my mom and dad's place. I had just told them the bad news of my experience with Tracy, and other shit I was going through. Niggas was trying to mess up my trap; no one was going to stunt my game. I had one chance to get Chino out these streets. He was a pain in the plan I had to make it to the top.

# To the Thug I Loved Before

The music was blasting in my car. I was rapping Lil Baby's '*Errbody*', and knew all the words faithfully. He was rapping something real. Everything he was saying was true. I came to my destination—Monica's. I parked my car in the drive way. There were two cars, Jai's and Monica's. I was hoping she would at least talk to me.

I got out of the car, and dusted off my clothes. I had to fix this shit. I was tired of bad shit happening to me. I sighed as I knocked on the door. My heart rate picked up. I checked my breath.

*Good.*

I checked my hair.

*Could be better.*

The door opened to a half-dressed Monica. Her body was everything. But she ain't like men. Well, according to her words, "men like me".

"What are you doing here? And how did you find out where I live?"

"Hello, Mon," I said, rocking back on my heels.

"Mm-hm? What do you want?"

"Dang. Didn't get any pussy last night?" I said, raising an eyebrow. Her face softened, and she nodded.

"Wait! That's none of your business. What do you want, JaKobe?"

"JaKobe? You usually call me jackass, asshole, or—"

"Just what do you want?" she said, crossing her arms over her chest.

"For you to put on some damn clothes. You making me sick."

"Jaidah! Come get JaKobe before I kill him!" she shouted. She let me in, and shoved me as she pointed at my shoes.

"Man, okay."

"Thanks, Jackass. Oh, and socks too. I don't want your sock fuzz on my black furry rug." I rolled my eyes and took off my socks.

"Where is Jai?" I questioned, as she switched her tall frame into the kitchen.

"In her room. She likes her privacy. So I suggest you don't go in there."

"Yeah. Whatever. Where is her room?" I asked.

"You'll find it. And it's your funeral." She spoke loud enough for me to hear. I jogged up the steps, and looked down the hall. Which damn hall is her room? I walked down the first one I looked at, and a cracked door got my attention.

"Mom, what do you mean you can't take care of her?" she said through the phone. Leaning against the door frame, I listened to the conversation. Yeah, I'm nosey,

"Mama, calm down please. Everything will be okay. Wait! I'm too young to be taking care of kids, ma. Don't cry, please," she sighed.

What happened is what I wanted to know.

"Auntie is in a better place now. I'll be over there later to talk to you. Just get some rest, okay. I'll see what I can do about Cousin Jackie. I know—I wouldn't want her in a group home either. Okay, mama, okay. Bye." She hung up the phone, tossing it over on the bed. She placed her hands in her lap as she looked straight ahead.

I pushed the door open lightly. "What's up?" I said, stuffing my hands in my pocket. She turned around and looked me up and down. Her eyes were puffy, and her brown skin face was flushed.

"Why are you here? How are you here? Wait! Bradley told you where I stayed, didn't he?" she said, giving me a look. I nodded.

"I'ma kill him."

"You okay?"

"Why? You're not the caring type. Why are you here?"

"I wanted to talk to you face to face."

"What if I didn't want to talk to you face to face?"

I threw my hands in the air.

"Can you just listen to me? Damn!"

"No need for your NF," she said, folding her arms over her chest.

"The hell is a 'NF'?" I questioned with a baffled face.

"A nigga fit," she said with a stone face.

"Man, just shut up and listen."

"Come again?" she said with a raised eyebrow.

"Man, can you just listen to me?"

"I'm not a man, JaKobe. Speak to a woman like she's supposed to be talked to." Her tone was damn sharp.

"Can you please listen to me?"

"My ears are open."

"Well, you were right about everything. I should have listened to you. Tracy was a hoe. I don't know why I didn't see it."

"You didn't see it because you was blinded by her overly inhuman huge ass. Her ass could block the damn sun and kill us. But please continue."

I rolled my eyes.

"She cheated on me with a woman. I'm sorry for what I did to you. I was wrong."

She busted out laughing.

"Where's the damn cameras?—Cos that was so phony," she said with a straight face.

"I'm serious! What I did was for real dirty, and I want to apologize."

"No flowers? Some apology."

"Don't make me hurt you," I said, squinting at her.

"You already did that."

I licked my lips.

"I'm sorry for real. How long you gon' throw that in my face?"

She stood up and walked over to her window. "Do you remember that night? And don't play with me."

"Yes. Yes I remember—" I remember that night as if it was just another day. I could never forget that. She turned around and stood there staring into my eyes—my soul, to be more exact. My mind dozed off.

"I'll let you think about that. Then I'll give you your answer." She turned back to the window, and my mind wandered off to the night in the hotel—

*I led her into the hotel room. I had butterflies out of this world. And she was way beyond nervous.*

*"JaKobe, what if—what if it don't fit? What if you don't think I'm sexy? What if I don't do you good?" Before she could think of another what if, I turned around and pressed my soft lips against her neck, letting my hot peppermint breath fan her neck, making her shiver. "Relax, baby girl." She was so trapped in her thoughts after that. She didn't even know that I had pulled off her shirt.*

*I had her so frustrated. Sexually frustrated.*

*"Um, wait!" she managed to say as I planted small kisses on her soft spot on her neck.*

*"What's the matter?" I questioned in a serious and caring tone. "Please don't back out now."*

*"Do you want me? You know, in this way?" I chuckled and nodded. I grabbed her hips and pulled her closer to me, making her breath catch in her throat.*

*"I've wanted you in so many ways—You wouldn't believe it, I want more than sex from you—You should know that," I said to her. Presently, I smashed my lips into hers, running my fingers through her blonde curls.*

*Her mind and mine was so cloudy after that kiss. I licked and sucked on her bottom lip, begging her to let my tongue in. She let me as I softly grabbed her ass.*

*"JaKobe—" She gasped.*

*"Hmm?" I hummed against her skin. I picked her up ever so gently like a feather, as she wrapped her arms around my neck and her legs around my waist. It just made me smile at everything she did. I put her down, unzipped her dress and pulled it down. I trailed kisses down her back. I pushed her on the bed softly, and placed kisses down her stomach, making her shiver and squirm.*

*"Be still, baby," I told her, as she crinkled her eyebrows. As my kisses came up her body, I kissed her cleavage, reached under her and unhooked her bra. She couldn't control the moans as I licked and sucked on her nipples, biting them lightly. "Wait!" She moaned as I took off my boxers.*

*"Relax, baby, I'll go slow," I said, as I looked into her eyes. I could not believe this was happening. I was having sex with my best friend. I was going to regret this in the morning. I kissed her slowly on her thighs. I was making her feel so good. After this, I had to end it.*

*"O—JaKobe, be gentle with me." I nodded and stared at the thong she had on.*

*"I will, baby girl, but when did you start wearing these? Huh? Who you been wearing these for?" I said as I kissed her pubic area, making her back arch.*

*"JaKobe! I ain't been wearing them for nobody," she moaned.*

*"Mhm—You sure about that?" I said, as I kept planting soft kisses there, pulling the thing to the side, licking her intimate area softly. I bet she could feel her heart beating in her ears because her breaths started to pick up as I got up from my knees.*

*"Get on the bed, Jai." She nodded and leaned back on the bed, and I pulled down the thong she had on completely all the way off. I came closer to her, wrapping my arm around her, and planting kisses all over her neck and breasts.*

*"Mmm—That feel so good, O."*

*I got in between her legs, and she could feel my hard member poke her lightly. I started to grind against her, and it was driving me insane. I drove her even worse.*

*"Relax for me, baby. I promise, I'ma make you feel it and feel good." She nodded, and Jaidah leaned up and push me back a little. Her eyes widened as my dick sprung up. I chuckled and rubbed her thighs, bringing her back to reality. "Just keep calm." She swallowed hard.*

*"B-but—It's so big," she said, as she looked me up and down. I grabbed her by her chin, and kissed her deeply. She was making me feel bad.*

*"You actin' like you ain't see it before," I said playfully.*

*"Shut up—" She groaned as I laid on her, putting my weight on her. Jaidah wrapped her legs around me as we began to make*

*out again. And I knew the moment was about to come. Could she handle this? Damn? Could I handle this—*

When I looked back up at her, she had this evil look on her face.

"I'm sorry," I confessed.

"Will your sorry fix what you did? I trusted you, believed in you, and you shitted on me! It was a fucking bet, a bet to nail me then throw me away like trash! My virginity meant nothing to you. And you expect me to forgive you for that? Taking my fucking innocence and fill my head with lies?" Her eyes were bloodshot.

"Jaidah, I was young and dumb. I'm really sorry." Her face was making a gangsta break down.

"Sorry won't fucking fix it! Want to know the damn truth?" She walked up to me and began to poke my chest.

"What will fix it?" I spoke. My mouth was dry as she gave me the evilest look ever made by a woman. It was called hate.

"Can I get my virginity back? And give it to the right one! No! So nothing can fix this shit! But I will tell you the damn truth." Jaidah's words crushed me.

"What is it?" I said hesitantly. She poked my chest repeatedly, with anger laced in her throat,

"I absolutely loved you! But you didn't even see that. JaKobe Rico Thompson, I don't know if we'll ever be friends again!" She slapped my chest.

"You loved me? When was this?" I asked like a dumb ass.

She rolled her eyes. "Are you stupid? I mean really?"

"I am, sometimes—I do dumb shit. I'm sorry." I grabbed her arms. "I really am sorry. But for you to say your virginity meant nothing to me, is a lie! I thought of that dumb mistake every day!" She looked away from me. I just wanted her to forgive me.

"I was a teenager. And I don't love you anymore. Let me go." As she asked, I let her go.

"You love me as a friend?" I asked, trying to get her to look at me.

"The fuckery!" She pushed me off her, and I grabbed her wrist.

"How did you love me?" I asked, I just needed to know.

"More than a *friend*. But nigga, you know what's up? I don't love you *anymore*. I buried those feelings a long time ago. And I made sure to never love another fuck nigga like you again in my lifetime." I let go of her wrist.

"That's harsh."

"I had to become harsh. You'll be alright. We gon' be alright. I'm fucked up, homie, fucked up. But if God got us, then nigga we gon' be alright." She smiled.

"Please don't quote Kendrick Lamar," I said, running my hand down my face.

"Do you hear me? Do you feel me!"

I shook my head.

"Can we try to be cool?" I questioned once again.

She shrugged.

I groaned. "Jaidah!"

"What?"

"Can we start over?" I said, grabbing her chin to make her look at me.

"I'll get back to you—I said we gon' be alright," Jaidah said coldly.

"This is going nowhere," I said with anger.

"Exactly."

"Can I call you? Try and fix our friendship?" I questioned. She looked up to the ceiling, and she cupped her chin.

"What friendship? We could never have one again. Maybe associates. Yeah, that'll work."

I ran my hand down my face again,

"Are you okay?" I asked.

"Peachy."

"Then why were you crying?" I said, sitting in her bed.

"Why would you care?"

I wanted to scream and yell.

"Man! Stop bullshitting me!" I yelled. She looked down at her phone.

"Goodbye, JaKobe. I'll think of letting you call me. But yo' big ass gotta go." She helped me up and pushed me towards the door.

"Why? Aye, stop manhandling me! Why you kicking me out? That light skin nigga—Rashad—coming over?"

"You're light skin too. And that's none of your business. Now go." I turned around and grabbed her,

"If you think that little big-lipped toothpick ass nigga gon' steal you from me, then you sadly fucking mistaken. Jai, you know how I am. And I'll put up with him being your little fucking boyfriend for a little while, then I'ma end that shit myself. Trust me. I'll do it." I spoke inches from her face.

"Your breath smells like pure shit. And if you think your words put any fear in my heart, you're dead wrong. I like him, I don't like you. Like I said, I'll tell you when we can talk. But until then you gotta bounce, JaKobe."

I smirked.

"Try me, Jaidah. Just fucking try me, yo'."

She stuck her tongue out at me.

"He was just over here last night. There's nothing you can do. Goodbye." She slammed her door in my face and locked it.

"No the fuck she didn't—Alright, Jai! We gon' see!" I turned around, walked down the hall, and jogged down the steps. Monica was sitting in a chair, sipping something.

"How did it go, Jackass?" She giggled.

"Shut up before I drop kick your giraffe ass."

"Ohh, I'm so scared," she laughed.

"Man, I'm out. Tell Jai I ain't playing with her ass either. That nigga bet not be touching in her either." I began to slip on my socks.

"You're too late, my friend. I think he ate her box already!" She busted out laughing when she saw my face. "Be gon', Jackass."

"Friends or not, he ain't gon' have her. I'm out."

## To the Thug I Loved Before

She shrugged as I opened the door. "Bye."
I shook my head as I jogged out to my car.

Monet Dragun

# Chapter 9

## Pain

*Jaidah O'Neil*

"Monica! Where you at, boo?" I said as I came down the steps. It was quiet in the house, and I hadn't spoken to her since JaKobe left.

"Moni!" I yelled louder, as I went into the kitchen to get me a small snack before Rashad came over. My mind was still wheeling, still jumbled from what my mom told me just an hour ago. My mom's older sister—Mahogany—had been sick. She passed away this morning from cancer.

I knew my auntie was sick. But I didn't know she was that gravely sick. I was torn up inside because when I needed someone, she was there. She was there when my mom and dad were at work. She was there for everything. She was just as strict as my mom, and always honest. She was my favorite auntie. My mom was the third child of five. All sisters had different attitudes.

Auntie M was so strong. Even when she was sick she never let anything get her down. I stood in the middle of the kitchen just staring at nothing. I didn't notice I was crying.

"Jai, you called me? I was in the back with my little boo thang. I think she's the—Jai? Are you okay?" she asked. I finally looked at her, as my knees grew weak. "Jaidah, are you okay?" she shouted as she ran to my side. She pulled the condiments out of my hands, and placed them on the counter. Monica took me in my arms as I cried. I was falling apart bit by bit.

"She's gone, Moni," I said as my voice cracked.

"Who's gone? Who, Jaidah?" she said, rubbing my shoulders.

"Auntie M. She passed away this morning. She lost her fight with cancer. I didn't even get the chance to say goodbye. I haven't seen her in weeks. And I feel so bad. So damn bad! She has a little daughter, Moni." I shook my head.

"Oh my god! I'm so sorry. How is your mom doing?"

"Not so good. I have to pull myself together and go see her. My mom needs me right now."

"Calm down. You need to relax. You're breaking again. Have you taken your anxiety pills?" I shook my head. "Is Rashad coming over?" I nodded.

"Why haven't you taken them?" I shrugged.

"I don't know."

"You can't keep doing this to yourself. What did your mom say about Auntie M's daughter? Will she be okay? Where's her dad?"

"He bolted like the scumbag he was. Lyric doesn't have any other siblings. And mom's other sisters don't give a damn about nobody but themselves!" I was growing heated.

"Calm down. Is your mom going to be able to take Lyric into her custody?"

"I don't know. My mom is older now. And she deals with kids daily. Plus, Lyric is young and such a handful. I don't know how my mom and dad would handle her." I rubbed my eyes.

"There's something you're not telling me—" Monica said as she looked at me.

"Moni! When you coming back to bed?" her girl shouted from the back room.

"Hold on!" Monica yelled back. "So what's the missing link?"

"She might want me to take care of her," I sighed, avoiding eye contact.

"But you're only twenty-three years old! You have your whole life ahead of you. What's going to happen when you go back to New York City?"

"I don't know, Moni. I just don't know." I felt my eyes water again.

"Don't cry. When are you going to see your mom?"

"My dad told me to come by later tonight. He wants her to get her thoughts together. So, I'll be here for a little while longer."

She nodded.

"Everything will be okay. You earned so much in your life. It won't be taken away. I promise." She gave me a tight hug, and I wished all she said was true.

"Thank you. Now go back to your girl before she has a hissy fit." I laughed as I wiped my small tears. Monica gave a short laugh. She sighed and gave me another hug before she walked away. I bit the corner of my lip, as I swirled around in the chair. I grabbed the chips and soda, which I shouldn't be eating because I'm on a no-carb diet. But with all the mess I'm going through, I deserve to splurge.

I walked up the black steps and down the hall to my room. I noticed my phone was lit up. Tossing the bag of chips on the bed and placing the soda in the dresser top, I grabbed my phone, looking through the text. I smiled when some of them were from Rashad. I had a few from my dad, brother, and even JaKobe. I didn't bother to open his, though.

I went to my dad's first, making sure to respond to his message.

Dad: *hey baby girl. Just want to see how you were holding up. Just be strong for your momma, okay? Love you. Talk to you later.*

I shot him a quick text and then opened up my brother's. His was about the same thing. I went to Rashad's, and smiled.

Shad: *what's up, dear?. I'll be there soon. Had to make a quick stop at my studio. Still trying to finish shit up for the promotion deal with O Harrison*—3:01 p.m.

Shad: *Jaidah! Meeting still running slow. You want me to bring you food? I know that damn diet ain't working for you. You too thick to be trying to diet. You know I love your curves*—3:20 p.m.

Shad: *You mad at a nigga or something? I thought I ate your pussy good last night. You ain't responding. Got me all in my feeling like a girl*—3:36 p.m.

Shad: *yo, sweetie? I miss you... I'll see you in a bit*—3:45 p.m.

I smiled at how into me he was. I didn't even know how to reason to all of that. My phone buzzed again, and I licked my lips, opening the text.

Shad: *Yo Jaidah! I'm outside!*—4:30 p.m.

I tossed my phone on the bed and hopped off my bed. Exiting out my room, I walked down the steps. I slowly stopped when I heard weird sounds coming down from Monica's hall.

"None of your business, Jai," I said to myself. I shook my head and skipped over to the door. I unlocked the top and bottom locks, and opened the door. He was walking up with some bags,

"What's up, J? Can't answer my texts and shit. Broke my heart."

"Boy, bye." I laughed.

"Stop quoting Beyoncé, man. Next thing I know you gon' be banging up my car with a bat and a yellow damn dress on." He laughed as he stepped in and closed the door behind him.

"Whatever. Queen Bey is a masterpiece."

He shook his head and placed the frozen yogurt bag on the counter top.

"You got me a frozy! You treat me so good." I laughed, as I jumped into his arms.

"Mhm. Says the person who can't answer my damn text."

"Kiss me," I said.

"Nah. I don't do what you say." He chucked as his silver grill shone.

"Why you gotta wear that?" I groaned.

"You loved it when I had it in last night. Didn't you?"

"Shut up."

"You liked it."

"Shut up."

His hands palmed my ass. "You really wanna be all commanding? Better check ya'self before I do it for you."

I bit my whole bottom lip. I got on my tippy toes and whispered in his ear:

"I love when you aggressive." I bit his earlobe, and he shook his head softly.

"Don't start none, won't be none. Let's go upstairs and chill, baby."

"Carry me!" I whined.

"What? Girl you got two good legs. Use them."

"No. Carry me, papi Shad." He walked up to me and cupped my chin.

He smirked. I ran my hand through his hair, and licked his bottom lip.

"Carry me. Please. I've been having a rough day." I sighed as my voice changed in the same breath,

"What's wrong, J—"

"Ohhhh! Moni! Baby, yes, right there!" He looked at me upon hearing those loud moans, and I gave him that *'Don't ask'* face.

"I'll carry you up there, okay?" I nodded, as he picked up my small body and grabbed the bag of food as well. I laid my head on his shoulder, as he walked up the stairs two at a time. I had no idea he was this strong. He made it to my room, and kicked the door open with his foot. He placed me down on my feet, and took off his shirt.

"Why you—"

"I just want to get comfortable. You gon' talk to me, right?"

I nodded. He handed me my food. I opened it and ate it.

"So? I don't know how to start."

He sat by me and wrapped his arm around my waist. "Just start where you want. Okay?"

I sighed. "My auntie M passed away today. It still hurts like hell. I haven't even seen her since I came back to ATL. I just wish I could have talked to her before she passed." I began eating the yogurt.

"Wow! Baby, I'm so sorry to hear that. How did she pass?"

"Damn cancer. Breast cancer to be exact."

He gripped me harder. "I know how you feel." I looked at him.

"What you mean?"

"My little sister died of breast cancer. I know how your momma feel." I looked at him. He was so compassionate, something JaKobe never was.

"I didn't know that. I'm sorry for your loss."

He was quiet.

"This is why I'm into art so much. Because she loved when I sent her photos of flowers or even paintings of her. She was my inspiration. Still is."

"Rashad?"

"Yeah, Baby?" He turned to me, and I got lost in his chocolate eyes.

"Nothing," I said with a smile.

"Nah," he chuckled. "What is it? Speak your mind."

"Well, I really like you. Always have. I don't want to be like how I use to hold my feelings in and lose what I could've had."

"You talking about o'l boy? You still never told me his name."

"Yes. I don't want that to happen with you. You're something special. And you don't need to know his name. He's not important."

He sighed.

"To be real with you, I still feel like you love him. Just be real with me. Be real with yourself." I looked at him and his body language. I wasn't lying, I was over JaKobe. Rashad was so sweet, caring, and loving. I couldn't mess this up.

"I am over him. He is irrelevant. We were teenagers. And I was the one who fell for his lies. Rashad, I want to make this work between you and me." I grabbed his face with my hands and kissed him. And kept kissing him till his hands were on mine and his forehead was pressed against mine.

He pulled away. "Damn! Baby, please be real with me. You want me?"

I nodded.

"I wanna hear you say it."

"Yes, I want you. No bullshit." His hand slipped under my shirt, and his hand laid on my flat stomach.

"I want you too. More than you know," he said. I grabbed the back of his neck, as he kissed me. He pushed my body down, lying on top of me, kissing me, making the yogurt spill on me. He pulled off my shirt and began to lick the yogurt off my body. He was what I needed.

*** 

It was late at night, and I pulled into my mom and dad's driveway. I saw their matching cars parked in the driveway as I slowly came to a halt. I got out of the car, locked it up, and walked up the path. I used my spare key to unlock the door, then I closed it behind me. "Mom, dad!" I said as I walked in.

"In the dining room!" my dad said back, as I took off my shoes. I walked in and hugged my mom and then my dad.

"You okay, momma?" She nodded but didn't say anything. I could tell she was crying.

"Your mom has been drinking. And I don't blame her. Her sister called and asked about Mahogany's financial state. Fucking broke bitches and blood suckers who want nothing but damn money!" He hissed.

"Braxton. Please—"

"Baby, I'm sorry but it's the gat'damn truth! They treated her like shit when she was sick. I hate those damn gargoyles!"

"Daddy, you crude like a sailor."

"Remember I used to be one," he said, raising an eyebrow. The phone rang, and my mom picked it up.

"Hello?" She sighed.

"Lyric? Lyric can stay the night with me. She needs her family." She sighed. I bit my nails as I walked over to my dad.

"Daddy, you think I'm responsible to take care of Lyric?" He nodded.

"Yes. I know you love kids. And I know you're young. You have your modeling career. We never knew this would happen, but your mom needs you." I sighed.

"I know, dad. I'll try, okay?" He nodded.

"June! No one asked you to be a damn bitch about this! You don't have to worry about her. You never cared for your niece! So please fuck off! Ahhh!" Mom slammed the phone and stormed up the steps as she cried.

"Mom!" I grabbed her hand.

"I'll take care of her. If they call, just answer and talk to them. Okay? The pain will be over soon. I promise."

I nodded. She walked up to the stairs and disappeared, then my dad followed her. I grabbed my phone and saw a text from JaKobe:

*"Gotta keep acting like I don't know you. For your damn little roach boyfriend. We gon' talk. We gon' be friends. Even if I gotta do anything in my power to show you. You feel me. But listen . . . I never stopped thinking about you, Jai. I really haven't. But I'll let you have your fun with little roach nigga Shaddy-doo."*

# Chapter 10

## The Event

*JaKobe Harrison*

## Three Days Later

I took the little comb out of my glove box, and combed the naps out of my beard. I had some things to handle before the event tonight. The event was going to be filled with games, music, and more promotion for the kids. That's all this was about; it was for the kids.

I was going to put all my hate for Rashad aside. Truly, didn't hate him until I knew he was fooling around with my Jaidah. I was just thinking of what Jaidah said to me, and it still cut me deep every time:

*"Will you're sorry fix what you did? I trusted you, believed in you, and you shitted on me! It was a fucking bet, a bet to nail me then throw me away like trash! And you expect me to forgive you for that? Taking my fucking innocence and fill my head with lies?" Her eyes soon turned bloodshot. I was trying to fight the urge to cry. All this anger I gave her and still I wasn't shit.*

*"Jaidah, I was young and dumb. I'm really sorry."*

*"Sorry won't fucking fix it! Want to know the damn truth?" She walked up to me and began to poke my chest.*

*"What will fix it?" I said, as my mouth was so dry. She gave me the evilest look ever made by a woman. It was called hate.*

*"Not shit! But I will tell you the damn truth."*

*"What is it?" I said hesitantly. She poked my chest repeatedly, with anger laced in her throat.*

*"I truly loved you! But you didn't even see that. JaKobe Rico Thompson, I don't know if we'll ever be friends again or even be cool with one another!" She slapped my chest.*

*"You loved me? When was this?"*

*She rolled her eyes. "Are you stupid? I mean really?"*

*"I am, sometimes—I do dumb shit. I'm sorry." I grabbed her arms. "I really am sorry."*

*"I was a teenager. And I don't love you anymore. Let me go." I looked down at her while trying to pull her face up to look at me.*

I sighed heavily as I walked up the path and to Brad's door. I had to talk to him about my feelings for Jaidah. I wanted to be her friend again. But inside, I don't know if I wanted more than that. I knocked a few times, hearing the giggles from inside the house. The door opened and there stood Dylan. "Hey, munchkin. Did your momma tell you to open the door?" She nodded.

"I looked out the window and saw it was you, uncle." She smiled

"Give me a hug then." She laughed and did just that.

"Where is your dad?" I questioned, as I stepped onto the house, closing the door.

"He is in the music room."

I nodded. "Okay. Go and play." She nodded, and her mom—Tia—came from out the kitchen.

"Hey, how are you?"

"I'm fine." I sighed.

"You are not fine, what's the matter?"

"Well, I broke up with Tracy. And Jai don't want nothing to do with me. It's just a lot going on in my life that I wanna fix, you know!"

"You know what I know, JaKobe?"

"What's that?"

"You're selfish. You don't know the half that Jai has been through. Me and you are cool. But I don't think you and her will ever be."

I nodded, I heard this all before.

"I'm going to fix all of this. For sure—I really am. I'ma go talk to Brad."

She nodded as she flicked her hair back and finished chopping up the food. I walked to the back, and down to Bradley's music studio. It was always his hobby to make music. Why he hasn't pursued his career, I have no idea.

I opened the door, and he almost snapped. "Aye! I'm in here, man? What you doing here?" He dapped me up.

"I need to talk to you." He nodded and cut off the beat.

"What's happening?"

"Well, it's about your sister. I need her back, man. I fucked up bad. I'm so gone without her, bro."

"But you never had her. She called me two days ago. She not doing well and you ain't making shit better. To be honest, I don't see a chance of y'all being friends." I knew I slipped up. But someday I had to tell him, he was my friend at that. I couldn't keep lying to him like her pain was from something else, and it was me all along.

"Man! I don't need to be patronized right now. I'm in need of help right now. She is the only thing that can put the pieces back together."

"But she don't want you. You ended what y'all had. You're pretty much dead to her. You know that woman can hold a grudge. Now you gotta tell me. What really happened between the two of y'all? And this time no more bullshit. Alright? We boys, so tell me what's up between you and my sister and maybe I can actually help you."

I was tired of lying so it was time for me to let this shit go.

"You really wanna know why your sister hates me so much?" I said, trying not to sound so nervous.

"Yeah, nigga," he said, pulling his hat back.

"Alright. So it was senior year of college—"

"Already know that shit. Fast forward, nigga. Speed it up, yo!" he said bluntly.

"Okay, well, frat night. We had stayed at the hotel. I had made a bet with the gang. And they said it had something to do with Jai.

She was so innocent, so free, and sweet. Everyone liked her, but she was never going to fuck none of them jocks or thug ass niggas I ran with. They all tried it, and I think you know that." He nodded as he looked at me with a straight face.

"Yeah, I had to beat some ass over baby sis 'cause of that. Continue—"

"Well, I was part of the bet. Man, they just threw me in it 'cause she was my best friend. I was stupid really. After she gave me that damn make-over, I had some sense of place in the world. I wasn't just some thug playing football and running the streets. Always hated how I looked, but Jai, nah. She never saw what I saw. And I lost her. Well, that night we were drinking, pretty heavy. Anyway, we went farther than friends should that night, and we had sex. She thought I was a virgin. So I lied to her. I had already had sex with Tracy. I made her believe that I had feelings for her.

I didn't see that she had deep feelings for me when we were having sex. After that night, I knew it was a mistake, and I pushed her away. I acted a damn fool for what I did. Damaging her was not my intention. That's why she hates me so much. All because of a damn bet to nail her and show the gang her panties. I was just trying to fit in for some shit that didn't make sense. I was stuck between the two. But in the process, I lost my best friend in the whole world. The one who actually gave a damn about me!" I began to rub my hands together as Brad was silent. For a moment I didn't know what his next words were going to be.

"So? You tell me you boned my damn baby sister and broke her heart?"

I nodded. "It was the worst mistake of my life, bro. I swear I ain't mean to do that shit. It's been eating away at me for the longest."

Bradley nodded as he rubbed his beard, then with a quickness he punched the shit out of me, knocking me off my balance for a second.

"All this time! Nigga, I trusted you with my baby sister! I thought my own sister was overreacting, and you fucking broke her like that! I gotta kill yo' ass! I don't give a fuck what you got on you. You know I get active about my blood, especially Jai!" He began to rain blows at my face. I didn't want to fight my best friend. But I had to defend myself. I tackled him, but that didn't even give me the upper hand. He head-butted me and gave me a hard gut shot, making my break down on one knee.

"You bitch ass nigga!" As I was trying to pull myself up I felt cold steel against the back of my head. "Nigga, fuck you and get out my house!" He had this hard mug in his face. I wiped the blood from my nose and punched him back. He gave me a cold stare.

"This is why I didn't tell you! It was the worst mistake. I never meant to hurt Jai!" I yelled as I continued to wipe the blood from my nose.

"Like hell you didn't! You are one selfish muthafucka! And to think I defended your ass! Get out my house before I really do something I'll regret!"

I nodded and wiggled my jaw. "I need her back. I crave her every day and I just can't live with what I did to her." I felt the sharp pain in my heart from thinking of how wrong I had done her. She didn't deserve it.

"She don't want your ass back! All the shit she been through! It was all because of you! I'm glad she found Rashad! Yo' ass really ain't shit! Now get your ass out and don't come the fuck back! Fuck you and your damn event!"

I nodded and walked out of his studio. I walked up the steps and through the foyer. I passed by Tia, and I knew she heard everything I said. The look of disappointment was plastered with it all over her face.

I just walked straight past her and to the front door. Out of all this I didn't expect to lose my last friend. I got to my whip, hopped in, and I stared at the road ahead of me. "I gotta fix this shit. And fast." I peeled out of the driveway, and drove to my house. I had to get rid of this thing tonight. I had to clear my mind of everything.

\*\*\*

"Hello, everybody! We got a field of games, food, and fun for all of you. I'm DJ Moondawg, and I'll be hosting this evening." The crowd cheered as I stepped out with the kids.

Everyone was impressed with everything I put together for the evening. Rashad was filming and taking pictures of the kids with Drake. He was to be performing for tonight. I looked around, and spotted the beautiful Jaidah O'Neil. I was tempted to talk to her. But I knew that wasn't right. She walked around, greeting the kids, and I couldn't help but stare.

She was with Monica, and I moved to take some pictures with the kids. The servers began to serve the food. Jaidah had walked over to Rashad, and he kissed her in the cheek.

"Oh my gosh! It's Jaidah O'Neil!" one of the girls shouted. "And she's with Kia Dunkin and Monica Haynes!" The girls went crazy and charged over towards them. I smiled as I grabbed me a glass from off the tray. I felt like drinking tonight.

I moved down to the floor, and Monica spotted me after she signed some autographs. "Sup?"

"Hey, JaKobe. Lovely event you have going on here." She sounded so fake, but I let slide.

"A little fake? Don't ya' think?" She laughed as she slapped my shoulder. "I can't curse in front of the kids. So deal with it." One if the waiters walked up and gave her a drink. "Drinking partners for the night?" she asked me.

"Sure," I said with a light smile. Jaidah was conversing with Rashad and drinking her favorite wine with him, as her hand caressed his forearm. It just made my blood boil.

"Why you staring at her? You should just be friends. Or try to be. Maybe it's best you move on!" I nodded. Over the course of the event, the guest speakers came out and talked to the kids. As for me, I wanted and needed to talk to Jaidah. Me and Monica split later through the event. I found myself making my way over to Jaidah.

The people just kept coming with love towards Jaidah. As I approached, I could hear the fans swooning over her. "Ms. O'Neil, can I take a pic with you?" The couple turned around as the photographer got ready to snap some photos of her with the fans. Rashad noticed me as I walked up. I didn't want to be rude, so I dapped him up to keep it cool.

"Haven't seen you all night, man. Jai, this is JaKobe," Rashad said as he *introduced* us. Nigga got the nerve to call her by the nickname I gave her. She waved as if she didn't even know me.

"I know, man, I've been busy being a host. So how is the event going for you?" I added, trying to hide my anger.

"It's going good! This is the best thing for the kids in the hood, yo. They idolize you." All his words went in one ear and out the other. The only thing that had my attention was Jaidah. She looked so goddamn fine. I wanted to pull her aside just to tell her how I felt and take her right then and there. But I couldn't; he was there, and he was the one she wanted. I had a plan to get with her back, and that plan was in full effect tonight.

Monet Dragun

# Chapter 11

## That Toxic Fling

*Jaidah O'Neil*

I just can't believe him. JaKobe just thinks he can do whatever he pleases. Ugh! He just makes me sick to my damn stomach. Here he is trying to play coy with Rashad like they cool. And the fact that I haven't even told Rashad that I know him from way back! "Haven't seen you all night, man. Jai, this is JaKobe." I waved as if I didn't even know him. I wanted JaKobe to feel that because I truly didn't care for him not one bit.

"So, how is the event going for you?" JaKobe said, trying to be chipper, like *nigga, just go 'bout your business and focus on this event you're hosting.* He was trying to hide his anger, and I tried not to laugh.

"It's going good! This is the best thing for the kids in the hood, man. It's really dope. They really idolize you." I looked at Rashad. He was dripped down in Gucci, just standing there looking so delicious. I just wanted us to leave this and go home so we could spend the rest of the night with each other. But I would never stop him from getting his money.

JaKobe had finally ended the conversation with Rashad, and left our area. He made his way to another group, and began having a conversation with some other people. And every once in a while, I would catch him staring at me. Shit was uncomfortable, to be honest. So I had to move around and mingle with the supporters. An hour had gone by, and I didn't see him. I wanted to talk to Monica. But I truly hadn't seen her all night either.

It was now twelve at night, and the event was still going. The kids had left hours ago, and it was now adult hour. I was sitting at the bar with my *Sex on the Beach*. Rashad was taking pictures of all the artists, and it amazed me how much he loved his work. And I could see all the passion that came along with it, especially the real meaning behind the love of art in him. It made me fall even more for him.

As my eyes were glazed with awe over this man, I felt someone bump into me. And I almost spilt my drink. "Hey, watch it! I nearly spilled this drink all over me." I looked up to who had bumped me and immediately felt disgusted. "David? What the hell are you doing here?"

"Well? If it isn't Jai O'Neil—Mphm, long time no see," David said with a grim smirk on his face.

"My name is Jaidah, first of all. Why are you even here? When did you start caring about kids? I mean, when did you grow a damn heart, dick!"

"Well, guess who grew a backbone. I heard Monica was going to be here. Seen her and we had a few choice words. I truly miss her."

I scoffed.

"Stop your lying, please. You hurt Moni to her core. It took her years to get back to the strong woman she is today."

"No, I didn't. We had a bad argument that turned ugly. And if you don't mind, I have things to do."

I rolled my eyes, and he walked away. Some woman with a banging body switched over to him, and they grabbed hands while walking away. Quickly I began to look for Monica and still didn't see her. I hope she didn't have any stress over this. Seeing the woman walk away with him, I knew Monica didn't give into his snake-like charm. I got up from the bar stool and walked around, mingling.

"Jaidah, I've been looking for you all night. I have a few things to tell you!" Kia said as she caught up with me.

"Yes. I have the time, Kia, what's up?"

"So, about the line—When you get back into New York, we can launch it because we got the deal. I'm so glad we got in touch because you're such a good applicant for the line and our campaign. You've been through so much and overcome a lot in life. And I'm so glad to be working with you." She gave me a hug, and I hugged her back.

"Thank you, Kia. I'm so glad you understand."

"I know. I almost went through the same thing. Modeling is such a hard thing to get accepted into. You're healthy, and that's all that matters. Especially for us."

I smiled.

"Again, thank you! And it took me a long time to get past all that."

"You're welcome! Thank goodness you got through it." I nodded, and someone called her. We said our goodbyes, and Rashad walked over to me.

"Babe, this event was such a success!—I'm glad you were here to support all this with me," he said, hugging me from behind. He kissed my cheek, and I smiled.

"I'm glad I could, too. By the way, have you seen Monica?" I questioned.

"She left with some dude." I sighed and nodded. "But we can go home. I really want you to myself." He kissed my ear, and I bit my lip. He squeezed me tighter, and I grabbed his hand.

"Yes. I have some things to tell you, too."

He kind of frowned.

"Is it good or bad?" he questioned, and he squeezed my hand.

"Both."

He nodded as the event was dying down. The DJ was starting to turn everything down. And Rashad had told a few of his partners that he was leaving.

"JaKobe left. So we gon' leave now. I want you to myself." He mumbled, as he looked me up and down. He didn't know how bad I wanted him. But I didn't want to rush things. We walked out of the hall, and the valet pulled his car around. He opened the door for me, and I got in. My stomach was doing flips. I didn't know how I was going to be able to tell him my dark secret.

\*\*\*

"So, do you want to go to my crib or yours?" he asked.

"Well, Rashad, I haven't seen your place before. So yeah, I'd love to go." He nodded, and his hand gripped my thigh, making me jump a little. He caressed it as he grinned to himself.

"It won't take long to get to my house."

"So you have two homes? One in New York?" His hand rubbed up my thigh, and I silently groaned.

"I have three actually. One in New York, one here in ATL, and another in Cali."

"Wow! Why one in Cali?" I asked.

"Because that was supposed to be my sister's house. But I use that as my guest home with all the paintings of her, ma."

"That's really sweet of you—Oh my god! Shad, stop," I said as his hand was inches from my area.

"It is? And why, why should I?" he said, as he continued to drive.

"Because it's driving me crazy."

"I'd love to drive you crazy." His thumb rubbed my thigh, as he pushed my dress back more and more.

"Shad, I'm not ready." *Bitch, stop lying! You know you haven't had dick in some long years.*

"It's okay if you're not." He moved his hand, and I mentally cursed myself out. We turned on 10th street, and his house was huge.

"Your house is outrageously huge."

"That's not the only thing that huge, baby." This guy was going to be the death of me. He got out of his car, and opened the door for me. We walked up to the house, and he let us in. The house was just gorgeous. "Make yourself at home," he said, closing and locking the door. I pulled off my heels, and sat on his fluffy couch. Rashad came back with two wine glasses, and the bottle. He sat the bottle in the silver bucket, as he filled it with some ice.

"So, do you mind if I smoke, Jaidah?"

"No, I don't mind," I said with a smile. He nodded and sat next to me. He put both of his arms in the back of the couch, as he held the joint between his lips.

"You said you had to tell me something good and bad?" he said with a raised eyebrow before he took a drag. "I'm all ears."

"Well, how do I start?"

"Anyway you want to."

I pushed my hair behind my ear and sighed.

"Well, I was twenty years old. I had got into the modeling industry and moved out to New York. I didn't have any friends, and I was a loner. The girls looked at me like a threat, and I hated it. The only girl who accepted me was Monica. Me and her had been down since college. And Joshua—he was not gay, despite how people talked about him. But anyway, it was hard for me to really get shoots and bookings because of my brown skin and my hips and boobs. I wasn't so skinny as I am now." I paused and took a deep breath,

"Continue, baby. I'm listening." He blew out more smoke as he moved closer next to me. I nodded.

"So, it got harder and harder for me. So I grew to hate my body. I became self-conscious and I had body disfigurement disorder. I became obsessed with the perfect body image. And then came the bulimia."

"Wait, what? Really. How long did this go on for?"

"Three years."

"No way!" he said in disbelief.

"Yes way. The person who got me out of it was Monica. She found out about my disease, and she helped me through it. So now I campaign for it. I'm healthy, extremely healthy now." He pulled me into his lap and rubbed my back as he saw the tears.

"What caused all this?"

"That guy I told you about? That had me in a very dark place."

"You gotta tell me who this guy was. I promise I won't be mad."

"I can't do that."

"Why?" he said with a frown.

"Because you already met him."

He paused and thought for a moment.

"Tell me. Please, please don't tell me it's—" I sighed and nodded. "It's JaKobe, isn't it?" He wiped my eyes, and I nodded.

"Wow! I'm not mad not at all. But that nigga lost some shit good." He kissed my cheek, and I ran my hand through his hair which harbored two braids. *Too damn sexy.*

"Yeah. But I'm healthy, and that's all that matters."

"Right. And I got you, I promise. I'm so glad you told me." He pulled me fully into his lap, and kissed my neck.

"Shad?" I moaned.

"Yes?" he said, as my eyes fluttered closed.

"You're high. Stop."

"I got control over my actions. I ain't that high, Jaidah. And I need you. I wanna make love to you. You make me crave you, girl. You need me as much as I need you. He unzipped my jacket, and my boobs popped out. His soft lips kissed my breasts, and I threw my head back. He shook his head, licking his lips as he tapped my thigh. He told to get up, and I stood up.

He looked me up and down. I could see his bulge. "Turn around." I nodded, and he unzipped my skirt. And I let it fall to my feet. I was about to turn around, but he stopped me. "Don't. You. Move."

"Why?" I questioned softly as his hands grabbed my hips.

"I want you to dance for me. I love these curves. You don't ever have to hate your body. I love everything you got." I felt his tongue lick on my back to my ass cheek. My body shivered.

"How can I dance to no music—" He clapped his hands, and soft music filled the living room. *Say It*—by Tory Lanez—echoed through the room.

"Move that ass. And I ain't gon' say it twice." He smacked my ass and sat back.

*Just keepin' it honest*
*You wouldn't want a young nigga*
*If I wasn't whippin' this foreign*

# To the Thug I Loved Before

*That's why I came back, top down*

*You gon' have to do more than just (say it)*
*You gon' have to do less when you (do it)*
*Tell mama you know I (show it)*
*Always want you to (prove it)*
*You gon' have to do more than just (say it)*
*You gon have to do less when you (do it)*

*Tell mama you know I (show it)*
*See you gon' need to do more than just (prove it)*
*And you know, you know*
*And you know, in this foreign car let it go*
*And you know, you know*
*And you know, in this foreign car let you know*

My hips moved to the music, hitting every beat as I moved my hands over my body. His hands wrapped around me, and he pulled me down on his member.

He stood up and tugged on my thin panties. We walked up to Rashad's room. I tugged on his shirt and pulled it off, throwing it somewhere in the room. Our lips connected, and we began to tongue each other down.

"Are you ready for this? We not rushing, are we—"

"Shut up and fuck me." He looked at me with lusty eyes. He picked me up and pressed me against his door, shutting it. Inside I had the most frightened look on my face. I hated when it came to this. I hadn't had sex since I gave myself to JaKobe, and I know this had to hurt. I just wanted to give him as much pleasure as possible. Just as he wanted to do to me. He didn't want to hurt me, and I knew that now.

"Are you ready, Jaidah? 'Cause I'ma fuck yo' little thick ass all across this house. And then some." He pecked my lips over and over again.

"Yes, fuck! Take these off—" I tugged at his belt, and he sucked in my neck again. "Yes!" I moaned as he undid his jeans and let them fall. Rashad let me down a little, as I had one leg wrapped around him. He pulled his manhood out as I stroked it with my hand. I had been drinking tonight, and I wanted and needed sex.

I pecked his lips as he stared into my eyes. He stepped out of his pants and got on his knees, kissing my stomach and then my clit, making my body jolt and shake. His tongue swirled around my clit. My beautiful moans filled his ears, making Rashad groan. "You ready?" he mumbled against my pubic area.

"Yes," I gasped.

"You sure? You sure you wanna give it to me?" he asked, as his tongue darted into me.

"Yes, Shad! Now stop asking me, baby."

He chuckled and came up to me, and tongue-kissed me, making me grab his head. He was making me taste myself. He was so damn freaky.

"You like how you taste?" He smirked, and so did I. I nodded, and I smiled as he rubbed his member against my clit.

"Baby, a condom—" I said shakily. He picked me up aggressively and slammed me on the bed, as his tongue licked in every inch of my body.

"I know, I wouldn't do it without one."

I cursed my damn self. He was making me feel so good. Rashad pulled a condom out of his drawer. He tore it open with his straight teeth, and pushed it slickly in his dick. I bit my lip.

He hovered over me as his chain trailed down my chest.

"Please, relax, baby. I know you haven't had sex in a long time."

I nodded, and took a deep breath. He slid into me slowly. I knitted my eyebrows together.

It felt painful but so pleasurable.

"Now, I want you to count to five, okay?"

I nodded and started counting.

"One—Two—Three—F-Four—fuck! Rashad!" I screamed as he pushed it in deeper. "Fuck!"

He moaned. The tears started to come down my cheeks. Rashad began to kiss them away.

"You okay?" he asked. I took another deep breath, and he kissed me deeply.

"I'm fine, keep going." He nodded, and my hand went straight for his back. I was making all types of marks on his back.

"Shit! Shit! You're too big!" I cried out. Rashad began to move in and out slowly, making love to me. He was moving so effortlessly, and it felt so good as his strokes grew faster.

"Fuck! Baby, faster!" I moaned as he gave me long deep strokes.

"You want me faster?" He groaned as he kissed me. He turned me around, making me lie on my stomach. He was deep-stroking me as I buried my face into the pillow, biting it and moaning loudly.

"Yes! Yes! Rashad, please don't stop!" I moaned and groaned louder as I wrapped my shaking legs around him tighter. "Baby, I can't—I'm about cum—fuck! Rashad!" He covered my mouth, as he went faster. I didn't even know he could go any faster. My area clenched around him repeatedly.

"Damn, don't do that, baby. Don't! Hold that shit, Jaidah!" He grabbed a handful of my hair. My hands dug into the mattress as his other hand smacked my ass. He kept beating up my spot, hitting it over and over as I came all over his member.

"I didn't tell you to cum, Jaidah." He leaned in my back as he spoke to me in my ear, making me moan over and over again.

"Shad! Please!"

"Please what, ma? Say it!"

"Don't stop. Shit feel so good." Shit gushed hard in his member, as he started going much faster than ever.

"Got me feeling you, girl. Shit. I don't want to ever leave you, or pull out this pussy." I thought I was going to feel bad having sex with Rashad. But it felt so right to me. He was all I could think about nowadays. His dick game was on point. The next moment I felt my body being lifted, and my pussy being banged out.

"I love you, Jaidah."
Did he just—?

# Chapter 12

## Lusting Mistakes

*JaKobe Harrison*

I woke up with a pounding headache. I didn't know what the fuck happened last night. Someone moved in my bed, and I frowned slightly, looking over to my left as I stared at a woman with purple hair. I smiled as I ran my hands through her hair. I can't believe she gave me a chance and is here with me now. The sun shone down on her as she turned over. She was so damn beautiful. Her eyes fluttered open, and we stared at each other.

"Huh—JaKobe, what did we do?"

"You don't remember?" I said with a smile, as I pushed her hair out of her face.

"No. I had a lot to drink—What did we do?" she said with a soft voice.

"We had sex. And it was some good wild sex too." Her eyes lit up. And she kissed my lips. I kissed her back as the kiss got passionate. I was enjoying it, I missed it.

"JaKobe! Wake the fuck up!"

I kept kissing Jaidah, tonguing her down, not hearing a word she said as my eyes were closed.

"JaKobe!" she said again.

"Shut up, Jaidah and just kiss me."

"Wake yo' punk ass up! JaKobe!" I felt a pop on my skin, and my eyes opened. I looked up at the ceiling.

"What, Jaidah?"

"I'm not Jaidah, Jackass! Get the fuck off of me." My eyes widened, and I turned my face slowly to the woman who was talking. The only person who called me Jackass was—

"Monica? What the hell you doing in my bed!" She rolled her eyes and began to hit me. I quickly grabbed her hands as she was crying.

"What the fuck! Stop putting your damn hands on me! Monica, just tell me what happened?" I said slowly.

"What the fuck you think happened? Look at us! We are both in your bed, *naked*!" She screamed, "I can't believe we did that."

"No, we didn't! All we did was drink at the party. You saw you ex and then—"

"Yeah, nigga! And then, then you took me here because I was too drunk. You didn't take me home because Jai and Rashad was going to be there! I slept with you, we had sex, oh my god—" She snatched the sheet off of me, and wrapped it around her. "I'm totally screwed! I betrayed my best friend! And I cheated on my fucking girlfriend!"

"Just calm down."

"Calm down? Nigga, don't tell me to calm down! Bruh, how the fuck do you think I'm supposed to calm down, bitch ass! This is all your fault!"

I tossed my legs over the side of the bed, and pulled on my briefs that were on the floor

"Hold up. My fault? Don't put all this on me. We were both drunk, bruh, it was a mistake. Do it look like I'd fuck you? Or even want to pursue you?"

"Shut the fuck up! JaKobe, me and Jai have a code. You know the damn girlfriend code. I have to tell her. That's my friend! I'd never do her like this."

"No! You can't tell Jai." She gave me a look.

"And why the fuck not? I am in a damn relationship, unlike you! I just got caught up!"

"What they don't know won't hurt them." I walked away from her. Without warning, she slapped me on the back of my head.

"What! You're fucking stupid!" she screamed, then shoved me over and over again. "I hate you, JaKobe, you're always ruining someone's life!" She slapped my face hard. So hard it echoed throughout the room. I grabbed her wrist and threw her on the bed.

"Yo, stop fucking putting your hands on me. I never meant for any of this to happen! I already know I messed up, and everybody hates me! Now for your sake, I suggest you don't tell Jaidah. Got it?" I turned away from her and walked towards the bathroom. "I'll call you a Uber or Lyft." She sniffed. I walked into the bathroom, slamming the door. I planted my hands on the marble countertop, and looked at myself in the mirror.

"You gotta change, man. You just got to." I stood there for a moment as the whole night went on instant replay in my brain. I placed my head in my hands, and just started to slap my head. I can't believe I fucked up again. I never wanted to do that with her best friend. I never even wanted to cross paths with Monica. But she was vulnerable, and we were both drunk. Everything just happened so fast I couldn't stop it.


Everyone was having a nice time, and I just couldn't stand her with him. So I needed someone to talk to. Scanning the floor, I saw Monica over by the bar drinking to herself. So I walked towards her just to have some conversation. I honestly didn't want to be alone. I grabbed another drink from the passing waiter that greeted everyone with drinks. "Thank you, great work tonight as well." The waitress smiled as she thanked me and made her way around to the other guests.

"Aye, what's up, Monica? How you doing tonight, girl?" She turned her head to me as she bit the cherry that was in her drink.

"Fuck do you want? I tried to be nice earlier but that's out the window now. The little kids are gone now. I can talk the way I want now."

"Damn, no more being fake, huh?"

She laughed. "Shid ain't no need to, 'cause do you see kids in this bitch now? I can talk how I want, so deal with it." Monica downed the rest of her drink, and the liquor slightly dripped from her bottom lip. The bartender brought over her next drink, but this one she passed to me. "Drinking partners for the night?" she questioned.

"Yeah, shorty, but I want something more strong," I said with a light smile. Jaidah was conversing with Rashad and drinking; the way the glass touched her lips made my heart skip a beat. Had a thug feeling like a punk.

"Why you staring at her? You should just be friends. Or try to be. Maybe it's best you move on!" I nodded. Over the course of the event, the guest speakers came out and talked to the kids. As for me, I wanted and needed to talk to Jaidah. Me and Monica split, then I found myself making my way over to Jaidah.

After the failed talking with Jai, I had sought solace in the bar. The kids were leaving, and I was downing drink after drink. I was pissed at all of this. I was trying to fix the situation, but it was getting worse and worse.

"Hello, Monica."

"David?" I turned around when I heard Monica call the dude's name.

"In the flesh. How you been with, like, vagina and all?"

"David, now is not the time for this. You left me, remember? Now excuse me."

"Nah, you didn't tell me shit. I loved you and you loved women," he said with hatred,

"So the fuck what! I was in a relationship with you—" I stood up with my glass in hand and stepped in between them both.

"Aye, this my party, man. I know Moni, so chill the fuck out, yo'." He laughed and looked at me.

"So you boning him now, Monica?"

"Stop, David! You know I never cheated on you. At all."

He looked at her, and shook his head.

"So, you leaving me for a fucking woman? That was cool, bitch? That's nasty—"

She tossed her drink in his face, and pushed him back. "David! You're so full of it. I love you, and you decided to dog me out! And abuse me! Did you not? So I don't want to hear that cry fool shit. I hate your ass." She walked away, but he grabbed her wrist.

116

"Bitch—"

I pushed him back and called my guards to get his sick ass out my place.

"Take his ass out!" They grabbed him up.

"Get y'all hands off me! I know my way out."

"Nigga, you better get yo' ass outta here before I beat your boney ass," I threatened.

He fixed his clothes, and smiled at Monica. "I'll be seeing you."

She walked away from him as she was crying. I shook my head as David walked away. Monica stormed off in another direction. I shook my head, and walked her way. I wanted to talk to Jai, but Monica was in need of a friend. I found her in the back, sitting on the bench, looking up at the sky. She had a drink in her hand, and was crying.

"Monica?"

"I always loved David. I never was a cheater, and I never will be. He hurt me so bad. Yes, he abused me. This is why I'm so tough. Why I don't trust that well. And then I met my girlfriend, Nicki. Well, she isn't my girlfriend. But I know she's the one. I've been ridiculed for being bisexual for a long ass time. I finally came to terms with myself. And I thought David did too. I was wrong."

"Moni, you cool. Even though I don't like you but you cool. He was an idiot to do you like that." I sipped my drink, and for the rest of the night we drank. She was drunk off her wits, and so was I.

I later had my driver drive us to my place because I didn't want her to be alone with everything that David guy had her feeling. And I knew Rashad would be with Jai. So I was just going let her chill at my joint.

"Ha, ha! This is so fun. Let's drink some more and play strip poker!" she shouted.

I laughed, and we stumbled into the house. We ended up grabbing another bottle and falling out on the couch. "JaKobe?

117

You're cool! Y-you know that? That's cool, ya know?" Her voice was slurred.

"Man, you alright too. You're funny as fuck, yooo—I'm so damn wasted it's a shame." Monica looked at me, and I looked at her, and we busted out laughing at nothing at all. "You know that rat, David, right? He got a damn grape fruit head," I said.

"What? I thought he had a damn watermelon head," she countered. We both broke out in laughter. She tried to get up, but fell down on me.

"Damn, girl! Get it together," I slurred. She got up, laughing and pulling off her clothes, touching me and all. "Monica— Damn!"

"Shut up—" She crashed her lips into mine, and I kissed her back. Monica opened her blouse slowly, twisting each button with her thumb and third finger.

When her shirt finally fell open, I studied her, then caressed her breasts. I grabbed her aggressively, and ripped her skirt off. I licked her nipples, then moved my lips slowly down her stomach, and a drunk Monica couldn't have cared less if I was. Monica removed her underwear. Kissing her just above her pubic bone, I slipped two fingers inside her. She moved into my hands until I stopped suddenly, removing my fingers as if I'd thought better of the whole thing. While she propped herself up on her elbows to see what had happened, I got up and opened my wallet. I was thinking about—or trying to think about—what I was doing. But right now I was lusting for Monica.

Instead, I removed a joint from the wallet, took a lighter from the table and lit up the joint, leaned over the bed, and passed it to Monica. She took a deep drag. She passed it back to me afterwards; I took another hit. Monica blew out the smoke, and unzipped my jeans. I wasn't wearing underwear, and Monica could see instantly that I had a longer, thicker dick.

I grabbed her waist as she wrapped her arms around me. After I had entered her and she wrapped herself around me, I picked her up and began to thrust inside of her. She allowed every sound to come out of her mouth. She let herself in that single moment to be carried. I began to pound her as I slammed her back against the wall.

"Shit! Shit!" She grabbed my face, and kissed me as I grunted into her mouth. She moaned into mine, as I sucked on her tongue. She began to claw and scratch at my back. But I wasn't stopping. I was hitting it so good our bodies were making knocking noises.

"Fuck! Yes! Like that—" I grabbed her hair and pulled it back, as I held her up with one hand, and took a deal of the joint.

"You like that shit!" I grunted, as I blew the smoke out and sucked on her neck.

"Yes!"

"Say that shit louder, Jai. Fuck—uh, I mean, Monica!"

"Yes, I like this shit! Damn!" We went at this all night. I didn't know what I was doing.

I heard the door slam, and I snapped out of my disgusting thoughts. "What the fuck have you done?"

Monet Dragun

# Chapter 13

## My Responsibilities

*Jaidah O'Neil*

I was sitting in my brother's living room. It was in the afternoon, and my mind was still in a spiral. I sat there swirling the glass in my hand as I stared off into nowhere, looking at the white covered walls. My brother called me yesterday and told me to come over his house. I had to go with my mom later on today; she had to go get Lyric from the girls' home.

It still pained me that Lyric would have to go through this pain. The glass became colder in my hand. But it still didn't pull me out of my heavy thoughts. The thought of Rashad popped into my head. And those sexual thoughts just came flooding back. This was just another juicy entry into my diary:

"Please, what ma? Say it."

"Don't stop. Shit feel so good!" Shit gushed hard in his member as he started going much faster than ever.

"Got me feeling you, girl. Shit—I don't want to ever leave you, or pull out this pussy." I thought I was going to feel bad having sex with Rashad. But it felt so right to me. He was all I could think about now and days. His dick game was on point. The next moment I felt my body being lifted, and my pussy being banged out.

"I love you, Jaidah."

Did he just—?

I slightly smiled at the sex memory between me and Rashad. But those words that came out of his mouth shocked me. I sighed as my head felt as if was going to explode.

"Sis?" I still sat there swirling the glass faster until it spilled onto my hand. I looked at my hand and sighed.

"You called me?" Bradley nodded and walked into the living room, and sat by me with a beer in his hand. I looked at him, and noticed he had a scratch on his face. "What happened to your face?" I asked, grabbed his chin and turned it towards me.

"Long story."

"Yeah, I got time, talk."

He looked at me, and gave me this look.

"You got nerve to talk? Why you didn't tell me you and JaKobe had sex?" My body tensed up, and I sighed. "Cat got your tongue?"

"I used to be in love with him."

"Awh, hell! That's why y'all ain't friends no more? Really? Why you put yourself through that shit!" I shrugged. "Nah, don't do that damn shrugging shit with me!"

I looked at my brother and started to talk. "Listen, he was my best friend. I used to love him, that's all. After he did me dirty and treated me as a bet, we went our separate ways."

"Is that why you were depressed, had bulimia?" I pressed the glass to my lips, and drank the remaining liquid.

"He was one of the reasons."

"Wait? One—"

I nodded.

"Sis, I'm your brother. You know I love you to death, now just talk to me."

"I had bulimia because I was a model. I wanted my body to be perfect, I wanted to fit in. I didn't feel like I was beautiful."

"Why you do that to yourself? Never let a man or anyone else for that matter bring you down. You're beautiful inside and out. Come here—" He opened his arms, and I leaned in as he held me tight.

"I know that now."

Bradley sighed. "I had to put the whoop on JaKobe ass. We ain't coo' no more."

"What? Y'all fought? When?" I said, getting up off him. I had a smile on my face.

"Why you smiling?" he said, laughing. "And yeah. I broke his ass off. He came over here the day of his event and told me everything. I was real heated and whooped his ass for it. Like, no one uses my sister." He ruffled up my hair.

"Hey, stop that. I just got my hair done. And, you're the best, you know that?"

"Yeah, I've heard it once or twice." He kissed my forehead and got up from the couch. I smiled and remembered what I really wanted to tell him. I got up and followed him. "You hungry?" he asked.

"No, I'm good. But I really had to ask you something. I need my brother's opinion." He took some food out of the fridge and placed it on the counter.

"What up? Speak your mind."

I sighed and pushed my hair back. "Well, me and Rashad knocked boots the other night. And he said he—" Bradley started coughing on the piece of celery he was eating. "You okay?" I said, running around the countertop and patting his back. Bradley snapped his head at me and swallowed hard.

"What the hell! You had sex with him?" He sounded shocked.

"Yes, was that a bad move?"

"Man, I don't wanna hear about my baby sister having sex. I don't wanna hear it. I like this guy. But no, no, I don't wanna hear it."

"Bradley! I need your help, we had sex and—"

Bradley placed both of his hands over his ears. "La la la la! I can't hear you! I can't hear my sister talking about fucking her nigga!" I finally caught up with him, and snatched his hands from his ears.

"He said he loved me!" Bradley's eyes were fixated on me, and there was silence. I gave him a look as I moved my hands in the air. "Hello?"

"Awh, he sprung. But I don't wanna hear your sex escapades!"

"Shut up, what should I do? He hasn't talked to me after the fact? Is he using me?"

"Nah."

I looked at him sideways,

"How do you know that?"

"Because unlike JaKobe, I've seen it in Rashad's eyes. He's just surprised that he let himself slip up. Just give him a few days. I bet he'll come to you." I bit my lips, as he patted my back and walked into the kitchen. Maybe he was right.

I walked back into the kitchen where he was. I had another thirty minutes before I had to go with my momma to the group home. I hope Lyric remembered me. I hope she was going to be happy to be leaving with us.

\*\*\*

Me and my mom didn't talk while we were in the car because she was still hurt over her sister's death. Besides, her niece didn't have anyone but her. I picked my nails, and bounced my knee nervously as she pulled the car onto the street.

"Can you please stop that, hunny?" she spoke. "You're making me nervous."

"I'm sorry, mommy. I'm simply scared."

"Everything will be okay. We are going to figure everything out and make your auntie proud." I nodded, and pulled my phone out. My phone was extremely dry; nobody was texting me, not even Monica, and she's usually blowing up my phone every day. She wasn't at the house this morning, and I figured she was with her girl.

"Mom? Maybe when I get my place, Lyric can live with me."

"Here or New York?" she said, looking at me then back at the road.

"I don't know, mom. I really love it up in New York." She sighed deeply.

124

# To the Thug I Loved Before

"You can't run from your problems forever. You understand, it's better to forgive and forget. I know what he did was wrong. But maybe he's changed. I know you're liking that Rashad man, and he seems good for you. But remember this—A man doesn't make you. You make *you*. You got that? I want you to write that on postage notes and plaster them everywhere in your room. You already went through so much, and I don't want this to happen again. If Rashad is the man for you—You know what you have to do?"

"No, what?"

"You really don't know, Jai?"

"No, momma."

She turned at me and parked the car. "You have to forgive JaKobe. Remember God made that saying for a reason. Now let's go." Before I could get any words in, she grabbed her purse, keys, and sunglasses and got out of the car. I groaned, throwing my head back as I got out of the car.

My mom was waiting for me as I closed the door and walked up to her. I looked up at the girls' group home, and sighed. I didn't want my little cousin to be in here at all. We walked up the doors, and I opened the door for my mom. I walked in after her, and the receptionist looked up the name for my mom.

She got up and gave us our visiting passes, as we walked to the back with her. I looked at all the little and orphaned girls. Even if they did have parents, they didn't know them. I shook my head as she took us to where Lyric was. She was sitting out in the swing, looking up at the sky.

"She's been out there every day like that. She doesn't talk to anyone or relate with the kids. I feel so bad for her. But I'm glad you ladies came. She really needs someone after she lost her mom."

"Thank you," my mom said. The woman nodded, and mom went outside to Lyric. She tapped on her shoulder, and Lyric looked up and hugged her tight. She started crying, and I felt some way inside. It wasn't fair. My phone buzzed; I took it out of my back pocket and looked at the contact name. The name showed exactly the way I had saved it:

The jackass: *hey uh? Can we talk tomorrow at some restaurant or somethin'? I need to tell you something.*

I closed my phone and walked outside, talking to Lyric. JaKobe could wait, and whatever he had to tell me could wait also. Lyric ran to me the moment she saw me.

"Jaidah! Why haven't you come to see me!" she yelled with tears.

"I'm so sorry. You're coming home with us. Believe that, okay? You're not alone. I promise." She hugged me even tight, and I rubbed her head softly. My phone buzzed and buzzed; it was interrupting this small moment. I pulled out my phone on our way back home as my mom talked to Lyric again. It was all texts from JaKobe. I sighed and just texted him back, saying: "Sure, we can talk. But not tomorrow, I have things to do, okay?"

I was going to take my mom's advice and try to mend things with him.

# Chapter 14

## My First Love

*JaKobe Harrison*

### Three Weeks Later

I was lying down on my back, with my hands behind my head. Just watching the ceiling fan as I thought about the past. Of course, Jaidah was in it. I was thinking of any way to get her back as a friend, and maybe more than that in due time.

I could picture her when we were younger. How she hadn't hit her growth spurt yet, didn't have all those curves. But she was still so fine. I didn't see that, though. I'd only seen a damn bet. She was the one that made me who I was. And I treated her like she wasn't nothing. Despite my smartness, I was dumb as hell when it came to women. I picked a hoe over a wifey. Jaidah loved me the whole time. And I bet if she had told me, I would have probably shot her down.

I shook my head as the ceiling fan kept spinning. She fully popped into my head as my eyes slowly closed. A flashback-like dream of us came into my head. And a low smile popped onto my face as I faded into sleep.

*The sound of shuffling made me open my eyes a bit. "O, when you get here?" she questioned as she came out of the bathroom with a towel wrapped around her. I rubbed my eyes. Her body was little but curvaceous. I licked my lips and shifted my eyes from her.*

*"I been here for a while, are you okay?" She shrugged.*

*"Don't know, my dad is just—it's just hard." She sighed. I nodded in understanding and fiddled with my thumbs.*

*"Jai, you can wear some of my gear if you like. Don't matter." I lightly shrugged.*

"Thanks. JaKobe, what are you staring at, silly?"

"Nothing, just hurry up, loser, so we can chill. You look like you need sleep."

"Yeah, I do need sleep. By the way, who is Patricia? Your girlfriend?"

"Huh? Uh, nah, she just a girl I talk to. She gave me her—" She put her hand up for me to stop, and she chuckled.

"I don't want to know, nasty!"

I shrugged. "Well, it wasn't nasty. We just talk but, when the right one comes around for you and he give you that good dick, you'll know why these girls fall for me." I laughed.

Her look kind of changed. But I didn't think nothing of it. "You are just too much, okay? Plus, you haven't even had sex yet yourself, sir."

I stuck my tongue out at her, and she shrugged in reaction.

"Anyways, ya' birthday is nearing in two more days, and I can't wait to give you your surprise. Well, both of our birthdays are coming up."

"JaKobe!" she whined. "I hate surprises, you know that!" She came out of my closet with one of my oversized shirts on. She looked good in it. Real good. Her wet blue-black curls fell on her shoulders and looked fine.

"Don't care, I'm giving you your surprise and that's final. Now, come get in the bed and go to sleep. You're in my house, so my rules, shorty." She rolled her eyes and pouted like a big baby. I flicked her bottom lip, and she giggled as she swatted my hand away.

"Stop that shit. You know how to make me feel so much better." I laughed lightly as I fell back on the bed. She laid on my chest but hurriedly shot up.

"You smell like pure sweat!" she said.

I shook my head. "Well, I couldn't hop in with you. Your ass took up all the hot water, anyways." I waved her off and got up. "I'll get in now."

"Yeah, with yo' stanky booty ass, you do that," she teased. She curled up on my pillow and pulled out her phone as the bright *light illuminated her face. She was my best friend—Damn, my best friend! This was why I couldn't fathom the feelings I was having. I didn't want to mess that up. As I got into the shower, I turned on the hot water, and let it hit the back of my head and shoulders.*

*"Jai, what are you doing to me?"*

My phone buzzed loudly, snapping me out of my reverie, making me jump and reach for it. "Talk to me," I said as I answered the phone with low eyes.

"Talk to me, you're so damn lame. This is Jaidah, water head!" My low eyes shot open as I continually stared at the ceiling.

"What's happening?" I said, trying to play it cool.

"You busy? I'm finally free from dealing with all the stuff in my life and my schedule is free." I bit the skin off of my lip as I listened to her talk.

"Nah. I ain't busy. And my day is free. What's up?"

"Meet me at *The Optimist* seafood restaurant. Cool?"

"Yeah," I replied, "that's a good idea. What time?" I asked.

"About—say, seven?"

I smiled.

"Is this a date? Why that Rashad nigga ain't call you?"

She smacked her lips. "This ain't no date, and don't worry about me and him. Do you wanna go or not? I won't beg you."

"Yeah, yeah. I was just messing with you, Jaidah. I'll meet you there, cool?"

"Yeah, that's cool. I'll see you." The phone beeped, and I looked at it, shaking my head. I leaned up out the bed, checking the time again. It was only five right now, and I had to decide on some basic shit to wear. My phone buzzed again. I ran my hand down my face and picked up my phone again. An unknown number was calling me, and I frowned as I answered it.

"Hello? Who is this?" I said into the phone, as I got up from my California King bed.

"Um—Tracy. Can I talk to you?" My head jumped back as her voice boomed through the phone.

"The fuck do you want? We ain't friends, I don't wanna talk to you after the shit you did. Go talk to your girlfriend."

"JaKobe, I really need to talk to you. This is really important."

I sighed. "I got somewhere to be. What you want? For some reason I feel like your fucking ass want something. It just feel like your ass bullshitting me."

"I went to the doctor and—"

I cut her clean off. "And what? Ain't no way your ass pregnant. Ain't no condom break, I wore the right size, and I used one every time we fucked, so what? I ain't giving you no money." I heard her sniffling. I ain't have no soft spot for her ass.

"I have a STD, JaKobe. I just wanted to tell you. I don't want you to get hurt. I already hurt you enough, I just want you to get tested. I'm so sorry, goodbye—"

*Beep, beep, beep!*

I pulled the phone away from my ear slowly and just shook my head, feeling like shit. All the time she was running around on me, I didn't think nothing of it. I ran my hands through my hair as I walked into my closet. There was so much running through my head. I rubbed my eyes, as I grabbed me some jeans and a button down shirt, and some shoes. I laid my stuff on the bed and went into my bathroom. I had two things on my mind: Monica and now Tracy.

\*\*\*

I pulled up to *The Optimist*. The valet opened my door for me and took my keys. I thanked him and walked in. I spotted Jaidah sitting alone and looking at the menu. I took a deep breath and walked over to the table.

"Hello, Jaidah."

She looked up and smiled.

"Hi, glad you could make it." She was being surprisingly nice. I sat at the table as the waiter gave me a menu.

130

"They got a nice beer selection," I said, as I eyed the menu and Jaidah.

"So? I'ma get straight to the point, okay?" she said. I nodded as I laid the menu down.

"Okay, I'm listening."

"We can be friends. I'm giving you a chance here, okay? I'm going to try and trust you, but first you gotta make up with my brother. Alright?"

"Nah. He ain't gon' forgive me. Do you forgive me?"

She stale-faced me.

"I'm his sister, just do it. And everything will be cool, okay? Just tell him the truth and be honest with him. And be honest with me as well."

I nodded. "I got you." I sighed and thought of how she was forgiving me. "You forgive me?" The waiter came to our table and asked us what we wanted to drink and eat. So I had to hold my tongue.

Jaidah began to speak. "Can I have another Southern Cat drink. And, I'll have the Arugula Salad, with everything on it for my appetizer, and for my entrée, I'll have the fish and chips." The waiter wrote down everything and looked at me.

"And you sir?"

I looked at my menu again.

"For my drink I'll have red wine. For my appetizer, I'll have the Fried Gulf Oysters, and then for my entrée I'll try the Lobster Roll; secret dressing on the side with Shoestring fries with the malt vinegar and garlic." He nodded, and he wrote it all down.

"Good choices, will that be all?"

"Oh. And the lady will have the Apple Cider donuts with the ice cream. Two actually." He smiled and nodded.

"I'll be back with y'all drinks."

I nodded, as he took our menus. I looked at Jaidah.

"What?"

"Nothing, why ole' boy ain't talk to you?"

"I don't know. We taking a break, I guess." Her phone vibrated, and she looked down at it.

"Is that him?"

"No, my brother."

I nodded.

"Can I ask you something?" I questioned.

"Sure? What is it?"

"How would you feel if your best friend had sex with one of your old friends?"

She sipped her waiter, and scratched her hand.

"I wouldn't care because if he or she is an old friend, then that means we are not friends anymore. If they fucked, that's on them. I wouldn't have shit to do with that."

I know I really fucked up now.

"Damn."

"Why you ask that?"

I shrugged.

"A friend of mine told me so I want to ask a female," I lied. The waiter brought us the food, and I couldn't bring myself to tell her what I did. The rest of the night was us laughing and more. I missed these damn times, but I had a feeling they weren't going to last forever.

"JaKobe?"

"Yes, Jai?"

She laughed.

"I think—I think I can finally move on and forgive you. So, I forgive you, JaKobe. All that is in the past, okay?"

"Wow! For real? Was I your first love?"

She sighed, and she swallowed her food.

"After that night, you'll always be my first love." Her phone buzzed. "But now you have to remember—We are friends. I truly am feeling Rashad."

"Is he your love now?"

"I don't know," she said, putting food in her mouth. Her phone buzzed; she rolled her eyes, answering it. "Hold that thought. This is Moni."

My heart began to thump.

"Hold on, Moni? What you mean you and your girlfriend broke up?"

I knew this night wasn't going to last forever.

Monet Dragun

# Chapter 15

## Who Cheated on Who?

*Jaidah O'Neil*

*JaKobe stopped singing some song by Chris Brown, and I knew he heard my sobs.*

*"Jai, are you crying?" he probed.*

*"N-no," I lied.*

*"You're lying. What's the matter, baby girl Jai?" That made me cry even more. Him just calling me the name he gave me so long ago made me cry even harder. I felt the bed dip in and JaKobe turned me over, looking at me dead in the face. He just still didn't get how much he meant to me. Yes, I read the messages in his phone.*

*"Really, what's wrong? Why you crying like this?" he said as he hovered over me.*

*"It's nothing really," I lied once again.*

*"Please, stop lying to me. Why are you crying like this?" He was my best friend, but how was I supposed to feel! He didn't know what I was going through. He didn't know that this time right now was the hardest thing I was going through. Because he was away when it happened, I was going through depression. And I vowed never to tell him. He wasn't there to comfort me when I needed him to.*

*"Jai? Talk to me," he said as he was still on top of me. I glanced down, and all he had on was a towel.*

*"Why, don't you have on any clothes?" I said through sniffs.*

*"Uh, I was distracted by you crying. Now please tell me, what's wrong?" His body was perfect and right now I was vulnerable. But I couldn't do that. Or could I?*

*"It's too much to tell. You wouldn't understand. And please g-get up, O."* I tried to crawl from under him. But he wouldn't budge.

*"What if I don't want to?"* Those words kind of hit me hard. I slowly closed my eyes and pushed him off of me. Then I walked to the bathroom.

I looked back at him. *"Stop being goofy. We're best friends."* To be honest I was conflicted myself. Did I want to reject JaKobe? Not really. But this was all way to new to me.

*"Jai, I'm sorry, okay? Come on, now."*

I was so confused.

"Jaidah?" JaKobe spoke as we ended the dinner a little early than expected.

"Yeah?" I answered as we began to walk out of the building.

"I had a nice time, maybe we can—you know? Do this again?" I half smiled as he extended his hand for me to shake. I looked down at his hand, but instead pulled him into a hug. He laughed and hugged me back, but I could feel the somewhat difference in the hug.

"What's the matter?" I said as I pulled away from him.

"Nothing, it's just I'm glad to have you back as a friend," he said as he looked at me.

"Sure, sure. We'll talk again later? Cool? I got to go handle my friend. She's in need of a pep talk. I just looked at her Snapchat, and she is on there ranting and crying." Presently, we stood out waiting for the valet to come around and bring our cars. We were having a nice conversation, and for once he didn't say anything that made me mad at him.

"Um, listen, I'm going to talk to your brother and fix that with him too. Alright? And when are you going back to New York?" He asked that question as he rocked back and forth on his heels.

"Well, there has been a lot going on in my life, so I don't think I'll be going back any time soon. My cousin needs me, and so does my mom. Plus the funeral will be this weekend—"

"Just know I'm going 'cause Auntie M was my backbone too."

I nodded with a smile.

"And, is Lyric alright? She can come to my camp for some counseling, food, and mingle with kids her age. So, bring her by. Cool?"

I nodded with a smile as the valet finally brought our cars around.

"Thanks, and I'll be in contact with you, okay?"

"Alright, I have to go check up Moni," I said to him.

"What's wrong with her?" he asked with a curious look."

"I think her and Nicki broke up." He almost tensed up but relaxed. I guess he was thinking about when his ex-girlfriend cheated on him. But I just let it go.

"Damn, but here comes your car," I turned around and watched as they pulled up. He stopped me before he spoke. "Jaidah?"

"Yes, JaKobe?"

"Why did you forgive me so easily?" I sighed as I turned away from him and walked around to me car. The valet handed me my keys as he stepped out. He smiled at me, and held the door open for me as I looked up at JaKobe.

"What would Jesus do?"

He smiled and didn't say another word. I stepped inside my car as I waved him off. I tipped the valet as he closed my door. JaKobe stood at the curb as I pulled off. I looked in my rearview mirror as he finally got into his car and pulled off in the other direction.

I turned on my radio as the smooth voice of Giveon blasted through my speakers. I continued to drive down the road as I sang along to the lyrics. My phone vibrated, and I ignored it while I was driving. I didn't live that far from the restaurant, but I knew that was Monica calling me. I wanted to know what made her and Nicki break up. Monica wasn't the type to cheat, or cause any type of distress in the relationship. But I didn't know. I wasn't sure what the cause of it was.

I knew she was stuffing her face with chocolate, skittles, and more. She did the same thing when she and David broke up. I didn't want to think that they had slept together, but when I saw him and didn't hear from her the day of the event, I couldn't help but wonder. I turned on the street off where Monica lived, and slowed down my speed as I turned into the driveway. I turned off the car and grabbed my small goody bag. I held my keys in my hand as I unlocked the car door and stepped out. I closed the door and walked around the car, and to the sidewalk.

I walked up to the front door and keyed myself in. The sound of somber music filled the house, as I entered and locked the door behind me. I walked through the foyer as I heard her crying. I placed the food on the counter, sighing. I knew she would be sitting up here like this. I haven't seen her in a few days. And maybe this was why?

I slowly walked in, and she looked up at me. Then she started crying even more. I sat by her, and rubbed her back. She cried on my shoulder as I rubbed her hair and back. "What happened between the two of you? You said she was the one?"

"I thought so but I was wrong, Jaidah. She cheated on me and I just figure out I'm not in love with her. I'm in love with someone else?" I looked down at her.

"Who?" I said as she shoved a cookie in her mouth. "It's not David, is it?"

"No, well, I don't know. Me and him talked and—" I shook my head now and stared at her.

"No, no! He used to abuse, lie, and cheat on you! Why would you wanna love him again?" I yelled.

"It's not him. I'm just so confused I don't know what to do. I just need to be alone, Jaidah, I'm so, sorry! I'm just in love with someone else, and I messed up with Nicki." She just didn't seem like she used too. She didn't talk to me, she didn't interact. She got up from the couch while crying, as she grabbed the food along with her. I sighed and rubbed my eyes.

"Monica?" Her door slammed, and I just shook my head. I wanted to know what had her so messed up. I know there is no way in hell she was in love with David. He was a monster. I was worried about her, and there was no way in hell I was going to let my friend go back to him. I pulled out my phone and got up from the couch. I wanted to talk to my mom and see how Lyric was. I called them as I went upstairs into my room and closed the door.

I called my mom and asked to talk to Lyric. I wanted to know what was going on, and if my mom was going to get full custody of her. I didn't know if I was going to take care of her, or if my mom was going to do so.

*** 

*2:39 a.m.*

I was lying in my bed. Up for no reason at all. I was wearing nothing but a Victoria Secret lace panty and bra set, and Louis Vuitton oversized tee shirt. I was looking at the new *Cosmopolitan* magazine.

I should have been going to bed, but why should I? It's Friday night, and I don't have nothing to do. Monica had shut me out, and didn't say a word to me after our conversation. My phone was buzzing. I didn't care to see who it was, there was nobody in my favor. It was just men who liked every last one of my pictures on Instagram.

And, the only man that I wanted to be laid up with and just have some conversation with, I haven't spoken to in days. And not even at work—I haven't had a photo shoot. I wanted to talk to him, call him, touch him—everything. But, I couldn't bring myself to do it. I couldn't bring myself to call him.

I was scared that he would reject me and what we did was only a one-time thing. My phone buzzed again, and I looked at the lock screen only for it to be an unknown number. I unlocked my phone, and went to my messages. It could be my agent, and just on my night off I might have to go into a shoot or a video shoot.

I looked at the message and it said: *"Meet me downstairs?"*

That shit was weird, so I got up and pulled on my robe. I tied it up, as my phone buzzed again. I looked at it and frowned. I closed my phone and walked down the dark hall, making my way to the stairs. The light rain beat down the windows, someone knocked on my door, and I tiptoed down the rest of the steps. I finally got to the door, but I was too short to look through the peep-pole, so I had to get on my tippy toes to look through it.

It was too dark outside for me to see who was out there. "Who the hell is it?"

"Rashad" My eyes widened, and I turned on the light. I unlocked the door and opened it.

"Rashad?—What are you doing here?—You haven't talked to me since that day," I said, putting my hand on my hip.

"Can you let me in? I'm soaked." I thought for a second and bit my lip.

"No, you haven't talked to me. So, go back to where you were."

He shook his head and pulled out something. "This is why I haven't been talking to you: I meant what I said when I said I loved you. I've known you for years and I always loved you. If I got to earn your trust, love and all that again, please, trust me— this is what I was doing for you. Now, a nigga is soaking wet. I haven't been with any hoes. I ain't like that, I promise I ain't like the nigga who—" I stepped aside and let him in.

"You can come in, Rashad." He stepped in, and I closed the door as he was standing there dripping wet.

"I'm here because I missed you. It's been a week and I need you, baby. I see you on damn Instagram and then niggas looking at what's mine. But, that's not all I want you for. I can't help but think about that night. I can't help but lust for you, baby." He pulled off his wet jacket, and I just licked my lips at how sexy this man was.

"Just take off your wet clothes. I'll dry them for you." He pulled off his clothes, and I tried to keep my composure.

"I'll be upstairs, I know where your room is. I promise I'll be the best boyfriend ever."

"Boyfriend? Rashad, you really wanna be my boyfriend?" He nodded, and walked upstairs. His Calvin Klein boxers were so damn sexy, as his pants hung low off his hips slightly.

"Lord! Give me the strength to not fall into the temptations of sex with this man."

I walked down to the laundry room and tossed his clothes in the dryer. After doing that, I hit the lights and went upstairs. I was mentally preparing myself for him. I didn't know what he was going to do. I had a sexy man in my room, and didn't know how to control myself.

I was all hot for no reason. He probably just wanted to relax and chill. But I knew what that would lead to.

"About time you came back up here. I was thinking you disappeared or something." I shook my head. "Why you so shy? You don't need to be. You're never shy around me. He got off my bed and walked up to me, making me back into the wall. He trapped me between his arms. His big muscular arms! His tattoos were so—damn, gawd!

"Do I make you nervous, Jaidah? I shouldn't. You're all I want, you're all I need. I shrugged and acted as if I didn't care.

"No, you don't. Now can you move? You left me for how long?" I was lying through my damn teeth.

"You're lying. I can tell, you can't fake your love for me, baby."

"Move, Rashad, I'm not fit to play any games with you—" His hand gripped my neck softly, and he smashed his lips lustfully into mine. His tongue danced in my mouth, making me moan. He pulled away from my lips and started to move his tongue on my neck, sucking all on my neck.

He pulled away from me and looked at me. Getting lost in his eyes, I didn't realize he had picked me up and pressed my back against the wall and kissed my shoulder blade. He pulled off my silk robe, and tossed it on the bed. Rashad stared at my body.

"I knew you wanted me. You are so fine, Jaidah. You should know you're the best thing in the world." He placed his hands between my head, and kissed my lips, making a sloppy noise as he kissed down to my neck, leaving wet kisses so good it made me moan. I missed Rashad so much.

# Chapter 16

## The Truth Will Set You Free

*JaKobe Harrison*

## A Week Later

I had made me a doctor's appointment a few days ago. I took her words into consideration and decided to get tested. I wasn't about to have a disease from a woman that cheated on me multiple times. I sighed as I wiped the soap off of my face, turned off the steaming hot water. I placed my washcloth on the counter, before walking out of the room.

It was quiet in my house. I wish I had someone here with me. I shook my head as I pulled on my outfit for today. I slid on my shades and grabbed the rest of my belongings. I walked out of my room, and turned off the rest of the lights.

After doing that, I walked out of the house completely as the morning sun beamed down on me. I walked down the sidewalk and to my car. I keyed myself in, and hopped into the driver's seat. Getting ready to pull off, I turned on the radio and backed out of the driveway, heading straight for the doctor's office. I was bound to get there in about twenty or thirty minutes top.

But I couldn't help but think about when Tracy called me, and what she had told me.

"Hello? Who is this?" I said into the phone, as I got up from my California King bed.

"Um—Tracy. Can I talk to you?" My head jumped back as her voice boomed through the phone.

"The fuck do you want? We ain't friends. I don't wanna talk to you after the shit you did. Go talk to your girlfriend."

"JaKobe, I really need to talk to you. This is really important."

I sighed. "I got somewhere to be. What you want? For some reason I feel like your fucking ass want something. It just feel like your ass bullshitting me."

"I went to the doctor and—"

I cut her clean off. "And what? Ain't no way your ass pregnant. Ain't no condom break. I wore the right size, and I used one every time we fucked, so what? I ain't giving you no money." I heard her sniffling. I ain't have no soft spot for her ass.

"I have a STD, JaKobe. I just wanted to tell you. I don't want you to get hurt. I already hurt you enough, I just want you to get tested. I'm so sorry, goodbye—"

*Beep, beep, beep!"*

I just became heated all over again. It wasn't right that she could do this to people. I don't know how many people she could have given an STD to. It was just shameful. I rubbed my head as I stopped at a stop light. I saw flashing, and knew it was some fans. I smiled and waved at them before the light turned green again. I pulled off, making a few turns and turned onto the street, pulling right into the street the doctor's office was on.

I parked and got out of the car. I beeped it locked, walking to the front doors. I looked at the sign next to the door, and I made sure I was going to the right floor. I opened the door and stepped in, going up the steps to the second floor. I walked down the hall, and opened up the door, going straight to the receptionist desk.

"Hello? How may I help you?"

"Yes, I have an appointment with Dr. Miles." She nodded, as I pulled out my papers and medical card.

"Name?"

"Harrison, JaKobe." She nodded, as she typed in the information from the papers.

"Okay, you're right on time. Just have a seat. The nurse will call you out in a moment."

"Thank you." She handed me back my papers and card. I walked into the waiting area, and sat down as I pulled out my phone. As I got a few notifications, I decided to text Brad. I let him know I wanted to talk to him, and apologize.

Me: *Hey, I just wanted to know if I could talk to you. And apologize?*

As I sent the message, I got another message—from Monica. I was wondering what she even wanted.

404-000-0000: *hey? Um, I was wondering if I could talk to you about something, please?*

I sighed, and decided to respond back. I don't know what I was getting myself into. I said I'd never text or talk to her again. But something was drawing me to her. My phone buzzed again, and I looked down at it:

404-000-0000: *meet me at the Red Room...*

The nurse opened the door, and called my name. This was going to be a long evening. I got up from my seat and walked to the back with the nurse. She showed me where my doctor's room was.

"I'm going to take some blood samples. But please tell me why you're here today."

I sighed. "I want to get tested for an STD." She looked at me and nodded. "Have you been having safe sex?"

"Not with my ex-girlfriend, no. She told me to get tested after she cheated on me."

"Wow, that's sad. Well, you're doing the right thing."

I nodded. "Can I rush the results? This stays completely confidential, right?" She looked at me, then my name.

"Yes, completely."

"Good."

\*\*\*

After coming from the doctor's, I pulled into the Red Room. I thought long and hard about what I was doing. I took a deep breath as I walked into the Red Room. I spotted her as soon as I stepped in. The Red Room was actually my second business. She was sitting there looking tired and anxious.

"Monica?" She looked up at me, and gave me a soft smile.

"Hi, I've thought long and hard about this. I'm just so conflicted inside." She didn't seem like the hard Monica she'd usually be. I waved for her to get up, so we could go to my office and talk private. We walked in, and she sat down. I sat on my plush, small couch.

"JaKobe, it's so hard for me to say this, awfully hard actually. Telling you what happened between me and my family is difficult. After I mentioned David to you, I think I should tell you what happened completely."

I was kind of confused.

"Okay. Go on."

"First off, me and my family don't talk at all, the holy Christians they are. They hate me for who I am because I'm— bisexual. They say, I'll be going to hell because of my gender interest. Well, the real reason me and Nicki broke up is because I'm conflicted with myself. I don't know if I really want to be in a relationship with her or—"

"David?" I butted in.

"No, not David."

"Okay, I understand."

"What do you understand? I haven't told you anything."

"I understand why, you've been through a lot. It can't be easy to just open up about your family to someone after dealing with it alone for so long."

She shrugged and placed her hand behind her head. "It's not that it's not easy, it's just I don't know what to share. I don't know what's too much, you know?"

I nodded with a slight smile.

"Sometimes there is no such thing as too much. If you wanna share what's on your mind, feel free. I'm not one to judge how much is too much. I'm sure I have a ton of things that could be deemed too much."

"Well, let's see—where should I start?" she said.

"The guy who are you conflicted with that made you and Nicki break up?" She kind of froze. I looked at her for a while. I guess she picked up on my confused expression. She didn't tell me his name. Well, I told her the name I thought she would say, but I was wrong of course.

"I meant, was he a friend? Is he a friend? Did you guys just meet?" I questioned.

"Yeah, not really a friend though. An enemy—more like— frenemy." I could see the look of regret on her face. My phone buzzed a few times. But I ignored it.

"What went wrong?" I said, frowning a little.

"There's this girl. She was in love with him."

I shrugged and chuckled.

"Oh, come on! You can tell me, have you told Jai?"

I watched Monica's face; her expressions are cute. I think it's pretty funny to watch her attempt to understand why things happen. No one knows exactly why someone does something but that person.

"It's scary to think of the all the things love will make people do."

"What? What are you talking about?" I asked her.

"Yeah, love is one hell of a drug. I still don't get it. He was someone I really thought I had a good friendship with. But all along he wanted my friend and because he couldn't have her, he cheated."

I smacked my lips.

"Come on! I have no idea what you're talking about. Who is the guy?"

She looked at me. Her hand fell on my knee, and she stared at me.

"Ever since the night we had sex, I've been going out of my mind. See, David—David was an asshole. He treated me like shit. He used to come home drunk, call me worthless, and do things no man should do. I loved him. Yeah, I was young. Very young and stupid, and I loved him so much that I would do anything for him. But, he went too far; he wanted me to sleep with one of his guys for money—Fun he called it. When I saw him that night, I saw the love and the hate. I tried to drink it all away, but it didn't work. I was very drunk when I came onto you. I knew what I was doing, I took advantage of you. And I was wrong, I was wrong to Jaidah. I was wrong to Nicki. But, Nicki couldn't satisfy me like you did. Neither could David. Even though I was drunk, I loved every minute of what you did to me. Jaidah is my friend. But I had to let the truth out—set me free, you know!

I could go on with lying to Nicki. Yes, I loved her too. I thought she was the one. She wasn't, to be frank. I love both genders. But the way you fucked me, made my body melt, made me crave it. I know it's shameful. I always said you were a jackass. Still are, but deep down inside of me, I've seen something more. What I'm trying to say is that—I need you."

I was shocked and appalled. I didn't know how to react to what she just said. I was never going to talk about that night. But here I was, here I was with Jaidah's best friend, betraying her again.

"Monica, I—"

"I understand if you never want to speak to me again. I can just tell Jai that I cursed you out or something. She'll understand that I don't like you, and she'll never suspect it. I just wanted to get it all off my chest before I exploded." She gave a small smile. My phone vibrated again. I pulled it out, my mind was everywhere. My eyes were blurred and confused. I just shut off my phone and looked at Monica.

She was gathering her things and leaving. "You just don't drop shit like this on people and expect them to accept it! What the fuck! You're saying you have feelings for me. Then want to say, 'Oh forget it!' Are you fucking nuts, Monica?" She turned back, and looked at me.

"I won't bother you. I mean it." Her hand touched the nob of the door. She pulled it open and was about to walk out. I walked behind her and closed the door with one hand.

"Wait," I said.

"Why?" she said.

"Because—"

"Because what!" she said, turning around so we were face to face. I sucked up all my pride and pulled her by that tight ass blouse of hers and slammed my lips into her. Our teeth hit a little bit, but our tongues saved the moment. Her hands ran through my hair as I lifted up her skirt. Picking her up roughly. "We can't," she said, pulling away from me.

"We are both already in too deep. There's no going back now." I untied her blouse in the front, and her breasts spilled out of her shirt. She groaned softly and wrapped her arms around my neck, as I hiked up her skirt and began to kiss all around her neck, making her throw her head back in pleasure. I carried her over to the couch, sat her down, closed the blinds and hovered over her. Her chest was heaving up and down as she yanked at my belt.

I swatted her hands away. She grabbed her purse and threw a pack of condoms at me. "Really? A whole pack?" She nodded as she bit her lip. Monica unzipped and unbutton my jeans, then yanked them down. She opened the pack of condoms.

"Eager, aren't you?" I said with a raised eyebrow.

"You have no idea." I felt the condom being slid on. I pushed her back on the leather couch, and pulled off her skirt. Next was the thinnest piece of underwear I'd ever seen.

My thumb ran across her center, making her moan softly. I yanked her body to the edge of the couch and entered her slowly, and she couldn't help but grab one of the pillows.

"Yes—"

"I haven't done anything to make you say yes—" I began to stroke in and out of her. Her moans echoed throughout my office room.

"Monica, what are you doing to me?"

"I don't know, jackass. What are *you* doing to me!" She moaned, I flipped her over and entered her wet pussy from the back.

"You gon' learn my damn name ain't jackass." I pulled her hair back, making her lick her lips. I was in for big trouble.

# Chapter 17

## November Approaching

*Jaidah O'Neil*

"Rashad, have you seen my keys?" I asked him as I entered my bedroom. The house was quiet, like it had been for the past few days. I've gotten scattered text from Moni here and there. I know she was going through something; she would usually close herself off to the world. Me knowing this, I didn't want to pressure her at all. I rubbed my hair as I held my phone in my hand. I was totally discombobulated. I had so much to do today. My mom had to work, and so did my dad. So, Lyric would be home alone, which neither of us wanted in her time of grief.

I asked Bradley if she could be with him today. But that was a no-go. He was actually not even in town. I hated when he left and didn't even tell me. I slapped my forehead as my phone buzzed, signaling that I had a text message from somebody. Rashad's voice pulled me out of my phone. I turned around to him shirtless and in a pair of briefs. Why did he have to wear those? Why couldn't he just wear some loose ass boxers? He knew he was blessed in that department, and he had nerve to be walking around here in this Versace briefs that hugged every blessed part of his bottom half.

"Baby, you good?" he said, snapping me out of my trance.

"Yeah, yeah. I'm good."

He smiled that priceless half smile as he dangled my keys in my face.

"Found them on the floor by the window. You say you have to be somewhere? Now?"

I nodded. "Mm-hm, I have to go by my mom's, pick up Lyric, then go to the modeling agency and talk business about my campaign, and business with Kia. I also have to meet her sometime this week. I don't know what I'm going to do with Lyric today. I think to cheer her up, I'll bring her around some of the positive people I know in the business." I grabbed my keys and looked at my phone.

"Well, damn! Daddy Rashad don't get no play today? Jeez! I'm not even busy, and I'm not in the equation." He spoke with his hands in the air.

"I'm sorry, it's just this week is really hectic for me. With the meetings for the fall fashion shows, to the fittings, to my own business, to the funeral. It's just been a lot for me to break down." I sighed. I could tell he was looking me up and down,

"Did you eat anything this morning?—It's almost ten to eleven," he said with genuine concern.

"Actually, I haven't had anything but some yogurt with granola on top," I said, still looking down at my phone, typing away and not really giving Rashad any attention.

"Baby, why when I made dinner last night you ain't eat it?" he pressed further.

"Wasn't hungry."

"Okay. What about the day before that?"

"I don't know. I was running errands. Had to do stuff for mom. I couldn't eat much but a half of club sandwich and a low-cal tea." I got up from the bed, where I was sitting for only a few moments.

"Hold up, where you are going dressed like that? Show that body, mmm. Nah."

I finally looked up at him.

"I'm dressed appropriately for today. What's the problem?"

He laughed.

"What?" I questioned with attitude.

"Baby, you only got on my tee shirt and I doubt it's even anything up under there."

I looked down at my body and groaned loudly.

"Shit, you're right." I laughed along with him. "I'll go change."

He grabbed my hand, and pulled me into his chest.

"It can wait. You need to eat. I don't need you passing out on me. You're going to be out all day; you need something in your stomach before you go."

I sighed.

"Rashad, I don't have the time, baby." He grabbed my phone and locked it, tossing it in the bed and holding me tight.

"Look at yourself! You're running yourself down. You've been up all night doing this and that. What about yourself? What about your health?" He did have a point.

"I'm just going through a lot."

"And I'm here to help. Like I said, I don't have anything to do today. I'm perfect to go with you, help out and everything. Plus, I think Lyric would like me." I thought for a moment, and he pecked my lips. "Come on! You know I'm good for it." I nodded, and he kissed my lips once more.

"Thank you, Rashad. I don't know how I was going to get through today anyway." His soft lips kissed my neck. I felt so weak at the knees. I ran my hand through his hair which still harbored the two French braids. His lips and tongue began to suck and lick at my neck at the same time. I bit my lip, slightly breathing out loud softly.

His hands held my body in a way I just couldn't fathom. He knew this was my weak spot. I turned my head, biting his earlobe. Feeling my body heat up, his hand slid under the shirt, his fingers soon finding my sweet spot. They grazed over the smooth lips, then the clit, making me hold my arms tight around his neck. He just wouldn't stop kissing and sucking on my neck, still making sure not to leave a mark but making it feel so pleasurable.

"Rashad?" I spoke softly, as my face started to turn up into a sexual frown. For some reason, Rashad could take away all my problems, fears, and anxiety. Not just by sexual favors but by his words and actions. I bit my lip, closing my eyes as my right leg wrapped around his waist. His free hand released his member from his boundary of tight fabric. The moment his tip and shaft entered me, I threw my head back, letting my mouth stay agape.

His other hand supported my back as I wrapped my other leg around his waist. How can a quick conversation turn into hot sex like this? I was in heaven, I was making every love sound known to man, as he bounced me down on his member with me clinging to him. My phone buzzed and rang. His hand tangled in my hair as he brought his lips to mine, giving me a hot passionate kiss.

"Rashad—I—have—to—get—that," I said through our wet kiss.

"Give me twenty minutes, baby." I moaned louder, as he slammed me down, making a wet squirting noise, but my phone kept ringing.

"You have one new voicemail," the ringtone said as the phone buzzed twice. Meanwhile, Rashad's strength never failed him as he was pounding with rhythmic strokes inside me.

"Hi, Jaidah, Auntie Jill just left. I'm scared. I couldn't tell her, but some boys have been bothering me, and not in a teasing way. I don't want to go back to that school. I just want to go home. I'll just sit here and wait for you. Bye."

I groaned loudly at Rashad. "We have to stop, Shad, please!" He rested his head in the crook of my neck. Trying to catch his breathing, his member pulsated in me. And I bit my lip to hold my eager moan.

"Fuck!" He dragged out as he slid his piece out of me with a pop.

"I'm sorry."

"It's not your fault, baby. I'll get cleaned up in the guest bathroom. 'Cause I know for damn sure if we get in there together I'll bend you over and hold your arms back, and make you take this thick c—"

"Stop it, Daddy. We have to get going soon."

"Man, don't call me that right now while we in this position."

I tried not to giggle.

"Well, maybe later?"

154

He looked at me, eyes still dilated with lust. "I doubt it. By that message we just heard? Lyric will probably be over here with you. So, I'll suck it up and not think about it. But damn, you just blow my mind. We haven't had sex in some weeks. A few days ago, that shit was just foreplay." He let me down, and I fixed the shirt as I pulled my hair into a tight ponytail.

"We will fit time in for us. I promise."

"Nigga stuck with blue balls and shit. Shit is a mother fucker.

I shook my head as I walked into the bathroom. My phone rang, and I didn't feel like going into the room to get it.

"Shad! Can you answer my phone for me?" I yelled as I hopped into the shower, letting the hot steamy water run down my skin.

"Yeah! I got it," I heard him say, as I was lathering up my body. I began to hum as I let the water run down my face. It was only a quick ten-minute shower before I got out. I dried my body off and walked into my room. Rashad had a towel around his waist.

"Who had called me?" He didn't say a word. "Shad? Did you hear me, sweetie?"

"It was JaKobe."

My body froze.

"Oh? What did he want?" I bit my lip as I slid on my underwear.

"Don't act dumb, baby? He asked when y'all gon' hang again. I guess he ain't know it was me on the phone. He said he talked to your brother and some more bull ass shit. Why you lie to me?" He turned and looked at me as I walked into my closet.

"I—I didn't lie."

He smacked his lips. "C'mon, man! Yes, you did. You told me you ain't know him. Right now all of a sudden y'all cool ass buddies?"

"Shad?"

"Don't fucking Shad me? Why you lie? You could've told a nigga."

I sighed. "We went to college together. That's it."

155

"Nah, that ain't it. I've know you for a long while. And I know when you lying, you get all fidgety and shit. What?"

I rubbed my forehead as he stood there.

"I don't wanna talk about it." He held onto my waist.

He held on to my wrist. "Nope, nah, uh uh. If a female called my phone and you ain't know about her, you'd have a full fit. Tell me, yo'. How you know him? I ain't gon' get mad."

"But you're fucking mad now! JaKobe is just an old friend. We rekindled our friendship. We just fell out and then got back talking."

He let me go. "You're leaving out fucking bits and pieces. We ain't leaving till you tell me—"

"We had sex, alright! You happy now that I said it?" I rolled my eyes and pulled on my shorts. He stood there without a peep, then he spoke,

"Is this the guy that you told—"

"Yes, that is him, Rashad. We have to get going." Rashad, didn't say anything else about it. I didn't want to tell him because he works with JaKobe sometimes, and I don't want any damn drama. When me and him left out of the house, he didn't say anything to me. We got in his car and drove to our destination. I called my cousin, and told her I'd be there soon.

Throughout the whole ride, Rashad was just behind the wheels, listening to Kanye West. I just looked out the window without a word.

\*\*\*

We were in the Red Room business building. I was hashing out business with Kia. This place was a nice establishment. And the room we were in was beautiful with the view. Lyric walked into the room, and I smiled. We both turned to her, and she didn't even notice Kia. "Lyric, this is Kia Dunkin. Kia, this is my fashion-loving baby cousin—Lyric." Lyric's jaw dropped as she stood there frozen in her spot.

"Oh my god! You're my idol!" she exclaimed.

"Thank you, dear. You're so beautiful. Don't let no one tell you different." Lyric nodded, as me and Kia talked about the outcome of our business. Rashad was doing some other stuff for me, and I was glad that he came.

"So, I was thinking. Since November is approaching fast, I think we should have the premiere of our business on your birthday week. How does that sound?" I wasn't too fond of my birthday. But a lot of my fans would come to this, and be happy to see me.

"Yes, that is actually a good idea, Kia."

"Can I be in the show?" Lyric said with excitement. We both laughed at her happiness. I looked at Lyric. She was exceptionally tall for her age; she had developed quickly. I now saw why the boys were messing with her.

"Of course, you can, love."

Lyric grinned; this was the happiest I've seen her since we had gotten her from that group home.

"Okay. We still out having it in New York, right?" I nodded, and Kia handed me some paperwork to sign. The day was ending, and I was glad I had gotten all this finished. I had two helpers, and I was glad for them.

"Yes, we have a month and a half to plan this. But, actually, I have planners starting on everything. So, we won't have any problems."

"Very good. I'm sorry to cut our engagement short. But I have to be getting back to New York, for America's Next Top Model casting. And, Lyric, when you reach sixteen to twenty, I want you to audition, okay? You have so much potential."

"Thank you, Kia. Can I take a picture with you please?" Kia nodded. My phone buzzed, and I looked at it to be my realtor.

Debby: *"There are some houses and condos available in ATL for renting. Would you like to check them out? Call me back when you have the time. Ciao."*

I bit my lip and replied her. Things were going well in Atlanta. Maybe coming back wasn't such a bad idea after all. Rashad had come up the stairs and handed me some important papers.

"Thank you, Rashad."

"No problem." He hugged me from behind and kissed the side of my face, "I'm sorry for overreacting."

I slightly smiled. "Sorry for lying."

"We good, baby. Damn. She reminds me so much of my sister."

I looked at him and kissed his lips. "Are you okay?" He nodded. Kia had said her goodbyes, and left. I looked at Lyric and how ecstatic she was.

"I'm going to treasure this moment forever! Thank you, Jai!" She beamed.

"You're welcome. Now, I was wondering—do you want to spend the rest of the day having fun? We can get food and go back to my place, or Rashad's. He has some cool stuff at his place." She looked at him and blushed.

"Jai?" she said, wiggling her finger for me to come closer to her, and so I did.

"Yes?"

"He's cute. Can we go over his house?" She giggled. I laughed and nodded.

"He is cute. And yeah we can."

She held onto her picture, as we began to walk out of the building. As we were heading out, I heard everlasting familiar voices. I turned my head over Rashad's shoulder. I noticed Nicki and David together, and talking over by the receptionist desk. Rashad didn't notice them; even if he did, he would not really recognize David. I frowned. I thought I was absolutely seeing shit. I blinked, and they were still there talking. I was wondering why they were even side by side. Two of Monica's ex's spelled trouble to me.

# Chapter 18

## Oh, How Things Change

*JaKobe Harrison*

The soft bed felt so good to my body as I laid under the silk sheets. The movement in the bed, the constant movement, made me raise my head up. My phone was vibrating against the bed; I picked it up, seeing that it was my trainer. I clicked off my phone, sending her straight to voicemail. Football just wasn't for me anymore. My money was growing from my business side, and I was proud of that.

I laid my head down, seeing the time in my phone. I had to get some rest. I was going to be hanging with Brad and his kids today. I had talked to him just a few days ago, and we patched everything up. I couldn't lose him as a friend, after we'd been friends for years. I could still see he was pissed about what I did to Jaidah. But if she let that go, then he did too. But I knew well enough to not push him either. The phone started to vibrate again. I sighed and picked up my phone, but this time it wasn't mine.

I looked over my shoulder to see Monica. I sighed. I'd forgotten she was even here. It's been a long while since I even had a woman in my crib. I shook her body, placing my hand on her bare back. "Monica? Get you phone." She groaned and just pulled the covers over her head. I snatched them back, shaking her again.

"Get your phone, girl!" She smacked her lips and extended her arms from under the cover and grabbed the phone, answering it before whoever it was hung up.

"Hello?" she said in a deep sleepy voice.

"What's up, Jaidah?"

I rubbed my eyes, as I turned on my back and looked up at the skylight. I listened to her talk, and it was like the pit of my stomach flipped.

"What do you mean why am I not at the house? Okay, just out, Jai. You don't have to be worried about me."

I shook my head. What was I doing right now? I got up from the bed, knowing it was three a.m. I couldn't listen to this.

"What you mean you seen David and Nicki together?"

I threw my head back and stepped out of the room. I had so much on my mind, and this was not helping at all. I walked down the steps, and made my way into the kitchen. I walked over to the fridge and pulled me out some water, then a pudding. I felt a pair of arms wrap around me, and I jumped a little.

"What?"

"Why the attitude?" Monica asked, as I pulled open the small container.

"Nothing, I don't have an attitude," I said, sitting at the island counter.

"I see it all on your face." She walked around the counter and hugged me from the side. "You changed as soon as you heard me talking to Jaidah on the phone." I pulled the drawer open, grabbing me a spoon. I scooped me out some pudding and placed it in my mouth. "JaKobe?"

"I said I'm coo'. Go back to bed." She smacked her lips.

"How are we going to be together if—What's this?" she said, picking up a piece of paper off the table.

"My business, put it down," I simply said.

"This is a damn test form! Why didn't you tell me you went to get tested for an STD before we had sex! Shouldn't that be fucking important to tell someone who you have sex with!"

"Aye! No need to yell. It's three a.m., do it say I'm positive for it? No! My fucking ex was a hoe. That's why I got tested. Damn, leave it the hell alone." I finished the pudding and threw it away in the garbage, then I placed the spoon in the sink.

"JaKobe, if you're going to be with me, you gotta tell me the truth."

I sighed.

"You know? I don't even know if we should even be together. This is too much for me. You're Jaidah's best friend! I already hurt her once. I just got in her good graces and here I am, sleeping with you, her best friend! You should feel bad too." She fiddled with her nails and shook her head.

"I have deep feelings for you. And it's just not from sex! It's not—it's not—" She ran her hand through her hair, and her face was soft and sad.

"It's not what?" I said, grabbing her wrist.

"When we were in college, I secretly wanted to be with you. I really did." My eyes widened. This was too much to take in.

"So? You're telling me that! Man, this is too fucking much! How many times I gotta keep fucking up!"

"JaKobe, please—"

"I don't know about this. I just think we should be friends." She wrapped her arms around me and kissed me. For some reason, she made me weak. And I didn't know where I stood with this.

***

Later on that day, I was with Bradley. We were at this amusement park with the kids. I had hit run down by a few kids for autographs, but I didn't mind at all. "JaKobe? So when you gon' try the dating game again?" he said as he watched his kids play the games.

"Um? I don't know. Shit is actually tough right now. I'm actually feeling someone right now." He looked at me and raised an eyebrow.

"For real? Who is she?" I had this look on my face, and he knew some shit was up. "C'mon! Don't lie, bruh. Who is she? I'm listening."

"You ain't gon' drop kick me, or body slam me on the ground, are you?"

He laughed, and so did I.

"Nah, man! Who?"

I slightly sighed.

"I ain't gon' lie. Her name is Monica."

He looked at me, looking shocked than ever.

"You what! Well, I never liked her. She was always against men. Men hater and shit! What spell she put on you, yo'? You fucked her, didn't you?"

"What? Noooo," I said, looking at the kids.

"Lying son of a bitch. She popped that tight pussy on you, didn't she?"

I sighed, rubbing my forehead.

"Yeah, she did, man. She said she liked me since college." Bradley patted my back and shook his head.

"You should have just got with my sister back in college and maybe you wouldn't be going through this. But in all honesty, I think you should just stop this right now. Before Jaidah finds out. You just might break her heart. Again."

I sighed, then we went over to the kids. He had his oldest along with Lyric. His little babies were with their mom. I wanted to spend some time with Lyric before the funeral. I just didn't know what to do.

I thought about what Bradley said. He was right, truly right. But I don't think I'd be able to get rid of Monica like that. We had a lot in common.

"Mr. JaKobe? Jaidah said for you to bring her a teddy and some candy—with your handsome head," Lyric laughed, and ran off before I could say anything. I shook my head. This was bound to get messy.

\*\*\*

I looked at Monica, and she swayed her hips to the music. She insisted on giving me a show tonight. I couldn't refuse. And I wanted her bad, after I confessed my feelings to her. I couldn't fail her. And, after she told me what happened more in her life, it's like, she was growing more and more on me. I knew I had to mend her heart in some way. But why? How? I need to slow this shit down. I needed to be thinking about other things but her! But I couldn't.

Monica had walked over to me and wrapped her arms around my neck. My heart rate sped up when her skin touched mine. I put my hands on her hips, and she closed her eyes. She was tempting, man, and she was grinding against my manhood, doing this shit on purpose.

"M-Monica?" She opened her eyes.

"Hmm?" she answered.

"You got me feeling some type of way. "Can you back up a little? We just going to fast with this." She frowned and leaned up. I was hard. Fuck! I felt embarrassed. How could she get me so hard like this? No woman ever did this to me by not doing anything. I shouldn't be feeling this way about her like this.

"I don't care. Maybe Jaidah wasn't meant for you!"

"What? How is Jaidah in this?"

"I just can feel it. You need to let her go. You don't have her anymore. Rashad does. I want you. I've told you my feelings. But you seem like you're not one with me. But you're fucking me! Me!"

I sighed.

"I don't wanna have this conversation. Hey, get up."

"No! You're about to stay put! I like you, I really do."

"You're rushing this shit! And I don't think we should keep sneaking around Jaidah back. This is sick."

"Just kiss me, JaKobe." I did as told without hesitation. The kiss was so good, I pulled her closer to me. I didn't want to rush this. I didn't even know what we were. But I wanted her, and I wanted her now.

"You happy? But I won't be one of your failed relationships. You need to slow down. Like right the fuck now before I tear that ass up!"

"Y-yes," she said as I gripped her ass and kissed her more. I had to have this girl. I didn't want anyone else to have her.

"JaKobe, oh my—" I kissed her, as my hand crept up her thick thigh, and into her lace panties, rubbing her clit.

"Shut the fuck up."

"You're mine?" I shook my head, but she didn't see it. I could never be anyone to another woman. I was always Jaidah's. Oh, how I could tell things were going to change!

# Chapter 19

## Fifty Shades Of Oh Hecky Nah

*Jaidah O'Neil*

"Mommy?" I said as I laid on her bed. My dad was off at work at his studio. He was a filmmaker, and a good one at that. I was just flipping the pages of my mom's new urban magazine. "*Mom!*" I said louder, as I swung my feet back and forth while I read the new column on my upcoming business. My mom came into the room with soap on her hands.

"What do you want? Jesus, girl, I am trying to wash Lyric's big mane. I swear you are worse than Bradley!" I smiled big and raised up the magazine. She gave me a face. "Now do it look like I can read that, or hold it?"

"Yes, you have your contacts in, right?" I said, raising my eyebrows at her.

"Don't make me pop you." I could tell she was seriously stressed out. Rolling half of the other page, I got out of her bed and walked next to her.

"See, it's a column on me and my business! Isn't that great?" She smiled as she read the article line for line.

Mom's smile broadened before she spoke. "This is amazing, I'm so proud—" She stopped talking when we both heard Lyric call her loudly.

"Auntie Jill! There is soap in my eyes!" Mom threw her hands in the air and walked out of the room. I shook my head as I sat back on her bed, while I continued to look at the magazine. My phone started to ring, and I rolled my eyes, like my phone had been blowing up from all my social media and calls. I pressed my lips to the side as I grabbed my phone off the charger. Seeing it was an unknown number, I frowned, wondering who could have gotten my number in the first place.

Me being me, I answered the phone, "Hello, this is Beck with the good hair. How may I help you?" The woman on the other end began to crack up. I waited until she was done so I could see who this was and how they got my number.

"Oh my gosh! You are really funny. Hi, Jaidah, this is Nicki. How are you?"

*Ohhh, isn't this a coincidence?* I thought.

"Hello, Nicki, who did you get my number from? Sorry, I just have to ask."

She sighed. "I got it from Monica a while ago. But I wanted to talk to you about her." I raised my eyebrows. If she was going to ask me about what she was up to lately, I wouldn't know; she's been so distant and off with me.

"Oh! Well, I haven't really been really that close with her lately. But I'll try my best." She hummed an *okay*.

"Well, you know me and her broke up. Did she happen to tell you why?" I pushed my hair out of my face and debated on if I should be nonchalant with her, act like I didn't know a damn thing, or tell her the truth.

"Well, to be frank with you, she told me bits and pieces. Why?"

She sighed deeply.

"I'm going to tell you why. Actually, she broke up with me because of some man. At first I thought it was David. But, I found out that was not the case. I know he had done some terrible things to her, but he confessed that he was truly done with her. Monica has actually lied to me and you. David is actually a Christian man. He was brought up to never abuse women. He told me about how she wanted to control their relationship, and actually do BDSM. She actually tried to do it with me. But I wasn't with it. You must not know who the real 'Monica' is!"

I was flabbergasted.

"Excuse me? No way this is true! I've known her since I was little and—"

"Believe me, I've known her for a long time too. Her parents really fucked her up for being bisexual. At first, I was going to try it, but then she became way too aggressive about it. I don't know if she's really confused about her sexuality or what. But, lemme tell you this. She's in love with some man, I don't know who but I know it is not good for her. You have to talk to her soon, or I think she'll really hurt herself, okay?" I was quiet, letting all of this soak in deep.

Then I spoke, "I can tell you really did love her. Are you sure about this?" I asked her.

"I am very sure about this. I'd never lie against her. We spent too long trying to make everything work. I really did love her." Then I knew that Nicki wasn't making up some obscene story just to get back at Monica. I sighed deep, shaking my head. This was just too much to take in.

"Okay, I believe you. I'll talk to her, okay?" She let out a breath of relief, before she spoke:

"Thank you, thank you. I hope she listens to you. I have to go."

I nodded as if she could see me.

"Okay, you're welcome. I have to be going now." She said her goodbyes, and I hung up. I tossed my phone on the mattress and shot up from the bed. I tied my hair up into a bun and slipped on my socks after that. Picking my phone back up, and slipping it into my pocket, I walked out of my room and onto the hall. I bumped into Lyric who was on her new phone that JaKobe bought her. He was spoiling her already.

"I'm sorry, Jaidah, but where are you going? You're leaving. Why you leaving?" she said all at once. I grabbed her shoulders and hugged her.

"Relax. Are you okay?"

She looked everywhere but me.

"What's up? What has been up with you lately?" She bit her lip and was mute. "You know you can tell me anything, right?" She nodded. "So do you wanna tell me?" She sighed and shook her head.

"Not—not right now. When I'm prepared, I'll tell you. Okay?" I nodded and gave her another hug. She smiled, but I knew inside she was hurting. I sighed and walked out of the house, ready to go off on Monica. I had some choice words for her.

\*\*\*

I pulled up to the house, and hopped out of the car. I was highly pissed off. I locked the car up. I pulled out my spare keys and keyed myself into the house. "Monica!" I said, as I walked through the foyer and to her room, banging on the door.

"What!" she screamed,

"Open up! Now!" It took her a while, but she opened the door, and she was half naked as always.

"Yes?" she said with attitude.

"So you're lying now? Really that's what we do?"

She smacked her lips.

"What are you talking about?"

"You lied about David, and what you said he did to you! Why did you lie? Huh?"

She laughed. "Get out my face with that. I don't have time for it."

"Nicki told me everything. Now why you have to lie especially to me?"

She narrowed her eyes at me. "Because you don't deserve *him*! You think you can have every man when you can't!"

I shrugged. "What are you talking about? You tripping for real?" She slammed the door in my face, but my foot was in the crack of the door. I pushed the door back open and walked into her room.

"Listen here, bitch. I don't know what the fuck you think you're talking about. But you need to chill the fuck out. We been friends for how long? Huh? You wanna lie to me and do all this other shit? The fuck is wrong with you! I don't know what's gotten into you. But you need to chill!" She stood there shocked, and then got heated, but I stopped it real quick. I slapped her, and she held her cheek, looking at me. "Get your shit together, Moni! And I mean it!" She didn't say another word. I flipped my hand up and walked out of her room. I had it up to here with the people in my life so far.

Monica came where I was, but I didn't have anything to say to her. "So, how many times are you going to lie to me? Huh?"

"So what! I've just been through so much in my life."

I shook my head. "So this is how me and you are going to be?" She just stared at me and shrugged.

"Cool. I'll be back over here to get my things. Since you want to be like this, why don't we just let our friendship be over with, huh? What about that?"

"Whatever. I'll be glad to have you out my house."

"Bitch, with your fake wannabe fifty shades of gay ass! Fuck you. Our friendship is over if you wanna be like this. I know you doing something worse than what Nicki told me. I'll find out for real." She didn't have words, but her face said everything. I flicked her off and stepped out of the house. I had too much to deal with. I didn't need any more negatives in my life. I had to worry about my auntie's funeral and my business.

Monet Dragun

# Chapter 20

## A Funeral and Secrets

*JaKobe Harrison*

It was raining heavily. We all sat in the chairs around Mahogany's grave, as the preacher said his last words.

"We commend her soul to you, Lord. Ashes to ashes, dust to dust. We pray to God that he takes Mahogany Jones into his open arms. This innocent soul was fighting against the devil—cancer. She had no fear in you, Lord.

Take her to the great pearly gates, and watch over her. Help her daughter fight the hurt of losing her dear mother. In the name of Jesus we pray, amen." I sat there holding Lyric as she had this stone-cold look on her face. I sat there in my black suit, hat and all. Everyone around me was crying and mourning her mom's death. She didn't shed one tear. I knew she was trying to stay strong, but this wasn't healthy.

The face she was making! It was just sad. She was at her mom's own funeral. I wanted to talk to her. But I didn't know how to do so. I don't know if she was bent on revenge, or if she was trying to be positive. I was going to do everything in my power to find out what was up with her. Every time she looked at a boy or man, she was either scared or furious.

Jaidah was dabbing her face with a handkerchief as we all walked up and placed roses on the grave. I walked over to her, and she gave me a side hug. Rashad had walked up next to her. She let me go to put my rose on her auntie's grave.

As the pastor got done praying, the raining finally stopped. The clouds began to let some sun light in. Lyric clutched onto the roses, the very red and white roses that her mom once loved so much. She walked up to the casket and placed them on top of the casket. "I love you so much, mommy. I'ma going to do everything you taught me and be the best young lady I can be. I'll see you soon." She planted a tender kiss on the casket and walked away. I looked at all the people crying and raising their hands to God. Jaidah's mom and dad tried to talk to Lyric but everything was blocked out. I felt so bad for the girl. "Jai? I'ma go talk to her, okay?" I said. She nodded, and I walked away from them.

"Thanks for helping her out, man, but I lost someone once important to me. I think—I think *I* should talk to her." I looked at Rashad, and nodded. I slid my hands into my pockets as I stood next to Jaidah.

"He has lost someone. And thanks for even coming. I know you said you'd be confused but still—" I slightly smiled as we walked to the limos.

"I had to. She was family to everyone. And she fought so hard to overcome the cancer. She was a strong woman."

Jai sighed.

"I just feel so bad for my mom and Lyric. They are both hurting. And, on top of that, I think Lyric is going through something really horrible. I just can't seem to break through to her. Every noise, every cry, everything is out of her mind. Nothing seems to faze her, and I mean nothing."

I shook my head as we all walked down the grassy hill. Talking with Jaidah was cool; it brought back the good memories. And at this moment she needed a friend.

We all waited at the limo while Lyric came walking down the hill with Rashad. I looked around and spotted Monica. But she didn't bother to come over to Jaidah and try and give her some love or condolences. I knew this wasn't right, and I couldn't keep doing this.

"JaKobe?"

"Oh, yeah? Yeah?"

Jaidah laughed at my confusion.

"I had said are you coming to my parents' for dinner? All of the family will be there." Lyric looked at me, and I couldn't help but say yes.

"I'll be there. How are you doing, Lyric?"

She shrugged. "I kind of feel empty inside." I opened my arms and she smiled, giving me a small tight hug.

"I'm here for you. Okay? I'm going to put you in my program, so you can be with some cool kids. How will you feel about that?" She looked up at me and smiled.

"That'll be cool." I let her go, and opened the door for her to get in the limo. Jaidah got in. Rashad looked at me, and extended his hand.

"That was nice of you. She needs everyone to help her. She needs a lot of people to stay on her, keep her out of trouble. I needed the same thing when I was her age. When I lost my sister, that was a terrible time for me." Rashad spoke those words as he shook my hand. He was true to his word, and I could tell he was a little different with being around me. *Did Jaidah tell him about me and her? Was he cool with it?*

"I understand, and you are good with her. Does she remind you of your sister?" I asked. He sighed.

"In a lot of ways, yes." With that comment, he got into the limo with the ladies. I closed the door, walking over to the limo where Bradley was. I could feel someone looking at me. But I knew it was Monica. I got into the limo, and we all drove off. Me and her had to be over with. She ignored her own friend. I couldn't live with that.

\*\*\*

We were all at the revival, at Jillian's house. Everyone here was happy but still mourning Mahogany. It was still a shame that only one of her sisters was at the funeral. It sickened me that they were too full of themselves to even go say their last goodbyes to their own sister.

I noticed Lyric was nowhere to be found. I grabbed a sliced piece of cake and walked through the people. I looked around, and finally noticed her sitting outside on the porch. She was crying her eyes out. I sighed deeply, as I slid the door open, stepping outside. She quickly wiped her tears away and looked the other way. I sat next to her and placed the cake on the table. "Hey? You okay out here?" She shook her head. "Is that a yes or no?"

"I just wanna be alone." I sighed.

"I don't think that's good. Talk to me, buddy." I nudged her shoulder. She looked up at me as the tears filled her eyes.

"I'm sick of being so afraid. I wish my mom was here. I don't want to go to that school. I just don't wanna be here anymore! You don't know what it's like, JaKobe." Her voice was deeply sad.

"I won't know unless you tell me, okay?" She stared at me, and fiddled with the cake,

"Well, some—some boys at school—they—" her lip began to quiver.

"They what?" I said, putting my arm around her shoulder, but she flinched a little. I squinted at her. She looked at me as the waterworks really came again. "What happened? I promise you can tell me."

"One day after school, they pulled me into the janitor's closet room—and—and raped me," she cried, "I don't know why I deserve all this bad. They said I wanted it! When I didn't want it! I don't even talk in any of my classes! I'm not a bad girl, I'm not a slut or a whore! I didn't want it, and they raped me! They said if I told anyone, they'd spread rumors around and get some people to jump me. I hate my life."

I looked at her, stunned.

"Lyric, have you told Jaidah?" She shook her head. "Do you want to tell her?" She nodded.

"Yes, but I don't—don't know how to. Can I just have a moment to myself please? I just want to be alone." I looked at her one time. Then I gave her a hug and kiss on the head, before I left. I was going to tell Jaidah. This couldn't go on any longer. I got up from my seat before I looked at her one more time. It was just sad that a young girl like her was getting sexually harassed and assaulted at school. She was only a freshman, and I knew the boys were way older than her. It hurt me so much to see her that way. Walking back into the house, I felt nothing but sadness for her.

I walked to where Momma Jillian was, and gave her a sincere hug. After doing that, I talked to Jaidah's dad for a bit. I wish I could tell them now. But how could I! That would be another heartbreak for them. I just wanted everyone to be happy from now on.

*** 

Later that night, I finally got home. I was tired and needed to lay down. I locked up my house and pulled off my tie and jacket. I walked into my kitchen, going straight to the liquor cabinet. I pulled out my favorite drink and poured the dark liquor into a glass. I rubbed my beard, as I placed an ice cube inside my glass. I walked out of the kitchen and through the foyer. As I sipped the liquor, it burned my throat a little, but I surpassed it.

Someone knocked on my door, and I sighed as I turned on my heels and walked to the door. I looked through the peephole and opened it. As I rolled my eyes, she stood there looking at me. "What you doing here?" I questioned.

"We need to talk."

"About?" I said, sipping the liquor down.

"About us."

I shook my head.

"There ain't no us. What's up with you and Jai?"

She walked into my house, and I threw my head back.

"Me and her are not friends."

I kind of choked on my drink.

"What! Are you crazy? Why? We can't be together, nah. This is getting out of hand."

She ran her hands down my chest, kissing my neck. "We can be together. She was in the way of us! Me and you can be a great couple, don't you think?"

"She wasn't in the way of us! You betrayed her. I'm betraying her! I'm not about to lose her again. You need to go."

"She has someone, she will never want you! But I want you. I wanna be with you, JaKobe. What don't you get? I confessed my feelings to you, and we had sex. You're just going to throw me away like this? Huh, JaKobe?"

I felt a little bad. I was going to feel even badder for Jaidah when she finds out. She was probably going to kill both of us. I pulled Monica into a hug, as she began to kiss my neck and touch me all over.

"I'm sorry, Monica. But we can't be together. You need to get yourself right. You really do. This isn't healthy for you. I know what that guy did to you. But I don't think I can fix that." Tears filled her eyes.

"You can't do me like this, JaKobe." Looking at her face, was it easy for me to break her heart? Or break Jaidah 's heart once again? I couldn't care with that.

"We have to stop this. Do you know we'll have to be a secret? We could never be a real couple, Monica. That would just hurt Jaidah, and you know that. You want to do that to her? You want to fuck her over like that?"

"Yes! I don't care about her, all I want is—" I pushed her back, and looked her square in the face; this all felt like deja vú.

"Get out, Monica! That's your friend, well, *was*! All this is some bullshit. Goodbye, Monica! This has all gone too far! We will never be together, we just can't!"

"You don't mean that! You don't—"

"Yes, yes, I do!" I pushed her out of my house and closed the door, locking it. This couldn't get any deeper.

# Chapter 21

## More Secrets…More Secrets to Tell

*Jaidah O'Neil*

*"Jai! Come on, I want to go outside!" she groaned as I sat on the couch and flipped through the channels.*

*"Jaidah! I know won't hear me!" she said as she stomped her foot and yelled at me. I knew she was about to have a temper tantrum.*

*Pop!*

*I looked at her, as she had a small mug on her face. "Ouch! Lyric, why'd you hit me?" I said, acting as if I didn't know why she did it in the first place.*

*"Because, you not listening to me! I want to go outside." She poked out her bottom lip.*

*I laughed and flicked the lip with my index finger. She slapped my hand and pouted more. She was always the fiery little kid. She got this from me. I'd usually babysit her in the summertime or when my auntie had to work.*

*"Stop pouting, Lyric. I'm going to take you outside right now, Lyric. Just say please." I smiled, making her pout even more.*

*"Please! I wanna play jump rope, and hopscotch!" She stomped her foot again. I rolled my eyes and got up, dusting off my pants in the process.*

*"Okay, okay! Come on, you big baby." I grabbed her hand as she skipped along the side of me. "I thought you were going to be my big girl. Hmm?"*

*"Well, you were ignoring me." She smirked. She knew how to get over someone real good.*

*I shook my head and opened the door, as I took my keys off of the hook. I had to watch after Lyric all day. But I didn't mind. I loved her to death. She was my best friend, the sister I never had.*

*"Jai, where is your boyfriend?" she questioned. I frowned.*

"My what?" I said, as she grabbed her jump rope out of the bin by the door.

"Your boyfriend—JaKobe." She smiled. "I like him, he's cute. He gives me candy when I'm over here." She giggled as she skipped out of the door, making her big curly hair flop everywhere.

"That's just my friend, Lyric. But, he's away right now. And, stay where I can see you. Don't run out there in the street either." I made sure my voice was stern. She nodded and skipped with the rope, singing a song as well. It was pretty hot out here today. I wasn't going to let her stay in the house and mess out in the nice ATL weather.

She waved at some of her little friends, as they came running into my yard. I sat there looking at all the kids, just day dreaming. I typed away at my phone, as I heard the ice cream truck approaching.

"Jai! Jai! Tha' ice cream truck, can we get some?" she pleaded with a pouty face.

"Okay, don't beg, you know I don't like that. I have to go get my wallet. Stay right here. Okay? I'm going to go get the money. Don't leave the yard." She nodded and stood there, swaying back and forth as I went back into the house to retrieve my money.

"Hurry! The ice cream lady going to leave!" she whined. I groaned, as walked into the house. I was trying to find it as fast as I could, then I heard her little voice.

"Oh! I have a dollar, Jai! I'm going—Ahhh!"

"Everybody, run!"

I stopped at what I was doing, stood up from my bent over position in my room. I ran down the hall as I heard my cousin's screams. I dropped everything and ran out of the house.

"Lyric! Where are you, Lyric?" I said in a frantic tone.

"S-she over there, Jaidah—She was running to the sidewalk when they started shooting!" the little girl screamed. I looked and saw Lyric lying face down in a weird and twisted position. Blood *stained her pink outfit, and I ran over to her, falling to my knees, wailing.*

*"Lyric! Stay with me, Lyric, so sorry I didn't protect you."*
*Everyone crowded around us as I pulled her into my arms.*

*"Someone, call damn 911! My cousin has been shot. Please!"*
*Her little brown eyes looked at me, and she smiled faintly. As her eyes closed, and her breathing wheezed, she was about to go into shock.*

*My heart stopped as I started screaming and yelling.*
*"Lyric, stay awake, please!" I yelled as tears ran down my eyes.*

*"Jaidah, get up, the ambulance is coming," I could hear one of the women say, as she tried to pull me up, as blood smeared my outfit.*

*"No, this is my cousin! My little cousin!" I said, rocking her body back and forth. "It was my fault. I shouldn't have left her! Lyric, wake up, Lyric, please!" She was hanging on for dear life.*

"Jaidah, wake up!" I felt my body being jolted, and I shot up out of my sleep. I looked around as I was in a cold sweat. I finally looked at Rashad. "Are you okay?" he asked, as I sat up completely in the bed, running my hands down my face. That funeral really had me messed up. I was glad my mom had finally gotten better. But it was as if I was getting worse.

"Yes, I'm fine." He gave me a questioning look. I sighed and pulled the second pillow into my chest, as I sat against his headboard. His room was huge, and everything was beautiful. I took a deep breath as I fiddled with the feather pillow.

"Okay, so maybe I'm not fine."
"Why? Because of the funeral two days ago?"
I nodded. "A little. Just looking at Lyric, I was heartbroken. I was having a nightmare about when I was just a teen and she was very younger." His hand rubbed my bare shoulder.

"What happened? You know you can tell me." He sat by me, as I laid my head in his lap.

"I blame myself for why she stayed away from me or why I stayed away from her for so long. One day I was babysitting her, and I was going to get her some ice cream. When I went into the house to get money, they started shooting and she got hit in the crossfire. I blame myself for that. That should have been me. Protecting her." He rubbed my hair as the tears rolled down my eyes.

"That's not your fault. You didn't know that was going to happen." I sighed.

"Every time I look at her I just wanna say sorry over and over again. Her life has been terrible ever since then." He sighed along with me.

"You know, I used to be just like you—blaming! Thanks to my sister's cancer."

I looked up at him.

"But you couldn't prevent that."

"When I was young, I thought all the junk food I gave her caused the cancer, I don't know. I blamed a lot of that on me. I was her protector. But I couldn't protect her from the bullet named cancer."

I rubbed his face as I pulled him down into a kiss.

"That wasn't your fault, Rashad."

"Neither was your little cousin getting shot." He kissed my lips, and we both pulled away as we looked at each other.

"You think I could be a good guardian for her?"

He nodded and smiled. "You'd be perfect. You know Halloween is coming up. We should throw a party or something?"

"That's actually Lyric's birthday. That would be perfect for her. I think it'll cheer her up." He nodded. "We can have it at one of your venues?" I added.

"Yeah, no doubt." He tapped my thigh for me to get up. So I did. He got up as those sexy briefs clung to all the right places. I smiled and bit my fingernail. He grabbed his phone as it was buzzing. His face frowned as he turned on a video. I heard the reporter from E! News talking:

*"Wow! So Monica Hayes has just confirmed that her and her ex-model best friend Jaidah O'Neil have stopped being friends because Jaidah has a crush on her!—"* I fell out the bed, and popped up as if nothing happened.

"What!" I said loudly.

"Don't act like you just didn't bust your ass on the floor."

I gave Rashad a look, and he held his hands up in defense.

"Oh hell nah! That bitch—" Rashad grabbed me, kissing me. I was trying to talk. He kept kissing me, making me calm down. I hated when he did that.

"Relax. You know it's a lie."

"Yeah, but she is about to ruin my rep. Hyperactive cat licking bitch!"

"Damn bae, relax! You're killing me, yo'!" He grabbed me as he laughed.

"This shit isn't funny." I pouted. Rashad pushed my purple hair out of my face, and pecked my lips.

"I love you. I know what you like, and who you like. Which is me, so chill ya' buns." He grabbed my ass as he kissed me. I mumbled into the kiss:

"I—uh—you—too," he laughed, and so did I as he pulled away. He pulled up his phone and took pictures of us.

"I'ma post these, and watch what my fans say. I will be having your publicist call E! News too. I smiled, looking at him as he typed away at his phone. After he was done, he looked at me weirdly.

"What? Why you staring at me like that?" I blushed and grabbed his face as I looked into his eyes.

"You make me happy." I pecked his plump lips as I grabbed his ass and turned around.

"Man, I told you about doing that shit. Feels gay."

"Gay means happy. So be happy, and feel happy." I grinned, and he waved me off. My phone buzzed, and I groaned as I skipped over to it. Nobody better be calling me about that gossip shit Monica said, which is a lie. I picked up my phone, noticing it was Lyric's school. I frowned and picked it up, knowing I was her second emergency number if my mom didn't pick up.

"Hello, this is Jaidah O'Neil!"

The woman on the phone announced herself as Lyric's Dean.

"Um? Hello. Something terrible has happened to Lyric. Some girls had jumped her, and she's pretty hurt badly."

"Oh my gosh! I'll be there. I'm her legal guardian." The woman said *okay*, and I hung up. I dropped my phone on the bed and hurriedly picked up my clothes, putting them on.

"What's wrong?"

"Lyric got jumped at school. I have to get over there!"

"Do you need me to come along?"

I shook my head.

"I got this, thanks, babe. I'll be back in a few, why would anyone want to fight her! This is just too much for her right now!" He shook his head, agreeing with me. I could only imagine how she felt.

# Chapter 22

## Tell Your Friends

*JaKobe Harrison*

After I left the gym, I headed over to the restaurant with Bradley. He had a free day, so we decided to hit the gym and then get some breakfast after that. The past days have been chill with no drama. And it felt good; that was until Bradley brought up something I didn't even know about.

"Yo'? Did you see what Monica told E! News?" he said as he looked up from his menu.

"Nah, I haven't seen it or read it? What she do?"

He raised an eyebrow at me.

"You seriously don't know? Or you really know? Stop messing with me. You knew already, right?"

I nodded. "Yeah, I did. It was just too much for me to handle. She was a cool girl, but I couldn't do that to Jai. If she was to find out, she'd have both our heads, and I'd lose her as a friend once again. I just can't have that. I believe that's why everything was going so wrong in my life. Because of how I treated her." He nodded in agreement.

The waitress came over, sitting some glasses of water in front of us, along with some utensils. It may have been TGI Friday's, but their food was bomb as fuck. "Hi, I'll be your waitress today. My name is Ginger. Could I get you anything to drink? Appetizers?" I looked up at her from my menu.

"Yeah. I'll have some potato skins as my app." She nodded as she wrote that down on her pad.

"And you, sir?"

Bradley smiled at her. "Yeah, Ginger. I'll have the wings as my app. Extra sauce." She wrote all that down.

"Okay? And drinks?" she said with a clear country accent.

"I'll just have a coke."

"Yeah, same here," Bradley chimed in.

"Okay! I'll get that for you, gentleman." She took our menus and walked away. It was noisy with all the people in here on their lunch rush. I sipped some more of the ice-cold water in front of me. Bradley typed at his phone before he finally looked back up at me.

"Yeah, so anyway, Monica told them that the reason her and my sister aren't friends anymore is because Jai has a crush on her. And I'm, like, what the fuck? My sister don't like girls, she strictly dickly. It was foul for Monica to even say some shit like that, discrediting my sister's rep. She better hope I don't be petty as fuck and hop on Twitter and get to putting her ass on blast."

I shook my head in disgust. *Maybe she took my breaking up with her the wrong way.* Jaidah didn't do nothing to Monica. Monica was the one buggin'.

"I feel you. I truly broke it off with shawty. She was getting too damn clingy. She gave some fire head, but damn, she was falling for a nigga too deep for my liking." My phone chimed a basic iPhone ringtone, signaling that it was an unknown caller. I pulled my phone out of my pocket and looked at it.

"Yo'? Who that?" Brad asked as the waitress brought our apps.

"I don't know, hold on. Hello" Brad shook his head at my change of voice.

"Nicki? What's up? How you get my number, mami?" I said, taking a bite out of my potato skins. Chewing, she spoke through the phone, saying some shit that almost made me choke.

"Hold up? What? What you mean, she was using me? Monica crazy. But she ain't that crazy." I was popping the straw into my cup.

"Oh? She is that crazy. Okay?"

Brad started laughing as he ate his food.

I flicked him off and leaned back in the booth seat. "So she lied to me? About all that David stuff? Wait, how I know you ain't jealous like her ass? Oh, damn. You ain't gotta curse at a nigga, yo. Lemme finish—" I poked the side of my lip as I kissed my teeth. "Alright, you can finish. I'll listen."

"Damn! Shorty shut you down real quick," Brad said, giving me a face. But when he saw I was serious, his facial expression changed. And I was getting pissed off at the same time. Like a nigga couldn't even finish his damn food, or enjoy it.

"Nicki, you sure all this true—" Before I could finish my sentence, Brad snatched the phone out my hand.

"Listen, chicken head, you fucked with Monica, right? You knew everything about her? Is that right? Yeah, I know that's about right. You blastin' a nigga for what? Because she broke up with—Just get straight to the damn point." I shook my head, knowing this was about to go south.

"Yeah. You check that broad before I do. I don't play about my sister, and she fucking with the wrong O'Neil's. You feel me?—A'ight." He hung up the phone and handed it back to me. I couldn't help but laugh when I grabbed it.

"So what she say after you scared her shitless?" I said, eating my last potato skin.

"She said Monica won't stop till she has you. Basically, the bitch sprung. She'll get over it. I'ma tell some friends, they'll handle it. She won't be messing with you or my sis no mo'." His words were deep and promising. I felt a little bad for her but not that bad.

*** 

I had gotten home, but it felt lonely to me. So, instead of moping around the house, I was going to go to the Dog Pound pet store downtown and get me a little pup.

But before I could even leave the house, someone had knocked on my door. I groaned and went to the door, opening it.

"What up? We need to have a man-to-man talk," Rashad said to me. I didn't know how this was going to go. But truth was, I had been waiting on this day.

"A'ight, come on in," I said with a humble smile. But on the inside, I was willing to clock this nigga if he got outta pocket. I closed the door. He sat on the couch, looking around at my place.

"What's this talk about?" I asked.

"I think you know what it's about. I know about what you and Jaidah had. And I wanna make some shit clear." I had this death wish for this dude, and in my head there was this image of me snuffing out his life as he was over here sitting on my couch.

"Yeah? And I wanna make something clear too. She won't be your girl for long. So have fun while it lasts—with yo' yellow crayon ass.

# Chapter 23

## Oh Shit, Gat'damn!

*Jaidah O'Neil*

Going up to the school, I felt as if my heart was going to explode out of my chest. I was really worried about her. After losing her mom and not have her dad around, I know she had to be going through it all. Now, being somewhere foreign to her and at a different school wasn't going down well for Lyric at all. I thought it would, I really did. I didn't think anyone would be bullying her. She was such a nice girl.

My head hurts just about it. I walked into the school with a hard mug on my face as I stomped through the hallway. Walking into the office, I saw my cousin sitting there with a bruised face. I really wanted to beat someone's ass for doing this in the first place. She sat there looking off into space. I walked over to her and tapped her shoulder. "Hey, Lyrical Miracle. You okay? You ready to go—" She looked at me and nodded.

But, before I could even get her up to leave, the principal opened the door and stood there with a sad look in her face. "You three can leave, your parents are waiting—they should be ashamed of you—And you should be ashamed of yourselves," she said, as the girls walked past her and then past us. All of them were noticeably older than Lyric. I gave them a stone-cold look like my dad. My dad could intimidate anyone with this look; all he had to do was turn the upper lip up. And you were done for. They saw my face and rushed out of the hall area, and to their awaiting parents.

"Are those the girls that did this to you?" I spoke aggressively. She nodded as she looked down at her fingers. Some of her nails were broken off. I knew she defended herself then. I shook my head in so much disgust. "I hope they got suspended." The principal nodded and asked for me and Lyric to come in. Lyric sat up, and I could now see the messed patch on her head. I was furious. She had very nice hair and these hoe ass little girl gon' have me go gangsta on 'em.

We went into the office. Lyric sat down with her hands on her lap. The principal shut the door, letting me sit down as she came around to her desk. "Well, first off, I'm sorry this happened to your cousin. I know she's been having a rough time. She's not a bad kid at all."

"I know that, I just wanna know something. Why did they target her? Why bully her?" I rubbed Lyric's back.

"Well, from what Lyric told me, the girls had been ranting and taunting her for almost a week now." I turned to Lyric with a surprised face. "Now I see. You had no idea about this—" she said.

"No, Ms. Harper. I didn't know that. Lyric, why you ain't tell me? You know I'm here for you 24/7." She finally looked up at me with watery eyes. "What's the matter? Tell me what's wrong. Is it more you need to tell me?" She sighed and shook her head. The principal looked at Lyric.

"She has been like this since the fight happened. But Lyric is also suspended for three days. Only because of the fight. The girls got two weeks and detention. Like they should." I nodded, knowing that she was going to get suspended. It wasn't fair on her part, but I understood.

"Will those girls mess with her again? 'Cause I'll be up here every day if I have to. I don't play about my family." She nodded in understanding.

"You ready to go, Lyric? I know you had a rough day." She gave me this look that only I could see. The principal didn't see it, and I knew something was wrong with her. I shook the principal's hand as I gave her a few more words. Lyric was all messed up inside, and it just made me so sad. I walked out of the office, and with Lyric right beside me. We both walked out of the student area and into the hallway. We heard some laughing, and I turned around to see a group of boys laughing and joking around.

Lyric kind of tensed up. She thought I didn't notice it, but I did. The boys walked past us, but one stopped and looked at Lyric. "Yo? I heard about that fight—you a'ight?" he said, as the guys stopped along with him.

"Y-yeah. I'm okay."

"There's no way. Look at your face, I swear if I was there I'd fuck 'em up."

One of the boys who were taller than the rest of them stood with his arms crossed over his chest. He had this mean demeanor on his face. As he looked at Lyric, I knew I had to speak up to why he was looking at her this way.

"Uh—You, no not you—*you*," I said, pointing at the tall older boy.

"What?" No he did not just *what* me?

"Boy, don't *what* me. Why are you staring at my little cousin like that? I saw that look!" He laughed, and the other boys started to whisper among themselves.

"Man, take your Barney ass on somewhere—She should know her place and shut the fuck up!—That's why the bitch got her ass jumped!" he said, getting fresh with me. I laughed lightly, and Lyric looked at me. She saw that crazy look in my eyes as I took off my shoes.

"Did you just call my baby cuz a bitch?" I said, flicking my nose with my thumb.

"That's what you heard, shawty. I didn't stutter, bitch should learn how to close her legs too." Lyric began to cry. I knew this girl her whole life, I know what and who she is. If she had interest in having sex—and she was so grossed out when she'd seen me and Rashad kissing—she would have told me. She was only thirteen. I know she's not having sex. I'm just like my momma—I can smell and tell if your ass had sex. And this little boy just crossed that white line. The line to get his ass whooped on.

"Call her that name one more time," I said, hopping around on my feet and popping my neck.

"Please, just stop it," Lyric said.

"You think I'm scared of you. You and that bitch can suck my—" my fist connected with his nose, and it was all over from there. I gave him a one-two punch to his jaw and nose again. He tried to grab me, but I kept my feet planted on the ground. I elbowed him in the back, and he groaned. I kneed him in the stomach and the crotch. I proceeded to kick his little ass before someone grabbed me.

"That little disrespectful fuck did something to my little cousin! When I find out, I'ma kick your ass some more!" I wiggled out the security guard's arms and began to pound on the boy some more until he was trying to cover up his face.

"Get off him, ma'am!" He snatched me up.

"Little bastard ass nigga! I know who your family is, and I'm tellin' 'em. Your cousin JaKobe is going to beat your fucking ass!"

He stood up and got a cheap shot in.

"That's why I bust your cuz pussy wide open, bitch!"

I kicked him in his groin, and he fell over.

"Let me go! Let me go!" I looked at Lyric, and the boy who was the nicest to her was trying to calm her down. "What did he do to you, Lyric! Tell me now! Right now!" My face was red, and the guard had me in some type of lock, so I couldn't pound that boy's dick in.

"He—he—"

"You can tell her, Lyric," the boy whispered.

"Tell me what Christopher did to you! Please, Lyric."

"He raped me! Him and his friend!" She pointed to Christopher and the boy who was tall but a little shorter than Christopher. He had a bigger build, and it made me furious. The guard was a little shocked at what he heard, and that gave me the chance to get out his grip. I ran towards the other boy and began slapping and punching him as I cried.

"Bitch! Bitch! Bitch!" I said as I punched the shit out of him, not caring how big he was over me. I was in full-blown tears, and two guards were trying to pull me off him. This was the second time I couldn't protect her.

Monet Dragun

# Chapter 24

### Shit Gets Shittier

*JaKobe Harrison*

I had gotten home, but it felt lonely to me. So, instead of moping around the house, I was going to go to the Dog Pound pet store downtown and get me a little pup.

But before I could even leave the house, someone had knocked on my door. I groaned and went to the door, opening it

"What up. We need to have a man-to-man talk," Rashad said to me. I didn't know how this was going to go. But truth was - I had been waiting on this day.

"A'ight, come on in," I said with a humble smile. But on the inside, I was willing to clock this nigga if he got outta pocket. I closed the door. He sat on the couch looking around at my place.

"What's this talk about?" I asked.

"I think you know what it's about. I know about what you and Jaidah had. And I wanna make some shit clear." I had this death wish for this dude, and in my head there was this image of me snuffing out his life as he was over here sitting on my couch.

Walking into the living room, I stood there slowly rocking on my heels before I sat in the chair. "Now what you gotta talk to me about?" I said with a look on my face as I sat back.

He began to laugh. "You should already know? I see the way you look at Jaidah. It's so obvious. She told me what you did to her back then. And bruh, that shit wasn't coo'. You feel me, son?"

"That ain't none of your business!" I said, leaning up in my seat.

"Yo', she's my girlfriend. So, yes, it's my damn business when she stuck on the way you did her! You did her like shit, pure damn shit! Some friend you was and you are now! You think you're fucking slick? Nigga, no! I know your ass is up to something, I know! And you better fucking hope I don't find out 'cause I swear I'ma' tell her so she'll know your ass hasn't changed! You fucking snake ass nigga."

I sat there, looking him up and down. I was ready to slap the shit out this pretty boy ass nigga.

"You think you know everything, huh? Huh?" He stood up, so I stood up. "Nigga, I know you ain't trying get buck in my *fucking* crib! I ain't did shit to hurt Jai!" Inside I was lying. Monica was my fucking mistake!

"Tuh! I don't believe that bull ass shit! She may believe your mark ass shit's gold but you truly is dog shit!"

I laughed and stepped closer to him.

"Say that shit to my face!" I said, getting heated. He smirked in my face and fixed his mouth to say some shit I ain't like. So I punched him in the face, releasing so much hate for this nigga. I continued to two-piece his ass till his got some cheap shots in. We were tussling on the floor now. This nigga forgot I used to be a football player. I body-slammed his ass to the ground. He elbowed me in the eye twice, making blood drip from my eyebrow.

I punched him as I gained some advantage. This little crayon ass nigga was good 'cause even after I busted his lip, he got some shots in. My house door flew open, and I heard her annoying voice, which threw me off. He got a hard shot in and punched me in the stomach. I fell over as she was screaming at us fighting. Like, bitch, this ain't no horror movie. He was about to be a punk ass nigga and kick me, but I grabbed his foot, making him fall.

"What the fuck is going on here? Stop!" She pushed Rashad, and I stood up. She pushed me back, and I moved her hands.

"The hell are you doing here? Who told you to come into my house?" I said, looking her up and down.

"I still have my key, asshole!"

"I ain't give you a damn key. Did you copy my damn key?" Rashad looked between me and her and began to laugh.

"Oh, wait till Jaidah finds out about this one. Nigga, the way she looks at you kits told me everything." I gave him a threatening look, and was about to kick his ass again. But Monica pushed me back.

"Stop it! Rashad. You can honestly do whatever you want. But do you really want to lose Jaidah? I don't think, so do you?" He looked at her with confusion.

"What does you and him have to do with me?" he questioned.

"If she finds out what me and him did, she'd become distraught and not want to be in a relationship. That's just how she is." Monica smirked. Now I knew she did all this shit on purpose.

"I don't give a damn about you or him. You a snake just like him. Period!"

"So you did this shit on purpose, Monica!" She looked back at me with a gleam in her eyes. And that's when I lost it. Tracy had played me, now Monica had did the same. "You made me betray my friend! Didn't you? You didn't care about if she was my friend or your friend, did you! Do you, Monica?"

"We can be together, that's why I came back. I knew you needed some space so—" I smiled that crazy smile and looked at Rashad.

"Lil nigga, you about to witness a murder!" Before he could say a word, I had wrapped my hands around her neck, slamming her against the wall hard, making her eyes shut tight and for her to gasp for air.

"Man! Don't get your ass arrested messing with this trick. Just let her go!" Rashad yelled, but everything was blurring, and my hearing was numbed. I wanted to kill her for the games she was playing. As I was squeezing her neck, all I saw was Jaidah's heartbroken face. I released her body; she fell to the ground, gasping for air. I kneeled down to her level.

"I swear—you better leave me alone, Monica. Leave Jaidah out of this! I mean it. You're so lucky, I swear your ass lucky! Now get out!"

"I'm pressing charges!"

"Oh? Like you did David?" Rashad spoke behind me. She rubbed her neck and looked at him. I was just so conflicted, I turned around and picked up the keys she had made. This crazy

bitch just had to get the hell out of my life. If Jai found out about this, I was done for. We were done for. I sat on the floor as Rashad pretty much pushed her out of the house, telling her some stuff he knew about her. They were arguing back and forth, and it was giving me a headache until I both heard them leave out of my house.

My house was a mess, and I was a bloody mess. "What the hell am I going to do now? *What have you gotten yourself into, JaKobe!*

# Chapter 25

### Rain Down

*Jaidah O'Neil*

We sat in my mom's dining room. My dad was pacing back and forth. Lyric was sitting in the chair, and she was just staring at the table. My mom was just rubbing her face as she looked at the both of us.

"I can't believe I had to bail you out of jail, Jai! What the hell? I know this is your cuz, but beating the boys—tell me what happened! Right dammit now!" My dad yelled.

"I don't know," I said, looking at Lyric. She shifted her eyes at me and I eyed her. She was going to have to tell what happened to her. She needed to tell them, not me.

"Answer me right now!" my dad yelled, making me and Lyric both jump.

"Okay, okay! I plead the fifth!" I semi-yelled, as I put my hands up at my dad.

"Girl, don't play with me."

"Uncle, it's not Jai's fault—I'll tell you what happened," Lyric said finally, looking up, meeting all of our eyes. She took a deep breath as she picked at her nail polish. My dad looked at her face and saw the concern and sadness. He sat down by mom and looked at her.

"Okay. We're listening. What's wrong, baby girl?" he said as he looked at her.

"About three weeks ago—these two boys, uh—They saw that I was the new girl. I didn't talk to anyone, didn't really participate because I was writing about my mom." She sucked in a deep breath as she swirled her fingers on the table. "So one day I was in class. The oldest guy, Trey, came up to me. He was being nice and trying to help me with some assignments I didn't understand. I took the kindness. We talked about sports, school, and just cool stuff. You know? I didn't think anything of it, then two days later I was in the gym. His friend—whom I didn't know was his friend—came up to me and told me I was pretty. I accepted with a smile, I didn't get all bubbly or twirl my hair like one of those girls who like attention. Because I don't like attention. I'm shy. I was just trying to make some type of friends." Tears started to well in her eyes.

"Go on, baby—" my mom spoke. "We are here for you." Lyric sucked in her bottom lip to try and keep it from quivering. She took a shaky deep breath and looked down.

"So the end of the week came, and me and the two boys were cool. So I thought. It was my study hall period, and I had to go to the bathroom. Usually, the teacher didn't let students go during her period, but she knew I was a good student. So, my teacher let me go. I went into the bathroom. A few minutes later after finishing my business I came out. It was a little walk to go back to class. There wasn't a short way to get back to study because it was in Narnia. While I was walking down the hall, I heard Benny's voice. I turned around and waved at him. He jogged up to me and was walking with me. He was being nice as usual, then the next thing I know his pushes me into a room. Trey is in there. I pushed my hair back as I looked back at the both of them. Asking them what's going on. They look at me, smirking, calling me a whore, slut, and the "C" word.

I try to push out of the room, but Trey pulls my hair, I hear the door lock and Benny slaps me in the face, saying: 'If you scream we'll leave you here to bleed out.' They both laugh like it's funny! They both unzip their pants and yank my pants down." Tears were running down her face, and so was I. My dad had this incredibly angry expression on his face. Worse look I ever saw. My mom was in full tears.

"What did they do to you, Lyric?" my dad said in a strained voice.

"They pulled their pants down, covered my mouth and shoved their penises into me. Taking turns like I was an animal! I'm a virgin, I never wanted that! I never flirted with them! They raped me, they raped me in school! Then after that they had me beat up because they thought I told a girl! Why would they want to do me like this! Why! I thought of killing myself and then I lost my mother!" I got up and pulled Lyric into my arms as she yelled in tears.

"Trey is related to JaKobe. When he finds out, he's going to kill that boy."

"I'm going to kill that boy! They raped my fucking niece—my niece! They're not getting away with this!"

Lyric shot up from her seat, screaming.

"No! No! They can't go to jail! Everyone will find out at school. I don't want to be labeled as a whore at school. Please! D-Don't!" She yelled, as she broke down to her knees.

"It's okay Ly, just take a deep breath. Nothing is going to happen to you. I promise you that. We promise you that." She looked up at me and hugged me tight as she cried. My mom and dad got up also.

"I've always loved you like a sister, Jaidah. I really do."

\*\*\*

Getting to Rashad's apartment, I had a lot on my mind. Lyric didn't want to part from me at the moment. So she was staying over here with me. Lyric had tired herself out, and was now asleep in Rashad's guest room. I rubbed my hair as I took my clothes and stepped into Rashad's room.

He was sitting on the bed with this look on his face. "Hey, babe? What's the matter?" I asked him. He pulled himself away from the phone and looked up at me. I missed my baby, but Lyric was weighed heavy on my mind.

"Hey," he said drily.

"Why so dry? You look like someone killed your bestie."

"Nothing. Just got a lot on my mind, bae. How is Lyric doing? She okay. She looked so broken when I saw y'all come in." I knew something was off.

"Um, no she's not. I had to beat up these two college boys because—because they raped her. Why would they do that to her!"

His eyes widened.

"What! No, not that poor little girl! So what happened? Are they going to jail?"

"I don't know, she doesn't want to press charges. She's scared. She don't want no one to find out about this." He frowned at me.

"Uh! Did you know JaKobe knew?"

I snapped my head at him.

"What! No, he didn't, he would have told me!" I yelled.

"I don't think it's something like that. Maybe she confided in him."

"Well, how did you know?"

He sighed. "I paid him a little visit. And let me say it didn't go so well." I noticed the scratch and bruises in his face.

"Talk to me. What went down?" I asked him, as I touched his face softly, kissing him.

"I think you should let him tell you. That's your friend." As I sat in his lap, I looked at him and he looked back at me. Things are just raining down on me, and I didn't like the downpour.

# Chapter 26

## They Don't Have to Know

*JaKobe Harrison*

Coming back home from the Dog Pound, I got this cute pit bull. I named him Tarzan because that was one of my favorite movies when I was a child, and because the little puppy kept jumping around. He was so happy to get adoptive that I just had to buy him. I had stopped at PetSmart, buying necessary essentials for Tarzan. I had this perfect place for him in my house.

He barked small as he trotted around the house. Walking into the kitchen, I was about to prepare something to eat when there was a knock on my front door. "Damn. Just got here." I groaned as Tarzan walked over my feet and barked again. I patted his head as I walked over to the door. I looked through the peephole and saw it was the police. I scrunched up my face as I unlocked the door. Opening it, two police officers stood there.

"Hello? Can I help you?" I asked, raising an eyebrow.

"Are you JaKobe Harrison?"

"Yeah, who's asking?" I said, standing in the doorway.

"We have a warrant for your arrest." My eyes widened.

"What! For—for what?" I said.

"The assault of Monica Haynes. You have the right to remain silent. Anything you say can and will be used against you in a court of law. You have the right to an attorney. If you cannot afford an attorney, one will be provided for you." As I was being Mirandized, I couldn't help but feel a little responsible for this. I should not have put my hands on her. But she had driven me to that point. They turned me around and handcuffed me.

"Who gon' take care of my—"

"Sir, we don't care about that."

Please, c'mon—" I smacked my lips as they hauled me out of my house. I was going to need someone to call. I had to call Jai, she was the only one who could help me out.

\*\*\*

The metal bar gate opened, and the lady officer called my name, "JaKobe T—"

"That's me. Can I make my one phone call?" I said, kind of harshly.

"Yes."

I nodded. I was pissed because I had never been in the system. Now I was, because of that dumb bitch. I moved around the woman as I walked over to the phone. Picking it up, I dialed Jaidah's number.

"This is a call from Fulton County Jail. Would you like to accept the charges for JaKobe Harrison?" I heard Jaidah 's sweet voice say *yes* into the phone. The next moment I was hearing her scream at me:

"What the fuck are you doing in jail, JaKobe Cornelius Harrison! What did you do?"

"Don't worry about that. Can you please bail me out jail? Please."

"Nigga, I just got bailed out my damn self! Why the hell didn't you tell me about what happened to my baby girl, Lyric? I thought no more—"

"Just hush, please! I need you to bail me out with my money, shit. Just do it and we'll talk!" She sighed over the phone and I ran my hand down my face. "Damn, thank you."

"Yeah, whatever. Keep your drawls on. I'll be there in an hour or so—"

"Can you come a little—"

"Don't *fucking* rush me! Where your money at?"

"In my house, in the safe. And, please feed my puppy, Tarzan—" She smacked her lips and before she hung up on me she said:

"You better fucking tell me the damn truth too. Or I'll cut your damn d—"

"End of call, goodbye," I sighed in relief and hung the phone up. The officer took me back to my cell as I waited for Jaidah to come get me. An hour passed as all these misfits were talking to me about football and whatnot. I was ready to get the hell out of here already.

"Harrison, you've been bailed out."

"Finally, I've been in here for ten hours. Nigga starving and shit. Fucking stomach touching my back and shit. Sure did take your sweet ass time, mama." I got up and walked down the hall as Jaidah signed some papers for me to be released. She looked at me, giving an evil look. She had heard what I said. I swallowed had as she yelled.

"Let's go, now!" I grabbed all of my things and walked out with Jai. She walked angrily to her car and got in, slamming the door. I got in as she began to yell at me while she drove away from the jail.

"So how the hell you get locked up? Huh!"

"Long story. Stop talking to me like you my momma." She snapped her head at me and popped me upside the head.

"Ouch, man! The hell!"

"Why you get locked up!" she screamed.

"Because a girl filed a—"

"What girl?" I smacked my lips. I had to tell her who. She was going to find out anyway. She always did.

"Monica," I said, a little above a whisper.

"Who? Why would she do that to you?" I rubbed my forehead.

"'Cause she obsessed with a nigga." She stopped the car and looked at me.

"Is there something you need to tell me? Why is she obsessed with you? Tell me the truth." She held the steering wheel.

"I don't know. She just tried to pull something but I wouldn't let her. That's all to it, she came over and tried something and she was trying to accuse me of shit. So I kind of manhandle her ass. And she pressed charges on me, I'm telling you the truth, Jai." She looked at me as if she was looking into my damn soul. I was wrong for lying to her like this.

"You telling me the honest truth?" I nodded. "Okay, then why didn't you tell me about Lyric? You know your damn sick cousin Trey did this to her. Him and his friend raped her in school!" Her eyes moistened with tears.

"My cousin? Hell nah, she didn't tell me all that. She made me swear not to tell you. She was so ashamed of what happened, don't blame her. She was scared." Jaidah nodded and pressed on the gas. She was so stressed out, I could tell. "You hear me, Jaidah?"

"Yeah."

I nodded as she drove down the highway in silence.

"Can you take me to my crib?"

She nodded as I leaned back in the passenger seat. I had a lot in my mind too. And it was about her. In about forty minutes of Jaidah 's speeding down the road, we were at my house.

"Damn speed demon," I said. She sighed and eyed me.

"Okay, goodbye. You can get out now."

I smacked my lips.

"You don't wanna come in?" I said, as I opened the door. She looked at me and shrugged.

"Only to talk."

I nodded, as we both got out of the car, and we closed the doors. She locked up the car, and we walked up to my house. I keyed us in, as I heard my puppy barking. He ran up to me a little frightened from being home alone. I went into the kitchen and poured me something to drink. Jai sat in the chair.

"So? Are you and Lyric okay?" She looked at me and started crying. I walked over to her side, pulling her into a much needed hug.

"It's so *fucking* sad. Why would they rape her? She's nothing but an innocent, smart thirteen-year-old. They took her innocence away, why would they do her like that? It's just not right, is all I'm saying, JaKobe. No girl should have to go through that! Never! I wanted to kill that boy, and I will be making Ly press charges. They need to go down for what they did to her." She sniffed as she spoke out in one breath.

"I know you're a little messed up about it. But everything will get better, I promise you that. Just get her a good therapist and she'll be better in due time. All these things take time." I rubbed her back. I looked at her as she cried over what happened to her cousin.

"She told me the whole story, every bit of it. She even thought of killing herself." Jaidah pressed her hand against her forehead as I pulled her head up.

"She will get better. Trust me, she has you. Remember?" She looked up at me and hugged me a little tighter. I pulled away and I brought her face to mine as I kissed her. I didn't mean to, but I did. Before I could stick my tongue in, she pushed me away roughly.

"Stop! You know I have a boyfriend, why would you do that!"

"I'm sorry, it's just, no one has to know! I'm sorry, I miss you. I made a mistake. I should be with you."

She pinched the bridge of her nose.

"JaKobe, I'll never feel the same about you again. I don't know if we can be friends after this. This is too much." I grabbed her hands.

"No, no, I'm sorry. I need you as my friend. I can do you better than Rashad!" She looked at me deeply and shook her head.

"I don't see that ever being possible. You were never the one, JaKobe. I've come to terms with that, and so should you. I have to go!" She pulled her hands away from mine and bolted for the door. I didn't bother to chase after her, because she was right.

Monet Dragun

# Chapter 27

## He Loves Me...He Loves Me Not

*Jaidah O'Neil*

It had been a few days later since JaKobe had kissed me. I had been a little distant here and there. I hope Rashad hadn't noticed because I didn't want him questioning me. I didn't want to lie to my boyfriend. I couldn't keep this from him. Just like he wouldn't keep anything from me.

Getting up from the couch, I went into Rashad's kitchen with my phone. About two days ago I had settled everything with E! News. But me and Monica was still not talking, and I was cool with that. She had been doing some way out shit that I was just not cool with at all.

Opening the cabinet, I pulled out some Cracker Jack. I may have been small but I could eat a hell of a lot of food. I was just about to go to the fridge when I heard someone scream.

"Ly! You okay? I'm coming!" I tucked my phone into my bra and ran out of the kitchen, into the hall, and flew up the steps. I went two at a time as I burst into the guest room. She was tossing and turning, and she groaned and moaned in her sleep,

"Baby girl, you gotta wake up. You're dreaming!" I said, shaking her as I crouched down on the balls of my feet.

"No! God, leave me alone! I—I don't wanna have that in me!" She screamed as sweat poured from her forehead.

"Lyric!" I said, slapping her face. She shot up from the bed and looked at me, crying. I frowned as I spoke to her.

"Ly? Are you okay?" She began to rock back and forth as she silently cried. "I was—was dreaming they were raping me over and over again! I can't go on like this, I can't even sleep!" she yelled. I ran my hands through her hair.

"It's going to be okay. Did you take your meds?" She started to shake a little.

"No, I didn't take them before I went to bed. They were making me sick, Jaidah. I can't do this anymore." I grabbed her face.

"You're going to get through this. We are pressing charges against those boys!"

"No, please no! I can't face them in court." I grabbed her face tighter.

"Listen! You have to. Or they'll do this to other innocent girls like you. They need to be punished! Do you understand me, Lyric?" She nodded. "I wanna hear you say yes. You will not be punished or ridiculed for what they did to you!"

"Okay, Jai. I love you so much." She wrapped her arms around my neck as she cried. I just rubbed her back and consoled her.

"Everything will be just fine. I promise you that. I owe you this." I kissed the top of her head as I laid her down on the bed. Grabbing the bottle of medicine off the table top, I opened it and poured two pills out. I handed them to her.

"Put these in your mouth. I'll go get you some water. You have to go back to school, Lyric. You can't let your perfect grades fail because of them, got that?" She nodded. I gave her a smile, and walked out of the room. I ran my fingers through my hair as I blew out a deep breath. I jogged down the steps, approaching the kitchen.

The door opened, and I stopped as Shad walked into the house with his photography bag on his shoulder. He looked up at me with a smile. "What's up, baby?" He beamed as he walked over to me and placed a kiss on my lips.

"Nothing, just getting Lyric some water."

He nodded. "How is she doing? Is she a little better?"

"Not so much. She was having a night terror, and I got her to take her meds. She's really broken, and I hate this. I wish I could kill them boys! I'm so damn glad JaKobe kicked that boy ass. His own family? Fucking unbelievable." He nodded in agreement.

"Go get her water. I got some things to tell you."

I nodded and skipped into the kitchen, grabbing the water bottle. I ran out of the kitchen and up the steps. Going back into the room, I found her sitting up with a nasty look in her face.

"I'm sorry. Did they dissolve?" She slightly nodded as she giggled. I handed her the water, then she quickly opened it and downed the water. "Better?"

"Uh, yeah," she said, letting the coldness go away. I smiled, and gave her another hug as she laid back down.

"If you need me call me. I'll come running right back in here, okay?"

"Yes, cuz. Thank you." She slid her hands under the pillow and closed her eyes. I sighed as I put the water bottle on the bed side table. Turning around, I walked out of the room, softly closing the door behind me. Rubbing my hair again, I walked down the hall to Rashad's room when I didn't notice the light on downstairs.

Walking down to the end of the hall, I entered the bedroom to see him laid up on the bed. With his phone and my Cracker Jack popcorn. I rolled my eyes and closed the door as I smacked my lips loudly.

"What?" he questioned.

"Those were mine, sir!" I grunted, as I stomped over to the bed. He laughed as he smacked in the popcorn and then smacked my ass. "Ouch!" I giggled, as he pulled me on top of him. Then he flipped.

"I missed your sexy ass today," he said, pecking my lips, again and again.

"I missed you too. It's been kind of a long day, baby. I had been looking for gifts for Lyric, for her party. I had to handle some business for my dad at his studio, and I cleaned up the whole house!" I beamed.

"You're a true wifey!" he said, biting his lips. He kissed me again as he slid his hand up my sheer loose tank top. His lip kissed the bare flesh of my neck.

"Shad—"

"Hmm?" he said, humming and sucking on my neck.

"I have to tell you something—uh, stop—Wait, shit that feels so good," I said, as his finger tip ran down my bare stomach, traveling down to the rim of my pajama pants. My mouth fell agape as he rose up.

"Tell me what, baby?" he said before he went right back to work.

"Wait, baby, stop, please. I really need to tell you something; it's important. Ouuuuu, fuck!" I yelped as he slipped his hand into my pants and tanga. His finger slipped in as he and swirled it in my clit. He began to say the nastiest shit in my ear, making me wet on impact. I could feel it coming down, could feel it clench.

"What you gotta tell daddy?"

I groaned as I rolled my head back and to the side. I found my strength to push him off a little. His face look a little shocked.

"It's really important, baby, please."

He nodded and slipped his hand out of my panties, making my body relax. I bit my lip and took both of my hands as I whipped my hair back.

"What's wrong, bae? You haven't let me really touch you for a week. What's up?" He pulled me close to him, and I was trying to find my words.

"Promise me you won't get mad, Rashad?"

He put up the Star Trek sign. "I promise." I started laughing, but this was supposed to be serious. I nodded as I kissed his tight jaw line. "Start talkin' to me, Jaidah—"

"Well, um remember how you told me JaKobe knew about Lyric. And what she went through, how I helped him get out of jail? Well, it was more to the story."

"Okay, go on, bae, go on. I'm all ears." I turned to him and grabbed his hand.

"Well, after I bailed him out with his money, I told him out, you know how I get. So he asked me to come over to his place for a few. I agreed." I paused, he looked at me and gave me an urging look to keep going.

"Keep going, Jai."

I sighed.

210

"So after I broke down about Lyric, he gave him a hug and then—then he kissed me. I'm sorry. I was scared to tell you, baby." His hands wrapped around my waist, and he pulled me on top of him.

"For your information, I ain't mad at'chu. 'Cause I know you ain't initiate that shit. I know you, I know you over this dude. I'd never just accuse you of any damn thing. I'm glad you told me and didn't keep it from me. Nothing else happened?"

"No, just that I pushed him off of me and gave him a piece of my mind. No one will ever take me from you." His hands crawled up my back as he kissed me, making me breathe heavily into our kiss.

"Baby, wait, please—" I begged.

"No, I wanna dick you down, baby. You mine, Jai, remember that—" he smacked my ass harder this time. And he wrapped his hands in my hair as his licked and kissed on my neck. Rashad pulled my pants off completely, slid my panties to the side, ran his hands down my thighs. Then he rubbed his thumb on all the sensitive parts on my tender skin, making goose bumps run down my body. I could feel the wetness grow even deeper between my legs. Rashad grabbed his dick, stroking it as he rubbed his tip on my clit. Moans escaped my lips while I could see him growing with every rub and stroke.

"Daddy," I cooed.

"What? What you calling my name fa', ma?" Rashad slid into my wet core slowly, causing my back to arch. He grabbed the ends of my tank top and lifted it over my head. He kissed my chest as he long-stroked me so slow I could feel my body tense up. His 6'5 muscular body flexed with every move he made. It just made me lust for him more. "You're making me so wet," I whined.

"I'ma give you this dick till you know who yo' man is, understood?" he said with a sexy but aggressive tone, and pulled out slow. "Roll over, get on all fours and arch your fucking back! You know how daddy like it. Come on." I did exactly what he said. Soon as my body was in position, Rashad smacked my ass once my ass was in the air.

While I was twerking my ass, Rashad pulled his boxers all the way down, grabbed my hips and went in deep. "Yes, daddy!"

"You gon' always be mine, Jaidah. If that nigga touch you again, I'ma beat his ass, ma." He ripped off my panties, tearing them in half, and continued to plunge into my wet pussy.

"Ahem! Are you going to buy me some more? Those were my fave." He gave me tight eyes, as he grabbed my chin, and tongued my mouth down. Then he pulled away and got down to my pussy lips.

"Man, this my damn pussy. I can do whateva I want. I'll get you some more lacey. Whatever them shit's called. Now lay forward with your pussy up and let daddy taste what yo' mama made." I giggled, as he gripped my ass cheeks and pulled them apart. My eyes closed as he began to lap and flick his tongue on my clit. He dragged his tongue from my clit to my open lips, and slurped.

"Put them pretty eyes on me, Jai," he said, slapping my thigh. I opened up my eyes, as he dove into my juices.

"Fuck, Shad, fuck!" I yelled.

"Keep ya' voice down. And you bet not come till I say so." He buried his face on my wetness, and shook furiously. My legs shook as I brought my hand around my back and pushed his head. That just made him go faster, even nastier. I couldn't contain my low moans, burying my face in the pillow as I got louder. Rashad was putting in some good ass work.

"Right there, daddy, please, yes! Don't stop!" He began rolling his neck, and I was going to lose it. My phone rang. "Bae, can—"

"*No.* Hell nah." He pushed me back softly, as my toes curled, and slid two fingers inside of me as he got my phone off the bed. He moved them in and out of me, and I breathed heavily. I put my hand over my mouth as he looked at my phone. He answered it as he rubbed on my clit with his thumb. I clenched my eyes tight as he was quiet. Then he spoke like the boss he was.

"Nigga? Why the fuck you calling my girl?" I knew it was JaKobe, then Rashad got gangsta.

"Nah! Ain't no talkin' to ha', wanna know why?" He sped up his finger pace, doing that trick I loved as he hit my spot, making me lose control, knowingly giving me permission to scream for him. And I couldn't help but to scream for real—"Ahemmm, uh—uh—uh! Mm, mhm, mm!"—as my juices made swashing noises. My hand fell off my mouth as I moaned loudly, uncontrollably.

"I'm fucking my girl, so don't call ha' no more, bitch ass hoe ass nigga!" He hung up the phone, turned it off and pulled his fingers out, licked them while he stared down at me. Then he rubbed the mixed juices all over his thick, long, hard dick.

"Daddy, oh ma god!" He smacked my thigh, making me flip over. He told me to hold my ankles as he entered my pussy so deep. My stomach caved in. He was stroking me, massaging my insides with his hard-on. He leaned on his side, gripped my thigh so tight his dick popped out. Quickly grabbing his dick, he pushed it in while circling my clit, and whispered into my ear.

"I love you, Jaidah. This daddy Rashad's pussy. You heard me?"

"Yes, baby, yes! Oh fuck, keep going, daddy!" He hummed as he massaged my titties. He made me forget about everything,

"I love you so much, daddy *fukdnfifndj*—"

"Got that ass speaking in tongue. Skinny niggas do it best." We were going to be at this all night. I wonder what tomorrow would bring us.

Monet Dragun

# Chapter 28

## Heaven Or Las Vegas?

*JaKobe Harrison*

A few days had passed, and I was still pissed that the gay ass nigga had did what he did over the phone. Now shit was war, he wanted his ass whopped and broke in half again! I sat in my office at The Red Room, looking through some paperwork when someone knocked on the door.

Pulling my glasses off my face and rubbing the bridge of my nose, I semi-yelled, "Come in!" The knob twisted, and the door opened to this little, tall angel—Lyric. I gave her a small smile as I sat back on my leather chair.

"Hi!" she said, waving at me. "Hey, Ly! How's everything going? Have a seat, angel." She nodded, then plopped down into the plush chair as she folded her hands into her lap.

"Well?" she finally spoke up, breaking our little silence, "The program has been going okay because I know you were going to ask that. I've been dealing with things, okay! It could be better. But you know how life is—"

"Your life shouldn't even be like this. Believe you me, I beat his ass! He was supposed to be brought up better than that." I shook my head, growing angry, but I calmed down.

"Thank you. I just wish this never happened to me. But I'm coping as best as I can. I have PTSD, and it's terrible. Jai wants me to press charges, but I'm scared, JaKobe. She's there for me a hundred percent, and so is Rashad. He's a cool skinny dude. But, sometimes I be thinking I wish I could be up in heaven with my momma. And I wish I knew were my daddy was." She smirked.

"I'm sorry, Ly—I really am."

"You don't have to be sorry. You didn't cause any of this. You have been a good friend and you've helped me so much. When I didn't want to talk to that therapist, you helped me." I smiled, matching her smile, and nodded. I knew she was hiding her true feelings, but I didn't want to push her off of the deep end.

"Well, let's talk about something positive. What are you doing for your birthday? It is approaching fast. You're finally going to be an official teenager!" She laughed at my facial expression.

"Yeah, finally, I can grow out of my awkward stage. But, Jai is throwing me a party and she letting me pick where I want to have it. And I was wondering if I could have it here!" She swayed back and forth.

"Really?"

She nodded. "Mhm. Jai can tell me no. Besides, I want you two in the same room for once. Just for me?"

"Well, I don't know about that. Your cousin doesn't want to talk to me." She flopped her head to the side as she pursed her lips.

"What! Are you crazy? She'd be happy to see you, please?" She straightened up and gave me the puppy dog eyes. I hated when she did it. Reminded me of Jaidah.

"Okay, play. Fine, fine. You're having your party this weekend on Friday?"

"This weekend! And is there any chance you can get a star to come to my party?"

"You're just using me," I said, fake pouting.

"No way! You're, like, my best friend, besides Jai. No way I'd use you, but I'd love to have *The Weeknd*. He is such a god!" She jumped in her seat. I shook my head.

"I can try. Only for you." She began to clap her hands and giggle uncontrollably.

"Thanks! You're the best! And by the way, the theme of my party is Halloween, of course. So make sure you dress up!" I threw my head back.

"I will, I promise. And are any of your school mates coming?" She settled down and sucked in her bottom lip.

"No," she said gently.

I sighed. "Lyric, I think you should invite some of them. All of them weren't mean to you, were they?" She shook her head.

216

"But everyone knows what happened to me. I feel like a freak!" She held her head down. I got up and walked over to where she was. I rubbed her back and raised her head up by her chin. Her eyes were slightly red, and her lip was quivering.

"Stop it. You're not a freak. You're a beautiful, intelligent, young lady. What happened to you does not define you. You understand me? You have to believe in yourself even when others won't do that for you. You have to stop digging yourself into this hole. I want you to walk with your head held high. Not down low. Lyric? What happened to you was not your fault. You didn't give those knucklehead boys permission or consent! They targeted you, and I'll do everything in my power to get you back to the happy young girl you were before. You got that?" I wiped her tears, and she hugged me tightly.

"Thank you, JaKobe. You're such a good guy. I wish Jai saw you this way." She sniffled. I rubbed her back in small circles as she calmed down. I wish she saw the change too. Lyric opened the door, and there stood Chino.

"Lyric, I'ma need you to go back to your cousin house. Here's some money for you to get some food and go shopping too. My assistant will have the car ready for you. Okay?" I had to hurry and get her out of here.

"But we were supposed to hang out today," she said with a sad face. I looked at her with a serious one, and shook my head.

"Yeah, I know. But we'll have to do this another time. You'll have to go home today. I have something important that just came about." She looked over at Chino who had a hard look on his face.

"Okay," Lyric said solemnly. I handed her the money, and she slid it into her purse. As I followed her to the door, I watched her go to my assistant. I gave him a nod, and he got her out of the building as quickly as he could. Turning towards Chino, I knew what this was about to be.

"Like I said, I knew you had something to do with my homeboy getting killed. One of us gotta go." Shaking my head, I knew it would come to this.

"I told you. I had nothing to do with lil' bro getting killed. You want the smoke, let's get it then." I spoke boldly. And meant it. I could tell his pride was hurt at how blunt I was. Chino thought he could ice me out, nah, I was one step ahead of him. Before he could reach behind his back and pull out his Glock, I retracted my pocketknife from my wrist and stabbed him five times in his gut. "Yeah, nigga. I told yo' ass. All that hot shit you was spitting was gon' get yo' ass put in the dirt." Chino began to cough on his own blood as I twisted the knife into his abdomen. Like I told his punk ass before, I didn't need him; he was just part of my plan.

I snatched the knife from his stomach; he slid down the door as the blood poured from his mouth. I bent down to his level, as his eyes were fluttering open and close. "Thanks for running the business for me, dawg. Go to sleep, nigga. You'll be joining your dead homies soon." I smirked.

Chino laughed. "Fucking your bitch was the best, yo'. Tracy knew some shit." He coughed but started to speak again. "And you got a nigga Rashad on yo' heels. You think you did some shit, bitch. Yeah, yo' ass ain't win shit."

My face went cold as I shoved the knife through his chest. "Bitch, I won either way. Ain't no nigga gon' get in my way. That's a fact. Now go be with yo' dead homies." His head slumped over as I snatched the knife from his chest, and the bright blood made a pool around him.

"If a nigga think they gon' get in the way of me getting my girl back, shit gon' get real." *It's high time I cleaned this shit up*, I thought to myself, mean-mugging the corpse.

\*\*\*

I took a deep breath as I sat out in my car. It had been exactly two hours of me sitting out here. I was at Jaidah's modeling agency. I needed to talk to her and fast. The shit I heard hours ago was weighing on me heavy. This was the only time I knew she wasn't with Rashad. My phone vibrated in my lap. Grabbing it off of my lap, I read the messages that were coming in.

"Why is she texting?" I said to myself, as I read the text from Tracy. She was sending back-to-back text that I really didn't understand or care about. Plus, I had changed my number so how did she even get it? Rolling my eyes, I slid the phone into the cup holder and pressed my fingers to my chin as I sat back in the car seat.

My phone buzzed again, and I picked the phone back up, looking at the next text. "What the fuck? Monica?" I seriously had to block these numbers. I heard giggling and loud talking, so I looked up from my phone.

Smiling, I sat up in my seat and started up my car, as I backed out of the parking space and slowly drove over to Jaidah.

"Yo' Jai!" I said out the window; she looked around and then at me. I pulled alongside of her and another girl. "Wassup?"

"Not you."

"Oh come on. Talk to me, yo." She rolled her eyes as she continued to walk down the side of the street.

"Oh my god! Is that JaKobe!" her friend said.

"Hi, how you doing? Loved your cover of—"

"JaKobe! What do you want? You are so embarrassing!" Jaidah growled.

"I just want to talk friend to friend. It's pretty important."

"What about?"

I gave her the eyes then at her friend. But she didn't see me 'cause she was looking at her phone.

"Uh, Reign, I'm sorry but I have to take a rain check. We can get lunch or dinner tomorrow?" Jaidah said as she stopped walking,

"Oh yeah! That's fine, Gigi is waiting for me so we can catch up tomorrow. And, you need to talk to him. So, Ciao!" They grabbed hands and kissed air on both sides of their faces. Reign waved at me, as she strutted off to her awaiting limo. I gave her a smile, and unlocked the car doors.

Jaidah got in the car and plopped down as she slammed the door. "What? I have nothing to say to you," she said, pushing her purple hair out of her face.

"I beg to differ."

"Whatever. I so don't want to hear your bull shit."

"Whatever my fucking ass! We need to talk for real. I'm sorry for the kiss but I couldn't help myself, yo'. You get me in my damn feelings. But your boyfriend is pushing it. He gon' get his ass beat! Again."

"Oh please! How could you do that to me? I'm faithful unlike you! I want to keep my relationship going. Me and Shad are going just fine. Here you go with this!" She yelled.

"Oh? So it's okay for him to be feasting on your damn box! That shit is mine, Jaidah!" She snapped her head at me and slapped me.

"The hell it is! You don't own me! I don't care if you did take my virginity. You ain't shit. Oh, I have been waiting on this fucking moment! You really wanna fucking go there?"

"Yeah, c'mon! Tell me how much of a fucking screw ball nigga I was back then!" I yelled, as I pulled into an empty parking lot.

"Oh? You have the balls now! Of course I haven't fully forgiven you for that shit! Who can! What girl can forgive some treachery ass shit like that! You think I'll ever let that fully go!"

"Oh, I've been wanting to say this—you were fucking easy. Okay? There I said it! Don't act like you weren't giving me damn consent! Everyday I'd be over your fucking house you'd have booty shorts on showing all types of fucking cheek! Yeah, I thought about dicking your uptight ass down! But I wasn't going to till I heard you and your damn friend talking one day!" I yelled in her face. I was sick of being called the bad guy.

*"How can you be dating that lame ass nigga?"* you said as you and Monica stood by the staircase after school.

*"No, how can you not be dating JaKobe? I see the way you look at him,"* Monica said to you.

220

To the Thug I Loved Before

*"Oh it's not like that. I'm trying to get him with Tracy just so I can steal him from her. I be throwing his stupid self hints all the time. Don't get me wrong, he is my best friend. But he is such a goofy nerd! I mean he is really cute but I want to score with him so damn bad!"*

Should I go on? Should I really! You wanna keep playing the victim! You were my damn friend too. And you betrayed me as well, so that why I fucked your ass without caring if you were a bet!" She raised her hand to slap me again. But I gripped her wrist.

"Can't face the truth, huh! I tried to let it go, but I'm sick and tired of the bullshit! What I did may have been hella wrong! But what you did was wrong too!" I shouted in her face as I held her wrist. She tried to fight against me but couldn't.

"Fuck you, JaKobe! I hate you, I hate you so much!"

"I hate cho' ass too!" I yelled with more venom in my voice. She pushed against me, and I flung her wrist. "Face that shit! You did what you did, and so the fuck did I! You can't play victim anymore!"

"Don't falter yourself, dickhead!" She shoved me. I wiped my hand down my face and looked up at the sun roof.

"You're such a bitch."

"So are you!" she screamed, hitting me again.

"Stopping fucking hitting me, yo'! Before I handle your ass!" She hit me again and again as she began to cry. She drew the line when she hit me in my crotch. I grabbed her roughly and got into her face. "Yo! You pushing me ova' the edge! Stop hitting me! Before I fuck yo' lil ass up!" Her face fell back, and she hushed up. She looked at me and grabbed my face, kissing me. She grabbed my head and stuck her tongue in my mouth as we were both breathing heavily. She bit my lip hard, and I groaned as I pulled back. Touching my lip, it was a little red.

My face was frowned up, as hers was too. I sat in my seat and pulled her on top of me as I grabbed her waist. What she had on was such easy access to her assets. She grabbed the sides of my face as we tongued each other down. I grabbed her ponytail, pulling her head back as she moaned. I kissed her neck, sucking her bare flesh.

She ripped my shirt open, and buttons flew all over for all I care. I let her hair go and raised up her velvet dress. I kissed her smooth stomach, as I lingered kiss after kiss. My hands raised up the sides of her body. I grabbed her braless chest, and squeezed.

Somehow, her hands went onto my waist band and to my zipper, quickly unzipping my pants. My nails grazed her skin softly, as I dragged them down her back. I grabbed the loose material that clung to her ass, and ripped it in half.

Tossing it into the back seat, I raised her small body up as she pulled my large hard member out of my boxers through the hole, and out of my pants. I pulled her head forcefully to mine and kissed her. "This shit gon' hurt. You bet not scream either. I'm a much betta' lover from back then." With that small speech, I shoved her down on my member, her wet tight cat sucking me in. She gasped and sucked on her lip as I ran my hand through her hair, letting the ponytail down.

Jaidah threw her head back, moaning. I pulled one hand out of her hair and slapped her ass. "What I tell you?"

"Mhm, fuck!" She never did listen. I moved my other hand and grabbed the lower part of her back. I slammed her down and watched as her face changed, and the sound of her juices flowed.

"What the fuck I say?" I said, slamming her down again, twice harder to hit her spot. Just to make her scream.

Jaidah screamed, "JaKobe!"

I smirked. "Didn't I tell you not to scream?" She nodded fast, and I slammed her down again. "Use your damn voice when I'm fucking you, Jaidah!"

"I hate you!" she moaned.

"I'ma change that preference real quick. This dick not even in all the way. Still got a few more inches to slide in this wet pussy."

She moaned softly, "Oh my! Fuck—God, help me—" She threw her head back; she wasn't going to know who Rashad was

or even the damn name. She gon' know him as a fuck nigga.
'Cause if I couldn't have her, neither would he or no one else.

Monet Dragun

# Chapter 29

## If Loving You Is Wrong

*Jaidah O'Neil*

"Oh, fuck O-Oh-Oh, JaKobe!" I screamed as he hit my spot on every stroke. He made me climax for the tenth time tonight. His strong big hands held my wrist tight down to the bed. I closed my eyes snapped shut, as my body convulsed over and over again.

His hot peppermint breath blew onto my neck, making the tiny hairs stand up all over my skin, "Please, stop!" I moaned, as he kept pumping with no remorse of my body giving out. "You're a fucking animal! God, I'm about to squirt—*Fuck!*" His fierce strokes of my pussy drew me over the edge. My legs clamped around his waist, and he plunged in deeper into my wetness, making my eyes roll into the back of my head. He just watched as my face contorted with pleasure.

"Oh, fuck! Keep pulsing that pussy on my dick I'm about to nut! Damn, I'm about to nut. Can I nut, baby? Fuck! Yo' shit so damn good." He groaned, he began to hit my spot harder over and over again, making my screams turn into sexy grunts of pain and pleasure.

"Yes, please, daddy, nut, nut for me! I want you to cum so bad for me." I begged as his strokes were about to make me cum all over again. And I really wanted to, but at the same time I couldn't take his big dick anymore.

"Goddammit, Jaidah!" he moaned out as he leaned up off of my body. Pulling his dick out of my area fast, he started to stroke his hard member fast as his seed spilled out on my thigh and stomach. "F-F-F-Fuck! Shit, damn girl, damn!" He grunted, throwing his head. I looked up at him, as I finally caught my breath myself. Finally coming down from his high, he bit his lip, looking down at me with lust-filled eyes.

"Clean this shit off, Jaidah, now—Right the fuck now, girl," JaKobe said in heaving breaths as he stroked. I leaned up and was about to grab his member when my phone started to ring and buzz. It was Rashad's ringtone. I looked over at my phone, "I need to get that?" I said, but he grabbed my hand and placed it on his dick.

"Nah. Just stroke it, Jai. Put them sexy ass lips on it." His chest heaved up and down. I looked up at him, and the freak in me got on my knees, and I gave in. I grabbed his thick dick with my small hand, squeezing it gently, stroking it up and down as I twisted. Wrapping my lips around the head, my phone rang again. He groaned as his hand laid on the back of my head, motioning me to just keep going, my lips softly wrapped around the head of his dick. I began to suck it slowly then, placing sensual kisses on the shaft of his dick. "Ahh, mmm, fuck!" he gasped.

Moaning softly, I pulled away. "Come on, let me get that—" He nodded and moved his hand as I extended my hand, snatching my phone from the table top dresser. Clearing my throat, I pressed the answer button, placing the phone to my ear. "Hello?"

"Where you at, ma?" Rashad began, yelling through the phone. "You know you had to pick up Lyric from her therapy session! She was trippin'. She didn't even wanna' leave with me to go home. I had to basically beg her. She needed her cousin and you got her thinking you not even there for her. She's so damn mad at you. You're going to fix this. You fucking forgot about ha'!"

"I'm sorry, I got caught up with Bella. I'll be home soon—"

"Nah, fuck that! You need to get hea' now! Lyric is freaking breaking down, and she won't even let me into her room! She's having flashbacks, and I can't even help ha'!" His voice boomed through the phone, and I ran my hand through my hair.

"God, I totally forgot she wanted me get her and spend time with her. I'm sorry, I'll be there now. I'm on my way—"

"Yeah, the fuck. Hurry the fuck up, no joke. It's one dammit a.m. I'll see you when you be here." Before I could say a word, he had hung up. I sighed, closing my phone. JaKobe's eyes were locked on me.

"If you gotta go, then you gon' head before ya little yellow crayon boyfriend come looking for you. I don't need to whoop no ass." He smirked at me, as he sat up against the head board.

"Shut up—I have to go," I whispered, as I got up from the bed. He grabbed my hand and pulled me so fast into his chest.

"But first before you go," JaKobe cupped my soaking pussy, making me even more aroused than before, "lemme eat that sweet pussy, right now." He pushed me down in the bed, and got on top of me. Pushing my legs apart, he dove into my extremely wet pussy and began to lick and suck on my clit, making me grab a head full of his curls. My heart was racing with love for Rashad. But my mind was lusting for JaKobe.

"Oh my gawd, JaKobe! Yes, right there!" I screamed. His tongue was doing magic, making me ache for more. I was on the verge of tears. The trick he was doing with his tongue had to be fucking illegal.

## Later That Day

Getting to Rashad's house, I had to walk in right or he was going to know something was up. My legs were all fucked up. Shit! My body was sexually damaged. I was caught in between. I had to forget about JaKobe. What happened this morning was never ever going to happen again. Walking into the bedroom, Rashad was standing in the big window. Looking at the rain that was pouring down.

"Hey, Shad," I said, being as much as myself as I could.

"Sup? Where you been, baby girl?" I placed my purse in the closet, as I took my hair down. He turned around, looking at me.

"I was with Reign—I told you, love. We had a few drinks and I lost track of time as we were working on the project. I didn't mean to skip out on Lyric. I just talked to her. She was upset with me. But I knew she needed me, and I apologize for not being there. It'll never happen again, she didn't mean to shut you out. She was just in a phase again. She's not sleeping, so she said she wants to talk to you." Rashad nodded, but he walked over to the bed and sat in the edge.

"I missed you today, you know," he said, holding out his arms for me. I walked over to him and sat on his lap.

"I missed you too." Before I could say another word, his lips kissed mine. "What was that for?"

"Just wanna give my girl some love," he smirked.

I immediately felt bad.

"Wanna take a bath with me?" I said, licking my lips. He licked my bottom lip right after I said that. He picked me up and carried me to the bathroom.

"I take that as a yes?"

He hummed a *yes* as he kissed and sucked on the pulse point on my neck. He really loved me, and here I was just hours ago. Cheating on him! He didn't deserve that. He sat me on the counter as he walked over to the bath cutting it on. My phone rang loudly in the bedroom. "Babe, I'll get it," I said, smacking my lips. Rashad pecked my lips one last time before he moved to the side and let me hop off the counter.

"A'ight, baby girl."

I jogged into the bedroom, went into the closet and pulled my phone out of my purse. The phone call was from JaKobe; my heart began to race as I watched it ring. Debating on answering it, I didn't want Rashad to come in here. So before the phone continued to ring, I sighed and answered the phone.

"Bonjour!"

"Sup, mama. Speaking the language of love to me, huh?" he said slyly on the receiver.

"No! Shush. Like I was saying, you can't call me. Okay? We can't talk to each other, okay? What we did, you know, was not right!" I whispered.

"You missing my dick right now, don't you?" I rubbed my forehead, and walked out of the closet with a normal face.

"No, I don't miss it!" I laughed. "Listen it'll never happen again. It was a mistake, man, remember I hate you!" I said, shaking my head as I placed my hand on my hip.

"Yeah. Yeah. Yeah. You'll be, soon enough. I don't need to fuck you to know I got in your head."

"We'll never have sex again, believe that!" I said before hanging up. I sighed and threw my head back, and tossed my phone the bed. I heard someone sniff. Turning around to see Lyric right there in the doorway.

"How much did you hear?" Scratching her head, she mouthed: "All of it." The hurt in her eyes showed it all. She loved the hell out of Rashad. Just as much as I did. I felt like complete shit. I was just so congested between the two. Lyric ran from the cracked door as she heard Rashad's voice coming from the bathroom. Rashad had come out of the bathroom with a towel wrapped around his waist and quickly wrapped his arms around me. I felt like crying because I was such a whore for cheating on him. With the man I knew I was over. Rashad loved me so much, but now I was questioning my love for him. But what if loving him was wrong? I couldn't believe I was questioning myself like this after everything we've been through.

Monet Dragun

# Chapter 30

## Waiting Game

*JaKobe Harrison*

I was looking at my iPad while I was sitting in my bed. My joggers were so damn comfortable. Who knew Louis Vuitton joggers could be great as shit. As I was in the midst of planning Lyric's party, I was going to make this the dopest party ever.

As I was doing so, my phone vibrated. Unplugging it from the charger, it was a text from Jaidah. I slid it open as I was looked at the tablet. Inputting my passcode, the message slammed down and I knew she was upset. But who cares?

My Soul & Oxygen: *So! You're planning Lyric's party? How dare you take my baby cuz from me! Traitor.*

I laughed at her message and brought the phone to my face as I began to type.

Me: *whatever, ain't my fault she loves me, like a big girl loves cheese burgers!*

I sent the message and laughed at my own foolishness. Slouching into the headboard, I began to type in my iPad again. I was currently emailing Drake through his business email about coming to Lyric's party. I was cool with him, so I knew he'd come through. He owed me this favor anyway. My phone chimed and vibrated again, and I picked it up off of my chest and looked at the message, shaking my head.

My Soul & Oxygen: *you're so funny ha ha. Stop spoiling my cuz, boy. That's all I gotta say, we really have to talk after this. For real.*

I laughed again at her *wanting-to-be-hard act.* But when she said we had to talk, I didn't know what that could be about it. But I didn't give a shit about that. Instead of texting her back, I began to face-time her on purpose. Even if Rashad was around, I knew she wasn't going to answer. I just wanted to fuck with her soul.

But surprisingly, she answered. "What do you want, JaKobe Cornelius Thompson?" Rolling my eyes, I tapped on my tablet.

"Hello? I'm talking to you, if you're not going to talk and make me look at a ceiling then I'm going to hang the fuck up," she said smartly. I picked the phone up and gave her a "I-wish-you-would" face.

"Man, you talking all this shit like I won't tear that ass up again. Stop fucking playing with me." Smacking her lips, she put me on pause, but I could hear her background. She was in the treadmill, but now she had stopped, and was breathing hard.

"Need some water? Or you need some *milk*?" I said, busting out laughing. She took me off of pause, and I was met with the middle finger. "When and where?" I said, raising my eyebrow.

"Shut up, where is Lyric's party going to be?" Jaidah questioned.

"At my venue, The Red Room. Why?" I could see her shrug.

"Just asking, mofo. Aye, Lyric, don't go so hard on your back like that—Ease up on your pull-ups," she said towards Lyric, making me peak towards the screen.

"My baby girl, Ly in there—lemme talk to ha'," I demanded quickly.

"Fuck no, this is me and her time."

I heard Lyric yell for her to give up the phone. I could tell Jaidah had some type of animosity towards her.

"I wanna talk to my Kobe Bear! Gimme!" She giggled loudly, and Jaidah stale-faced me.

"Dang, what's that face for?" I wondered. She just rolled her eyes, and didn't say a word. There was some shuffling, and I could see her hand the phone to Lyric.

"J-Dawg!" She beamed in the phone.

"Sup, shorty. How you doing?" I asked. Drake had emailed me back about being available for an appearance at her party. Things were going perfectly. I couldn't wait to see her face. With an extra surprise for her as well. Lyric was telling me how her day had been going so far. And she said something that caught my eye and almost made me choke. Did the same to Jaidah.

"Yeah, of course I missed you. After you just canceled our day and made me to go home. But, I can't believe you kicked me to the curb. I can't believe you and Jaidah had sex! How could you be such a fuck boy, JaKobe! She with Shad, you just don't want to see her happy? Your ruining her life, and you don't even care." I could hear Jaidah yelling.

"What the fuck! Little girl, give me that damn phone now. Don't make me pop you! Watch your mouth. You don't see me cursing around you, that is not cute for a girl your age!" Jaidah scolded.

"Aye, yo. Nah. Don't you ever talk like that again. Ly, you need to stay in a child's place. What me and Jaidah do is our business. Don't let me tell you that shit again. You hear me?" She looked at me and sighed.

"Yes," she said with an attitude.

"I said did you *hear me*. Lyric, let me say it again!" I yelled. Lyric jumped and quickly said an audible *yes*.

"Yes, I hear you. You know I love you, JaKobe but *no*. I love my cousin to death. But, you should not have interfered in her relationship with Shad. I told you he's a cool dude, and he actually treats me like a sister he never had. Just like you do. I may be young, but I'm not stupid. You two are really playing games. I see my cousin crying more than you. And you make her cry. You're putting Jaidah in an uncomfortable situation. It's sad and I don't like it." I was stunned at how mature she was talking. But one thing, a kid was not about to stand in my way of what I wanted.

"Lyric, I'm sorry. Okay, but that doesn't give you any right to talk like this."

"I know but this is too much. Don't be sorry to me. I'd love for you two to be together. But you should really let her figure things out. I'll let you talk to her, she's over hea' spazzing. She might pop me too." She passed the phone over to Jaidah. And sure enough, I heard Lyric get popped. Jaidah said her last few words to Lyric before her face appeared in the camera.

"That exactly what I wanted to talk to you about. I didn't think this was going to happen. That was some unexpected mess." She wiped her hand down her face and sighed.

"Yeah. It kind of was. I think we should really be a good example and not do this. Truth is, I've never cheated in my life because I never gave a guy a chance. Rashad is truly my first boyfriend, my real boyfriend. Love isn't a toy and I really care about him. I really am wrong for cheating on him. I haven't been able to sleep and it's just too much." I nodded, I didn't let what she said faze me. I was going to get her by any means. A smirk appeared on my face, "Why the hell are you laughing!"

"*Hell* is a curse word, Jaidah!" Lyric shouted.

"Little girl, hell is in the Bible! Stay in your lane and take you ass to your room. But back to you, O."

"Ain't no 'back to you'—you think Rashad is as good as me? You think he can give you the life you deserve? Ha! I got you in my hand like fucking puddy. We will see how long you can stay away from me. Bye, baby girl, hope you don't have wet dreams about this D!" Her jaw dropped, and I hung up.

Putting my phone on the charger, I closed my tablet and got up from my bed. I was about to do something when someone rang my doorbell. I looked at my phone, and then waited a moment. The doorbell rang again. I slipped in my Nike Slides. Walking out of my bedroom, and down the hall, I hopped on the railing and slid down the railing of the stairs.

Hopping off at the end and skipping a little to catch my balance, I looked through the peephole, cursing and rolling my eyes. "Who is it?" I said on purpose.

"It's Monica. Open up, please?" Monica said in a sweet tone.

234

"Why the fuck should I?" I heard her groan.

"Just open it up, please!" I didn't want my neighbors complaining, so I opened the door and stood there looking at her. My dog ran up between my legs and began to bark at her,

"Good, Tarzan! Get the bad lady." I chuckled.

"Stop playing. Please, we need to talk—"

"Have you talked to Jaidah?"

She shook her head, and I was about to close the door.

"Wait! Why would I need to talk to her?" she yelled, and that only made Tarzan growl at her.

"Because you almost ruined her. The fuck you mean?" I said loudly. Monica laughed.

"I could tell her about us—She disappears, and we can be together," she said and stepped closer, but Tarzan was about to bite her. "Get your damn dog!" she yelled.

"Then stay in yo' place. I don't care what you say, she won't believe you. Now what you want?"

"I need your help. Nicki is stalking me." I stale-faced her.

"What? Ain't no way. She ain't stalking you, bitch, stop lying. What are you really here for? I can see right through you." I folded my arms over my chest while examining her.

"I'm thinking it over. The way you make me feel all sexy but it's causing me shame. I wanna lean on your shoulder. And not feel no pain. I wanna fucking love you. Don't you see? I wish I was in love but I don't wanna cause any more pain. And if I'm feeling like I'm evil, we've got nothing to gain."

"The hell are you talking in song lyrics for?" I said, crossing my arms over my chest.

"In better words, *I'm pregnant* and I'm not keeping it. I have a career to worry about. And now a child on the way. That's yours." Monica cried.

"How many times do I have to tell you, I wrapped it up. Ain't no way that's my baby. Besides, if it was, you wouldn't kill it." I frowned, and looked her up and down.

"Condoms break, ya know. I don't care what you say. You're the only man I have been with. The second or third time we had sex, I poked a whole into the unwrapped condom." She laughed.

"The fuck! You are crazy as fuck. Why are you playing damn games? Nah, man, nah."

She smirked, as I began to panic but would I let her see me fold? Hell nah.

"I can't just let Jaidah be happy, so I'm going to destroy everything she loves. She thinks she can have everything? No! That little boyfriend of hers—well, you or a little Rashaddy seed is in me."

I shook my head.

"He's too much of a goody-two-shoes. Ain't no way he fucked your nasty ass. It's probably David's; knowing your whore ass, you slept with the whole Atlanta city. Don't go doing something that'll get your ass stomped out or killed. Leave Jaidah alone, man."

She shrugged.

"Believe what you want. That bitch won't have a fucking man, a life, a soul, a love one, nothing. Bet on that. She played you too, remember? Or you still wanna love her?" I waved her off and was about to close the door.

"Don't think I won't ruin you too."

I squinted at her and grabbed her by her throat.

"Is that a damn threat? You really want to do that shit, huh? You must not know what the fuck I'm really about, you think I'm pussy? Bitch, you got my ass in the system. Don't think I won't fuck you up again! This time it's gon' be worse than before."

"Do it then, daddy. I like that shit rough. Hit me—"

This hoe was crazy. I let her go, then flicked her body back.

"Hold on a second." I closed the door half-way and grabbed the taser I had gotten Lyric for her birthday. I came back and buzzed it at her ass. "Come over hea' again and my dog gon' bite the fuck outta' you and I'ma buzz your crazy ass to death. You lucky that's all I do. Don't push me. Try me, you trippy ass bitch.

Now, take a few steps back because I'm about to slam the door in five seconds."

"JaKobe, don't do this shit."

"Five!" I slammed the door and shook my head, as Tarzan wagged his tail. He was happy she was gone, and I was happy as well. I had to talk with Brad and figure a way to get rid of this psychotic bitch. And fast. I didn't mind getting my hands a little dirty.

Later on in the day, I had made it to my other place of business—The Red Room.

The waitress, Camila, was cleaning the tables off as the club was starting to fill up. I honestly didn't even want to see Bradley's face. I knew he was going to be, like, *"What the hell"*, Brad thought I was crazy. But I wasn't the crazy one; Monica was.

"Hey, Camila. Come here real quick." She looked up at me, and grabbed the towel from off the table.

She walked over to the bar where I was posted. Niko looked at me and got the pint. "What?" Camila said sweetly.

"One of my guys is coming in. His name is Brad; just send him up to my office." I came around the bar and grabbed a glass. It was my club after all!

"Okay, got it. Anything else, boss?" I poured the liquor into it, and spooned one ice cube in. Then I added in a little sweet flavoring.

"Nothing, that's all. But if a chick come and she won't refuse to leave, just call security and then I will handle it. I don't like no cops in hea'. They already don't like me as it is." She nodded in understanding. She was about to walk away, but she turned around.

"One more thing: Do you want to—you know—hang tonight?" she said, biting her lip. I downed the rest of the drink as it burned a little.

"Ahhh, that some good shit. But if you want to keep this job, I think you should stop worrying about my dick and get on someone else's. Got it? I got a girl." And with that, I walked away from her. She for sure had to pick her face up off the ground. After the

Monica situation was sure to be handled, I had one more to get rid of this light skin ass nigga, Rashad! I was so close to earning my Jai back; it was just a waiting game. No one was going to stop me from getting her. *No one.* My phone buzzed. Sipping my drink, I looked at the messages as they came in. A smirk crept on my face. I told that bitch to not fuck with me. And now look at her about to be a dead body.

I didn't know what was going on with me, but I was madly in love with Jaidah. If I couldn't have *her,* no one *will.* And I meant that with every bone in my body. I always said the gangsta in me would never turn me into a bad person, but Jaidah always did something to me. My love for her had turned me into a different person. Something the streets never did. People would say my love for her was toxic. But no matter what, I had to have her. The urge to have her body against mine was just too strong to ignore. Looking off into the distance, I could feel myself warping and morphing into a different man: a man *crazy in love.* So—

*Dear Jaidah,*

*If you're reading this, your love made me this way. You were made for me, and I was made for you. I don't know why I didn't take the chance to have you in college. But the moment we shared was more valuable to me than you know. You're the air that I breathe every time I see you. But know this: If anyone tries to stop the love I have for you, it won't end well. I've worked too hard to get back to how we used to be. I'm not going back to the old JaKobe. Ain't nobody gon' come in the way of what I fixed. And trust, the day you're my wifey is near. It'll be nothing but bloodshed if I don't have you. No one—and I mean no one—will stand in my way from having you. And if you deny me, that'll be your last breath. Because hell freezing over won't be able to stop me from hunting you down.*

*Sincerely,*

*The Thug You Loved Before.*

*To Be Continued...*
To the Thug I Loved Before 2
Coming Soon

# Submission Guideline

Submit the first three chapters of your completed manuscript to ldpsubmissions@gmail.com, subject line: Your book's title. The manuscript must be in a .doc file and sent as an attachment. Document should be in Times New Roman, double spaced and in size 12 font. Also, provide your synopsis and full contact information. If sending multiple submissions, they must each be in a separate email.

Have a story but no way to send it electronically? You can still submit to LDP/Ca$h Presents. Send in the first three chapters, written or typed, of your completed manuscript to:

**LDP: Submissions Dept**
**Po Box 944**
**Stockbridge, Ga 30281**

*DO NOT send original manuscript. Must be a duplicate.*

Provide your synopsis and a cover letter containing your full contact information.

Thanks for considering LDP and Ca$h Presents.

**Coming Soon from Lock Down Publications/Ca$h Presents**

BOW DOWN TO MY GANGSTA

By **Ca$h**

TORN BETWEEN TWO

By **Coffee**

THE STREETS STAINED MY SOUL **II**

By **Marcellus Allen**

BLOOD OF A BOSS **VI**

SHADOWS OF THE GAME II

TRAP BASTARD II

By **Askari**

LOYAL TO THE GAME **IV**

By **T.J. & Jelissa**

IF LOVING YOU IS WRONG… **III**

By **Jelissa**

TRUE SAVAGE **VIII**

MIDNIGHT CARTEL IV

DOPE BOY MAGIC IV

CITY OF KINGZ III

By **Chris Green**

BLAST FOR ME **III**

A SAVAGE DOPEBOY III

CUTTHROAT MAFIA III

DUFFLE BAG CARTEL VI

HEARTLESS GOON VI

By **Ghost**

A HUSTLER'S DECEIT III

KILL ZONE **II**

BAE BELONGS TO ME III

A DOPE BOY'S QUEEN III

By **Aryanna**

COKE KINGS V

KING OF THE TRAP III

By **T.J. Edwards**

GORILLAZ IN THE BAY V

3X KRAZY III

**De'Kari**

THE STREETS ARE CALLING II

**Duquie Wilson**

KINGPIN KILLAZ IV

STREET KINGS III

PAID IN BLOOD III

CARTEL KILLAZ IV

DOPE GODS III

**Hood Rich**

SINS OF A HUSTLA II

**ASAD**

KINGZ OF THE GAME VI

**Playa Ray**

SLAUGHTER GANG IV

RUTHLESS HEART IV

**By Willie Slaughter**

FUK SHYT II

# To the Thug I Loved Before

**By Blakk Diamond**

TRAP QUEEN

RICH $AVAGE II

**By Troublesome**

YAYO V

GHOST MOB II

**Stilloan Robinson**

CREAM III

**By Yolanda Moore**

SON OF A DOPE FIEND III

HEAVEN GOT A GHETTO II

**By Renta**

FOREVER GANGSTA II

GLOCKS ON SATIN SHEETS III

**By Adrian Dulan**

LOYALTY AIN'T PROMISED III

**By Keith Williams**

THE PRICE YOU PAY FOR LOVE III

**By Destiny Skai**

I'M NOTHING WITHOUT HIS LOVE II

SINS OF A THUG II

TO THE THUG I LOVED BEFORE II

**By Monet Dragun**

LIFE OF A SAVAGE IV

MURDA SEASON IV

GANGLAND CARTEL IV

CHI'RAQ GANGSTAS IV

KILLERS ON ELM STREET III

JACK BOYZ N DA BRONX II

A DOPEBOY'S DREAM II

By **Romell Tukes**

QUIET MONEY IV

EXTENDED CLIP III

THUG LIFE IV

By **Trai'Quan**

THE STREETS MADE ME III

By **Larry D. Wright**

IF YOU CROSS ME ONCE II

ANGEL III

By **Anthony Fields**

FRIEND OR FOE III

By **Mimi**

SAVAGE STORMS III

By **Meesha**

BLOOD ON THE MONEY III

**By J-Blunt**

THE STREETS WILL NEVER CLOSE II

**By K'ajji**

NIGHTMARES OF A HUSTLA III

**By King Dream**

IN THE ARM OF HIS BOSS

**By Jamila**

MONEY, MURDER & MEMORIES III

**Malik D. Rice**

CONCRETE KILLAZ II
**By Kingpen**
HARD AND RUTHLESS II
**By Von Wiley Hall**
LEVELS TO THIS SHYT II
**By Ah'Million**
MOB TIES III
**By SayNoMore**
BODYMORE MURDERLAND II
**By Delmont Player**
THE LAST OF THE OGS III
**Tranay Adams**
FOR THE LOVE OF A BOSS II
**By C. D. Blue**

## Available Now

RESTRAINING ORDER **I & II**
By **CA$H & Coffee**
LOVE KNOWS NO BOUNDARIES **I II & III**
By **Coffee**
RAISED AS A GOON I, II,  III & IV
BRED BY THE SLUMS I, II, III
BLAST FOR ME I & II
ROTTEN TO THE CORE I II III

A BRONX TALE I, II, III
DUFFLE BAG CARTEL I II III IV V
HEARTLESS GOON I II III IV V
A SAVAGE DOPEBOY I II
DRUG LORDS I II III
CUTTHROAT MAFIA I II
By **Ghost**
LAY IT DOWN **I & II**
LAST OF A DYING BREED I II
BLOOD STAINS OF A SHOTTA I & II III
By **Jamaica**
LOYAL TO THE GAME I II III
LIFE OF SIN I, II III
By **TJ & Jelissa**
BLOODY COMMAS I & II
SKI MASK CARTEL I  II & III
KING OF NEW YORK I II,III IV V
RISE TO POWER I II III
COKE KINGS I II III IV
BORN HEARTLESS I II III IV
KING OF THE TRAP I II
By **T.J. Edwards**
IF LOVING HIM IS WRONG...I & II
LOVE ME EVEN WHEN IT HURTS I II III
By **Jelissa**
WHEN THE STREETS CLAP BACK I & II III
THE HEART OF A SAVAGE I II III

# To the Thug I Loved Before

By **Jibril Williams**

A DISTINGUISHED THUG STOLE MY HEART I II & III

LOVE SHOULDN'T HURT I II III IV

RENEGADE BOYS I II III IV

PAID IN KARMA I II III

SAVAGE STORMS I II

By **Meesha**

A GANGSTER'S CODE I &, II III

A GANGSTER'S SYN I II III

THE SAVAGE LIFE I II III

CHAINED TO THE STREETS I II III

BLOOD ON THE MONEY I II

**By J-Blunt**

PUSH IT TO THE LIMIT

By **Bre' Hayes**

BLOOD OF A BOSS **I, II, III, IV, V**

SHADOWS OF THE GAME

TRAP BASTARD

By **Askari**

THE STREETS BLEED MURDER **I, II & III**

THE HEART OF A GANGSTA I II& III

By **Jerry Jackson**

CUM FOR ME I II III IV V VI VII

An **LDP Erotica Collaboration**

BRIDE OF A HUSTLA **I II & II**

THE FETTI GIRLS **I, II& III**

CORRUPTED BY A GANGSTA I, II III, IV

BLINDED BY HIS LOVE

THE PRICE YOU PAY FOR LOVE I II

DOPE GIRL MAGIC I II III

By **Destiny Skai**

WHEN A GOOD GIRL GOES BAD

By **Adrienne**

THE COST OF LOYALTY I II III

**By Kweli**

A GANGSTER'S REVENGE **I II III & IV**

THE BOSS MAN'S DAUGHTERS I II III IV V

A SAVAGE LOVE  **I & II**

BAE BELONGS TO ME I II

A HUSTLER'S DECEIT I, II, III

WHAT BAD BITCHES DO I, II, III

SOUL OF A MONSTER I II III

KILL ZONE

A DOPE BOY'S QUEEN I II

By **Aryanna**

A KINGPIN'S AMBITON

A KINGPIN'S AMBITION **II**

I MURDER FOR THE DOUGH

By **Ambitious**

TRUE SAVAGE I II III IV V VI VII

DOPE BOY MAGIC I, II, III

MIDNIGHT CARTEL I II III

CITY OF KINGZ I II

By **Chris Green**

## To the Thug I Loved Before

A DOPEBOY'S PRAYER

By **Eddie "Wolf" Lee**

THE KING CARTEL **I, II & III**

By **Frank Gresham**

THESE NIGGAS AIN'T LOYAL **I, II & III**

By **Nikki Tee**

GANGSTA SHYT **I II &III**

By **CATO**

THE ULTIMATE BETRAYAL

By **Phoenix**

BOSS'N UP **I , II & III**

By **Royal Nicole**

I LOVE YOU TO DEATH

**By Destiny J**

I RIDE FOR MY HITTA

I STILL RIDE FOR MY HITTA

By **Misty Holt**

LOVE & CHASIN' PAPER

By **Qay Crockett**

TO DIE IN VAIN

SINS OF A HUSTLA

By **ASAD**

BROOKLYN HUSTLAZ

By **Boogsy Morina**

BROOKLYN ON LOCK I & II

By **Sonovia**

GANGSTA CITY

By **Teddy Duke**
A DRUG KING AND HIS DIAMOND I & II III
A DOPEMAN'S RICHES
HER MAN, MINE'S TOO I, II
CASH MONEY HO'S
THE WIFEY I USED TO BE I II
**By Nicole Goosby**
TRAPHOUSE KING **I II & III**
KINGPIN KILLAZ I II III
STREET KINGS I II
PAID IN BLOOD **I II**
CARTEL KILLAZ I II III
DOPE GODS I II
By **Hood Rich**
LIPSTICK KILLAH **I, II, III**
CRIME OF PASSION I II & III
FRIEND OR FOE I II
By **Mimi**
STEADY MOBBN' **I, II, III**
THE STREETS STAINED MY SOUL
By **Marcellus Allen**
WHO SHOT YA **I, II, III**
SON OF A DOPE FIEND I II
HEAVEN GOT A GHETTO
**Renta**
GORILLAZ IN THE BAY **I II III IV**
TEARS OF A GANGSTA I II

# To the Thug I Loved Before

3X KRAZY I II

**DE'KARI**

TRIGGADALE I II III

**Elijah R. Freeman**

GOD BLESS THE TRAPPERS I, II, III

THESE SCANDALOUS STREETS I, II, III

FEAR MY GANGSTA I, II, III IV, V

THESE STREETS DON'T LOVE NOBODY I, II

BURY ME A G I, II, III, IV, V

A GANGSTA'S EMPIRE I, II, III, IV

THE DOPEMAN'S BODYGAURD I II

THE REALEST KILLAZ I II III

THE LAST OF THE OGS I II

**Tranay Adams**

THE STREETS ARE CALLING

**Duquie Wilson**

MARRIED TO A BOSS… I II III

**By Destiny Skai & Chris Green**

KINGZ OF THE GAME I  II III IV V

**Playa Ray**

SLAUGHTER GANG I II III

RUTHLESS HEART I II III

**By Willie Slaughter**

FUK SHYT

**By Blakk Diamond**

DON'T F#CK WITH MY HEART I II

**By Linnea**

251

Monet Dragun

ADDICTED TO THE DRAMA I II III
IN THE ARM OF HIS BOSS II
**By Jamila**
YAYO I II III IV
A SHOOTER'S AMBITION I II
**By S. Allen**
TRAP GOD I II III
RICH $AVAGE
**By Troublesome**
FOREVER GANGSTA
GLOCKS ON SATIN SHEETS I II
**By Adrian Dulan**
TOE TAGZ I II III
LEVELS TO THIS SHYT
**By Ah'Million**
KINGPIN DREAMS I II III
**By Paper Boi Rari**
CONFESSIONS OF A GANGSTA I II III
**By Nicholas Lock**
I'M NOTHING WITHOUT HIS LOVE
SINS OF A THUG
TO THE THUG I LOVED BEFORE
**By Monet Dragun**
CAUGHT UP IN THE LIFE I II III
**By Robert Baptiste**
NEW TO THE GAME I II III
MONEY, MURDER & MEMORIES I II

# To the Thug I Loved Before

By **Malik D. Rice**
LIFE OF A SAVAGE I II III
A GANGSTA'S QUR'AN I II III
MURDA SEASON I II III
GANGLAND CARTEL I II III
CHI'RAQ GANGSTAS I II III
KILLERS ON ELM STREET I II
JACK BOYZ N DA BRONX
A DOPEBOY'S DREAM
By **Romell Tukes**
LOYALTY AIN'T PROMISED I II
**By Keith Williams**
QUIET MONEY I II III
THUG LIFE I II III
EXTENDED CLIP I II
By **Trai'Quan**
THE STREETS MADE ME I II
By **Larry D. Wright**
THE ULTIMATE SACRIFICE I, II, III, IV, V, VI
KHADIFI
IF YOU CROSS ME ONCE
ANGEL I II
By **Anthony Fields**
THE LIFE OF A HOOD STAR
**By Ca$h & Rashia Wilson**
THE STREETS WILL NEVER CLOSE

253

**By K'ajji**

CREAM  I II

**By Yolanda Moore**

NIGHTMARES OF A HUSTLA I II

**By King Dream**

CONCRETE KILLAZ

**By Kingpen**

HARD AND RUTHLESS

**By Von Wiley Hall**

GHOST MOB II

**Stilloan Robinson**

MOB TIES I II

**By SayNoMore**

BODYMORE MURDERLAND

**By Delmont Player**

FOR THE LOVE OF A BOSS

**By C. D. Blue**

**BOOKS BY LDP'S CEO, CA$H**

TRUST IN NO MAN

TRUST IN NO MAN 2

TRUST IN NO MAN 3

BONDED BY BLOOD

SHORTY GOT A THUG

THUGS CRY

THUGS CRY 2

THUGS CRY 3

TRUST NO BITCH

TRUST NO BITCH 2

TRUST NO BITCH 3

TIL MY CASKET DROPS

RESTRAINING ORDER

RESTRAINING ORDER 2

IN LOVE WITH A CONVICT

LIFE OF A HOOD STAR

Monet Dragun

CPSIA information can be obtained
at www.ICGtesting.com
Printed in the USA
BVHW090959240521
608000BV00012B/2900